A Special Blend of Crazy

A Mundane Affair of the Heart

Lynne Maris

REGISTERED SquarePeg Books
A Special Blend of Crazy   A Mundane Affair of the Heart
Lynne Maris
Library of Congress Control Number: 2025909464
ISBN 978-1-965891-01-8

For everyone who said I could do it, even when I thought I couldn't, Thank you.

Here we go.

!!!!!Content/Trigger Warning!!!!!

While Regina, a primary character, shows signs of prior abuse at the hands of her ex-husband throughout the book, in Chapter 15, there is a section in which Regina briefly recounts her memories of physical and sexual abuse she experienced at the hands of her ex-husband. This section is marked with ~~~ for those who would prefer not to read it. Skipping this section does not significantly impact the story.

A Special Blend of Crazy

A Mundane Affair of the Heart

Lynne Maris

Chapter 1

Wake-up Call

There's a window in the bathroom, just above the toilet. I don't worry about leaving it open because it's a tiny window and I'm a man who owns a gun. I can see the trees, and the slope of the hill going slightly up into my neighbor's property. I can see a corner of her house and a part of her yard through the trees. The aspens bordering our properties clap their leaves in the moonlight, while the windchimes she's got up everywhere tinkle in the breeze. It's a nice mountain night.

And there's a naked woman in my neighbor's yard.

Not a sight you expect at three in the morning.

Of course I stare. *It's got to be a dream.*

She's wearing some kind of mask, and while she's far enough away that I can't see the details, I can see that she is naked. She shivers in the breeze. It's summer, but in the mountains it gets chill when the sun goes down. Her blurry body isn't perfect, but most real women aren't.

She snaps her robe to lie it flat on the ground, and then she lays on it in the tall grass. The details are fuzzy, but my mind can fill in the blanks.

For the first time in nearly twelve years, I am suddenly very interested in the female body. I can imagine quick gasps. Her body moves, her back arches slightly.

When she finishes, she gathers her robe from the ground and hustles it back inside. I hear a door open and shut again. It blows my mind that my neighbor—*my neighbor*—a nice, quiet lady—seems to have some kind of . . . what? I don't even know. If you've got a nice house, all temperature controlled and all, why would you go outside to do that? Is it some kind of naked pagan thing? I've heard stories, but they're all Hollyweird stories, so that doesn't count as actual knowledge.

Whatever it is, in the five years she's been in that house, I've never seen it before.

She could just have a kooky houseguest.

It takes my body a few moments to relax. I'm a little ashamed because I intruded on a woman's intimate moment. True, she was outside, but still, you don't expect people to see you at three am in a neighborhood where plots are measured in acres and trees block the view of most every house.

When the sun comes up, I'm back in the bathroom. The spot in the yard where I clearly remember seeing a naked woman is trampled down, but there are also some deer having breakfast, so it's hard to say what, if anything, actually happened.

I convince myself it's a dream. In my kitchen, I frown at my coffee. The house is quiet, because when a man lives alone, that's how the house is.

I throw on some music. Heavy metal fills the air, doing

nothing to drown out the quiet. A goodly portion of my favorite music comes from an era now referred to as classic rock. I'm not sure how the rebellious music heroes of my adolescence would feel about that classification, but it's definitely weird to think about most of them taking up golf, too. Almost as weird as last night.

It was just a dream. No one does that kind of thing outside of Hollyweird.

Jenny died in a car wreck twelve years ago. Maybe that's where the dream came from. I'm so lonely my mind made up something for me to see. I can almost hear the voice of my dead wife. *"You need a hobby, Shit-wit,"* she tells me.

I hear a key rattle in my front door and Simmons' voice a moment later. "Fall in for inspection!"

I turn to face him, holding my coffee in one hand. "Mornin', Sarge."

"Scram, Beaumont," the gruff Santa knock-off tells me. "It's inspection."

I nod, and head out to my back porch. It's hard to argue with the man who saved you from the joys of being an alcoholic. In early May the morning is chill as I sit in a plastic chair with my coffee. My neighbor's windchimes are quiet now, but the birds have made up for them with their chattering.

I wait for Simmons to find nothing, and join me out back. I'm not certain he even looks anymore, but random inspections are a ritual now, and old military grunts like us enjoy their rituals. It's been, what? Seven years since I drank?

Something like that.

I frown through the trees in the direction of my neighbor's yard. *Am I going insane?*

The thought is terrifying. I don't want to fall down that hole again. My wife's death sent me over the edge once, and I nearly lost my son in the process.

I prop my bare feet up on the railing. *No. No. I am not going over the edge, I tell myself. One stupid dream doesn't mean a damn thing.*

Simmons stomps outside and settles himself in the other plastic chair, holding a mug. He takes a sip, then pulls a face. "When will you learn to make coffee?"

"You're drinking it, aren't you?"

Simmons snorts. "Because I have to make sure," his muffled voice comes from the mug. His hair is nearly gone on top, but his beard is full and stark white, except for the coffee stains around the mouth. "You Army grunts wouldn't know good coffee if it bit you in the ass."

"You jarheads would drink cold mud and call it coffee."

"Drop and give me twenty."

"Did I pass inspection?"

"Yes."

"Then fuck off." We're both retired. I can say whatever the hell I want.

Simmons raises both bushy eyebrows at me. "Dizzems cranky 'cause your footsies is cold?" he asks sarcastically. He's got about ten years on me, and likes to rub my nose in it when I lip off.

I shake my head. "Didn't sleep well."

Simmons huffs then sips his coffee. "Want to talk about it?" he asks after a moment.

"Not really."

Simmons finishes his coffee without another comment. "It's okay to miss her, Jim," he says, getting up from his chair. "Just don't try to find her in a bottle again."

I nod, still staring at my neighbor's yard.

***

I call my son after dinner and we chat for a bit. Lucas has been trying to nudge me into the dating scene, but dating feels . . . fake, somehow.

"I think you need to get out, Dad," Lucas starts again. I didn't tell him about my dream, just that I'm noticing the quiet might be getting to me. "Why don't you come with us to church-"

"No." I say it a little sharper than I mean to. I love my son, I really do. I'm glad his friends helped him get through the dark times when his mom died, but I do sometimes wish the religion thing had been more of a phase rather than a life choice.

Of course, when my dad died I enlisted in the Army just as soon as I could, and when Jenny died, bourbon was my best friend for five years, so I guess I can't throw stones. I realize I'm staring through my kitchen window towards my neighbor's yard again. I scowl and turn away, pacing into my living room.

"Dad, I'm not trying to thump you with a Bible-"

"I know, son. I just . . . a man shouldn't go into a house of worship if he doesn't believe that way," I say, planting myself in front of the big picture window, looking out on my driveway. "It's disrespectful."

He sighs. "Can you think of it more like a social gathering?" he asks. "The ladies would chat for hours on end if it wasn't for the service."

I shake my head. "No. I am not going to church. Thank you, but no." *Especially not to meet women.*

"Tommy's supposed to get baptized in July. Will you at least come to that?"

Shit.

Tommy's my grandson. When did I get old enough to be a grandfather? "Yes. Okay, I'll come to that," I say, running a hand through my hair. It's so long now I can pull it into a small ponytail. A far cry from the short military professional look of my youth. "But I am not making a regular habit of church."

Lucas gives me the date and I scribble it down in my calendar. The kids these days use their phones or whatever to make their calendars but I still use paper and pen. It fits in my pocket, and I don't have to fight with a keyboard made for frickin' fairies to punch in my dates.

Lucas and I talk a bit longer before a baby starts howling in the background. Little Rosy sounds pissed about something. I let my son go so he can take care of his family.

I frown at my quiet house.

***

I'm something of the local handyman. I'm not certified for anything more than engines, but when you've been twenty years enlisted, you learn all sorts of things. People call me to paint their houses or fix a fence. I've worked some minor plumbing and electrical. I can even do tree removal as long as it isn't too close to anything important. One guy got pissed because I wouldn't touch a tree that was about five feet from an electrical line.

The power was out for a day in our neighborhood because the idiot tried to take it down himself rather than pay the money to call in a pro. Rumor has it he got stuck with a bill from the utilities company for fifty grand. Something about permits, happening on a Sunday, and the need for a bucket truck.

My truck is big enough to handle hauling most things,

and of course I clear snow from driveways with my blower. I don't like it, but I do it. If someone gets locked out of their house in my neighborhood, I'm usually the first one to get a call. No one seems to wonder much why I have picks, but that might be because I'm cheaper and faster than calling an actual, bonded locksmith to get back into the house. I also don't flap my yap at the spouse about how the wife (or a few times the husband) had to call me to their rescue.

This is not to say that my calendar is filled. It's pretty open, but I have a job or three to keep me occupied for a few days, and before long I'd almost forgotten that moment of my neighbor's. I'd convinced myself it was just a dream brought on by a bad case of the lonelies. Just to shake things up, I'd started going to the local coffee shop, playing a few games of chess or checkers during the day with anyone who'd come along.

About a week later, I'm in my bathroom at three again, like most nights. My body is nothing if not consistent. I hear her back door open, and I look through my window.

Her house is dark. Even the porch lights are out. It seems darker tonight than it was last time, but I can still see a bit. She's wearing her little mask and her robe is long, but thin and dark. I can see how it moves and the lack of bulk. I suppose it could be silk, but whatever it is, it's definitely not a girly pink.

A woman after my own heart. I hate pink.

She steps into the tall grass and sheds the robe. Her arms go up to the sky, almost like she's welcoming someone. Maybe she's pleading. I don't hear anything, though. She lays down and I can't move. I don't want to move. I can imagine what she's doing, but I don't want to imagine it. I want to see it.

I want to know if I'm going insane.

My body doesn't care if it's insanity or reality. It likes the show, even if two-thirds of it is only in my head. When she finishes I find myself aching for the first time in years.

***

To prove to myself I'm not insane I start getting up every morning around two-thirty to stakeout my neighbor from my bathroom. I put a tiny "x" on my calendar for the mornings she shows up. I start in May and by the middle of June I've got her pattern. She waits a week and then tacks on another day. Then she has her moment in the grass.

I'm not proud. I feel dirty actually. I'm not willing to go on a date. or even to the local Christmas party, but I'm more than happy to peep on some lonely woman's personal time.

I can see the grass rustle. I imagine her shuddering in desire. In my head she pinches her nipples, and strokes her skin with her fingertips. My breath quickens when I think about her hips gently rocking in the grass like she has a partner.

I'm fifty-seven and I've seen some shows in my time, but I've never been so turned on as my neighbor has me right now.

I pull my gaze away from the window and scowl. *This ain't right. I need to tell her; warn her off somehow.* A gentleman doesn't let a lady think she's safe and private when she's not.

***

My neighbor's house is a single level like mine, but painted dark blue with purple trim. I always thought it looked silly, but it's her house so she can do whatever the hell she wants with it. It isn't like we have a lot of covenants in ShadowPines.

I've been working myself up to confronting my neighbor all day, and my hand shakes a little when I ring her doorbell. It's Saturday afternoon and I'm fairly certain she's home because her car is under the metal carport at the end of her driveway. In the five years she's lived here, we've never talked other than to say "hi" if we bumped into each other while checking our mail at the neighborhood box.

It's the end of June and hot enough to hide my nervous sweats.

At least that's something.

I can't remember what she looks like. I know she isn't ugly, but I couldn't pick her out of a crowd if my life depended on it. The mask she wears during her woodland frolics is just a strip of black fabric tied around her head, but it doesn't help with trying to remember her face.

I mentally rehearse what I'm going to say. *Hi. I'm Jim, from next door. Anyway, you might want to check your property because I think I saw some kids messing around in your yard last night.*

It's short and simple. It gives her a way to know that, yes, while the trees might block everyone else's view, I still seem to have one. It also allows her some dignity in that I'm willing to assume it wasn't her, but rather some dumbass horny kids giving me one hell of a show.

When she opens the door, I'm lost. Her face is familiar, but I can't remember why. She's not drop-dead gorgeous, but she is attractive. Just looking into her eyes makes my mouth go dry. They're brown, warm and friendly. Her hair is brown and long, pulled into a braid with strands of grey streaking through.

All I can think of is how I want to feel that hair with my fingers.

I don't want to tell her now that I've seen her face up close, but I can't run away like some kid playing at annoying the hell out of people. I hook my thumb over my shoulder. "I'm Jim, from next door." It's a stupid opener, but it's all I can think of.

"Oh, hi, Jim. What's up?" She looks wary, but still willing to be neighborly.

Shit.

What's up? My cock? Yeah, that would be a great answer. "I was hoping you had a chainsaw I could borrow," I blurt out.

She wrinkles her nose. "Oooo. . . no, I don't."

Damn, she's pretty. "But you keep the trees pretty well off the house," I say to keep the conversation going. "You've got to have something like that."

She shakes her head. "I hired someone to mitigate the property for me when I first moved in. Now I just try to maintain it or call someone if it's something I can't do."

"Damn. Mine's got to be sharpened, and I've got a dead tree on my lot." It's a bald-faced lie, but our properties are large enough that she might not notice that I don't have any such problem. Fire mitigation of property is almost a religion in the Colorado mountains what with all the wildfires, so it's a valid excuse to knock on her door. I frown at the porch like I'm trying to think of my options.

It's a cheap shot to check out her legs in the shorts, but I'm not disappointed. They're long and well shaped. A little pale, and there are some scars and fresh scratches typical of life, but they are nice. "Oh, well. I guess I'll have to actually sharpen mine, then." I turn to leave her porch with a friendly wave. "Thanks."

She smiles and lifts her hand back at me before her door closes.

***

The next day I realize why my neighbor is familiar—she owns and runs Java Books, Honesty's only coffee shop, where I've been hanging out to take my mind off of the things I've seen in her backyard.

Aw, shit.

I order my coffee from the girl with the green hair, and find a place to sit, picking up a random book from a table, pretending to read while I sort out my options.

I could stop coming to the coffee shop, but then what would I do? It isn't like I'm intentionally stalking her. The shop is a nice place to relax and socialize for a bit.

One of the kids behind the counter starts singing along with the radio. He's got a good voice, and he's learned how to use it for the ladies. It's some love song or other that's popular now, and he's gesturing at the small gaggle of teenage girls at a nearby table. They giggle, pulling out their phones for pictures or what not.

The neighbor lady smiles at him as she restocks the fridge under the counter before starting another batch of coffee, and heading back into her office to do manager things.

"Small black coffee, up!" the singer calls out.

I fetch my coffee from the counter and retreat to my table. The girls leave, and one of the shop employees starts busing tables with the death of the teen summer lunch rush. I get invited into a game of canasta by the older card-codgers in the café corner.

I sort the cards in my hand, frowning. I like coming to

11

the shop. True, I survived well enough before I tried to make it a part of my day, but I realize I'm tired of the hermit gig.

I pay more attention to my personal situation than my hand, and get creamed by the geezers in the first game. I shuffle the deck and deal out the cards for the next round. There's a small racket behind me in the shop. The green girl behind the counter yells "Boss!"

I turn to see a small invasion of shorts-wearing travelers destined for Cripple Creek or points further on dominate the café. The boss comes out of her office and effortlessly handles the horde. It's somewhat mind-boggling for me to watch as she fills a million orders and rings up books at the same time, all with a smile.

I turn back to the cards. These old guys don't screw around. It might only be canasta, but they can smell blood in the water. It's a good thing I don't know how to play bridge or the card-codgers would be utterly ruthless when they're shy a player.

I'll just stop watching her. She's a nice lady, and she deserves her privacy.

How hard can it be?

***

In early July, I've caught another show courtesy of my neighbor. My knees are weak by the time she gets in her robe and leaves for her house. I look at my shadowed face in the mirror. I can just make out some of the grey in my hair and the blue of my robe, but there isn't enough light to see the look of disgust I'm throwing at myself.

I still don't know her name. I somehow managed to forget to ask for that little tidbit when I talked to her last, and the kids at the shop all call her "Boss."

I try to avoid her at her store when I'm there. She seems to get prettier and I feel dirtier every time I see her. One time she tried to take the empty mug from my table. When I saw the hand reaching for it, I naturally looked up and there she was—smiling at me. I jumped so high I spilled the chess game I was playing with some eight year old kid and his dad.

It's just as well. That kid was kicking my ass.

I think I should talk to her though. I know she's not married, and her antics make me think she isn't seeing anyone either. A good looking woman wouldn't be acting like some forest nympho if she had a boyfriend who did his job. Or a girlfriend.

I try to be open-minded about such things, but the thought that she might play for the other team is a real downer. That makes my chances of getting her on a date pretty much nil.

A date? Where did that come from?

Probably because even though she's got me hotter than I've been in a long time, I still feel dirty spying on her. I feel like I should at least know her favorite color or something, now that I've seen intimate bits of her anatomy.

What would I say to her? *Hi, it's me again. I was wondering if you'd like to go out sometime. After last night's show, I figure I at least owe you a lobster dinner.*

When did I become such a dirty old man?

My doorbell rings, and there's a pounding on my door. I freeze.

Shit.

She must've seen me. But how? My house is dark. If I don't answer, maybe she'll think she's mistaken and go away.

The doorbell rings again, followed by more pounding.

It might not be her. It might be someone else with a minor crisis.

Yeah. Someone else. Like Simmons. *Hi, Jim. Sorry to wake you but I was wondering if you had any snacks lying around. At three am. Because I just got the munchies something fierce.*

The pounding gets louder, and the doorbell rings several times in a row. My left arm under my tattoo tightens in defiance. Well, it might be time to face the music, but I sure as hell am not going to give up in the first round of interrogations.

More pounding. "Awright, I'm comin'!" I shout back at it. "Keep your pants on!"

I dash into my bedroom, and grab my gun from the nightstand. It might be my neighbor or it might not. Some habits just don't go away. I get to the door and open it just a crack, keeping my gun behind me.

It's her. My neighbor. My little nymph of the woods.

"What?" I grunt out. If I'm going to act like I just got dragged out of bed, then I'm going to play it for all it's worth, but my heart is pounding so hard my ears are ringing.

"I'm locked out," she says.

I rub my head with the hand holding the gun, and her eyes widen slightly. "I'm sorry," I mumble, trying to hide my sudden relief and confusion. "What?"

"I locked myself out of my house." She's starting to shiver. The robe she has on might go to the ankles, but it's thin and I know she's not dressed under it. She's holding it closed at the neck and the crotch, but she's definitely cold. Her nipples are like diamonds under the thin fabric, and my flannel pants suddenly don't feel big enough to hide my interest.

I pull my door all the way open and gesture for her to

come inside, as I fumble my robe closed. Fortunately, she doesn't seem to notice my clothes because her eyes are on the gun I'm waving around.

She hesitates for a moment, and I deposit the weapon in the pocket of my robe and successfully close it. "Well? You're cold aren't you?" I grouse at her. I really don't want to be rude, especially not to my nymph in distress, but if I'm going to sell my innocence, I've got to play the part.

She shuffles in, holding her robe tight. My front door leads straight into the living room, and I point to my couch on the left, all of two steps away, with a wool blanket tossed on it. She practically dives under it before I can say anything.

"You're locked out of your house?" I yawn.

She nods, the blanket pulled up around her neck.

"What were you doing outside?" I know very well what she was doing, and it was pretty damn hot, but if I don't ask, it'll look suspicious.

"I thought I heard something and I went to look," she says without missing a beat. Smart lady. "Nothing's there, and my door closes on me."

I rub my eyes and blink before going to my desk in the corner to paw through the drawers. "You're lucky that's all that happened," I say to her. "You could've found something with claws under your window. Or an intruder."

I suppose I fall under the second category, but I try not to think about that. I dig out my pick wallet and my reading glasses before heading to the door.

"Shoes?" she suggests.

I look at my bare feet. "I probably should, huh?"

"It would help," she says. "The rocks are pretty sharp."

"Hmmmm. . . " Is all I'm willing to let myself say. I go to my bedroom for my boots and bring out a pair of loafers for her. "They're too big for you," I say as I drop them near her, "but at least your feet won't get hurt on the way back."

The shoes are too big for her but she slides her feet in them without a word. Worry creases her forehead. I know she's trying to figure out how she can get out without revealing too much more. A pervy part of me is hoping that the robe just falls open when she shimmies out of the blanket, but the gentleman takes over.

For once.

"Keep in the blanket and come on," I say. I snatch a flashlight I have near the door and troop out with my relieved nymph following me.

The gravel of the road crunches under our feet as we walk to her house. I head for her front door when she stops me. "Can you turn deadbolts?"

"I'd rather not," I admit. "They're something of a pain."

She sighs. "Back door."

I'd figured as much. I just grunt and swing my flashlight from side to side along the path around her house so we don't trip on anything. When we reach her door, it is well and truly locked. It has a deadbolt on it, but since this is the door she came out of it isn't engaged. I have her hold the flashlight while I work.

"You know, you should at least keep a gun on you when you poke your head out at night," I start lecturing her. "At the very least, a shot or two off to the side in the ground is enough to startle a bear and maybe scare it off."

"I've got one," she says. "It's a rifle, though."

"And you left it inside because?" I'm actually glad she left it inside. As nice as it is to watch her at night, I would be very disturbed if her rutting partner was a rifle.

"I wasn't thinking," she says.

The door snicks open and I stand aside to let her in. In a

moment of utterly corny behavior, I bow at the waist, waving an arm towards her door. "My lady."

She laughs before stepping inside. "Thanks," she says, handing me my flashlight back.

"Not a problem." I start walking back around her house to the road when I hear her door close, and I stop in my tracks.

Shit.

I didn't ask for her name. Again.

Chapter 2

Dare to be Bold

My door won't open. It's bad enough that the only place I'm able to get off is in my backyard, but why couldn't I remember to unlock the door, or at least bring my keys with me? Windchimes tinkle gleefully in the breeze, making me hate them. If it wasn't so dark, I'd find them and rip them out of the damned tree. I jiggle the handle again, knowing it won't work.

"Stupid fucking bitch," I hear in my head.

I instinctively make myself smaller when I hear the words, real or not, before forcing myself to stand up straight. *Come on, Regina. Think. Options. What are my options?* I could break a window. There are plenty of rocks around, and of course I find one with my toe.

I curse and sit on the ground, holding my foot in frustration. Breaking the window won't work. I don't have any shoes on, and glass is bad when you step on it.

The windchimes tinkle again. I take a breath, listening

to them, remembering why I hung them all in the first place. He hated windchimes. Because of that, I've hung so many my property it's probably almost considered a public nuisance.

My shoulders bunch up with tension. No. I don't have to panic. I can breathe. I can think. Options. The neighbor. Whats-his-name. John. No, Jim. The handyman guy. Jim has lockpicks. I remember someone telling me about it last Christmas at the Munn's.

I look down at what I'm wearing. I just want to crawl in a hole and die. A satin robe and nothing else except my mask. Another breeze reaches me through the thin fabric, and I shiver. I can't stay out here too much longer. Summer in the Colorado mountains is nothing like the Appalachians— it's actually cold after the sun goes down. People bring winter coats to wear at night in the Rockies during summer. And I have to get to Java Books at five just to be open in time for the morning rush at six.

The absolute ridiculousness of holding my business equal to, or greater than, the risk of hypothermia, makes a hysterical giggle slip from my mouth. I can feel the panic rising again, and I step on it with another breath.

This isn't impossible. All I have to do is wake him up, tell him I heard something and got locked out. Clean, simple and neat.

"He's never gonna fall for that shit, you stupid bitch."

The voice makes me want to shrink. The windchimes tinkle again, and I don't hate them anymore. I put them up because he hated windchimes. I straighten my shoulders, and march to the road.

Well, I march until I step on another rock. Then I walk as carefully as I can with no light to his house.

The gravel road seems to glow in the starlight, and I'm

glad I don't have to worry about threading through the trees to find his front door. I find the first step of his porch with my already offended toe, and hop up the remaining two steps, making a mental note to take my keys and a pair of boots outside the next time I need a midnight adventure.

I ring the bell and pound on the door before I realize I'm still wearing my mask. I tear it off my face, bundling it in a fist before pounding on the door again.

"Awright, I'm comin'!" I hear faintly through the door. "Keep your pants on!"

I wish I had pants right now. I feel bad that I'm waking him up, but doors don't open by themselves, and it's better to do this now, than to wait until sunrise when he can get a real eyeful.

I imagine myself letting a leg slip out of my robe for him to see and really wake him up. I stifle wicked giggles when the voice in my head calls me a fucking slut, and the locks on Jim's door start to rattle at the same time.

His door opens a crack, and he's positioned himself mostly behind it, peering out at me. "What?" His hair is long and dark and tangled, and he blinks at me a bit like an owl. Now I really feel bad. I dragged this guy out of bed just because I was too damned horny to think first. I pull my robe closed even tighter. "I'm locked out."

A hand with a gun appears and rubs the shaggy mane on his head. *Mental note: He takes Colorado's castle doctrine very seriously. Always announce your presence.*

"I'm sorry," he mumbles. "What?"

I can't very well expect him to be bright-eyed and bushy-tailed when the sun hasn't even had its coffee yet, but I don't like repeating myself. "I locked myself out of my house." I try to make my voice sound like something approaching normal, but it comes out more as a pathetic squeak. I tell myself it's the chill setting in, not years of training.

He opens his door and waves me in. Fear clenches my gut. I'm practically naked, and I'm going into a strange man's house.

"So pretending to be a whore stops at the door, huh?"

I shake the voice off with a visible shiver.

"Well? You're cold aren't you?" he grumbles, fumbling with his own robe. There's a bulge in the robe pocket where he's deposited his gun, and I shuffle into the house as fast as I can without losing my grip on the mask or the robe.

His front door opens straight into his living room. He points to a couch with a blanket, and I'm under it before he has a chance to say anything. He may not have noticed the details of my condition yet, but he will when he wakes up a little more.

He yawns and scrubs at his hair again. "You're locked out of your house?"

I nod, since there really isn't anything else to say.

"What were you doing outside?"

My heart leaps into my throat before I remember my excuse. "I thought I heard something, and I went to look. Of course, nothing's there and my door closes on me."

He blinks at me, then rummages through the drawers of a desk. "You're lucky that's all that happened," he says. He sounds genuinely concerned for having been rudely woken up. "You could've found something with claws under your window. Or an intruder."

I nod—accepting the lecture seems safer than saying anything.

"Where the hell-oh. There it is." He stuffs a flat wallet and glasses into his robe, and starts for the door.

I look at his bare feet. "Shoes?"

He looks down and wiggles his toes on the carpet. "I probably should, huh?"

"The rocks are sharp," I agree, having just experienced them.

He tromps off to find some shoes, and I look at his house for the first time. Only the foyer light is on, but I see a neat house, if a little cluttered. There's a central fireplace that acts as a border between his living room and the back of his house. To the right in the back is a kitchen with the light on over the stove and a small table. The back left is covered in shadows, and I can barely make out a hall leading away. If I was truly rude, I'd ask to use his bathroom to snoop more, but I'm kattywampussed enough as it is. I don't need to know the intimate details of his life. I just need to know that he can get me back in my house.

His living room has a picture window curtained over on the same wall as the door and couch, and he has bookshelves covering every wall. They are literally crammed with books stacked on their sides and then in front of each other to make more room.

A man after my own heart. I love books.

"Bullshit," the voice says again. *"You show up naked on his doorstep, and he doesn't even want your pussy."*

I scowl at the bookshelves, scanning the titles, recognizing old friends. Fantasy. Science fiction. Urban fantasy leans against alternate history. Newer authors I've never read are stacked next to 1930's pulp collections. Somehow *An Examination of Cherokee Myths* fits next to three volumes of *The Complete Annotated Shakespeare.* Do-It-Yourself and home repair manuals have three shelves all to themselves, and there's a serious collection of upper-division history books as well. The Vikings. Rome. Russia. Asia and Arabia.

On his desk is a small stack of library books. The Celts. The Druids. Another three fiction books.

Is there anything this guy doesn't read?

I don't see any romance novels, so I guess he has some preferences.

Jim comes back carrying a pair of shoes, his own feet clad in a pair of scuffed up boots. It looks silly with the robe and the flannel pants, but I can't laugh. It's almost four in the morning and the guy is coming to my rescue, after all. "They're too big for you," he says, putting house slippers on the floor near me. "But at least your feet won't get hurt on the way back."

I'm relieved that I don't have to cut my feet up even more. The gesture is sweet, even if I will look silly with his big clod-hoppers flapping on my feet like a pair of clown shoes.

The problem is that I don't want to leave the blanket. It's cold outside, true, but I'm more concerned about the view Jim's going to have now that he's fully awake.

He starts for the door. "Keep in the blanket," he says.

I'm absolutely thrilled with his suggestion, and I flop along behind him, wrapped in his blanket and shoes, his flashlight making the rocks on the road look smaller and less pointy than they felt in the dark. We're halfway down my driveway when I remember something about locksmiths. "Can you turn deadbolts?"

He looks at me, his eyes bright and alert. "I'd rather not. They're something of a pain."

Well, dammit. "I went out the back door," I admit.

He shrugs and leads the way around my house, his flashlight sweeping back and forth. He offers his hand for a rough patch of wobbly flagstone but I shake my head. I smile at his back because it was a gallant gesture.

But the voice in my head is determined to ruin it for me.

Jim hands me the flashlight and kneels in front of my door, pulling on his reading glasses. He examines the lock and opens his pick wallet. "You know," he says as he works, "you should at least keep a gun on you when you poke your head out at night. At the very least a shot or two off to the side is enough to startle a bear, maybe scare it off."

I smile. It's nice that he's concerned about a woman he doesn't know, even at four in the morning. "I've got one," I tell him. "It's a rifle, though."

"And you left it inside because?"

"I wasn't thinking." It sounds like the safest answer. The truth is that my little acts of defiance would feel . . . less, somehow, if I took it with me. It's stupid, but it's true.

The locks turn, and he opens my door. With a flourish he rises and bows at the waist, sweeping his arm towards the kitchen inside. "My lady."

I try to stifle a laugh, and I'm thankful for the dark that hides my blush. I hand him his flashlight as I step inside. "Thanks," I say, smiling.

"Not a problem."

I close the door softly as he turns to leave, then collapse against it, my knees shaking uncontrollably. I pull his blanket tighter over my shoulders, focusing on the rough feel of the fabric. My heart hammers and my head feels light.

Breathe. Breathing is good. We like breathing. The blanket. It's not woven. My fingers scratch at the fabric. I rub my cheek on it, trying to stop the runaway panic.

There's a smell on it I can't identify. Not a laundry smell, or a smoker's, but different. A unique smell. A comfortable one. One that makes me feel safe.

***

I only have room for six tiny tables in the front café of Java Books, but the card players managed to convince me to keep the one large table for their games, shoved into a corner to the left of the counter as people come in from the door. I think they surrender the table to their wives at night, because I keep seeing a small group of women showing up after dinner to knit and what-not at the same table.

The used bookstore takes up the right half of the shop. It's more of a draw than a profit because it's so small, but it's always a treat to see some kid discover a book that can drag them away from their phones for a while. It took me a long time to get my bachelor's in Literature, and the bookstore gives me hope that the future won't be populated by illiterates.

Most teenagers show up to pretend like they're adults with their over-sugared coffees while they're trapped without a car in nowhere-Honesty. Morning and evening commute crowds, tourists and the occasional lost shmoe all end up in Java Books at some point during the day. My café and bookstore isn't much, but it has managed to become a social spot for Honesty, even though my wi-fi isn't the best.

A day after he came to my rescue, Jim strolls in, and waits in line. It's got to be at least ninety-five in the shade outside and he's wearing jeans and boots while everyone else is trying not to die in shorts. When he steps up I nudge Cheryl out of the way to take his order myself. "What'll it be?" I look up at him. I didn't remember him being quite this tall from the other night.

He looks startled seeing me behind the counter. I don't know why he's surprised. I own Java Books, for crying out loud. He's seen me here before.

He recovers, pulling out his wallet before I have a chance to think about it further. "Small coffee, regular."

"How do you take it?"

"Black and bold, Ma'am."

He offers me a five and I push it away. "This one is on the house," I tell him.

He looks down at me with a strange expression on his face. "Thank you," he says before stuffing the bill back into his wallet. He steps to the side of the counter to wait, letting the next customer place an order with Cheryl.

I smile, wondering if he would drink my personal brew. I start pouring the boldest coffee I have ready. "Did you get your things?" I ask him. "I left them on the porch?"

"Hmm? Oh, yeah. Thanks." He's reading the riddle of the day chalked up on the board next to the register. "Lady Jane Grey."

"What?" I ask.

He points at the board, his gaze now drawn to the brochure rack I have nearby, studying the local attractions under his mane of salt-and pepper hair in a short ponytail. "Who ruled England for only nine days?"

I lean over the counter to look at the board. "Hey, Steve?" I call out. "Did you pick today's question?"

The kid shakes his head as he buses the tables, his long blonde hair pulled back into a braid. "Mikie did, Boss."

"Mikie?"

"S'up, Boss?" My brown-haired singer comes out of the storage room, carting another two gallons of milk to shove in the mini-fridges under the counter.

"Is the answer *Lady Jane Grey*?"

"Aw, man!" he glares at Jim. "That question's only been up for two hours!"

"Pay up, sucker," says Cheryl, my oldest employee at

nineteen. I'm convinced she's the only reason that Mikie and Steve applied for a job at Java Books. Even with the green hair and the heavy eye-liner, the girl is a stunner. I think they'll stay on after she leaves for college at the end of summer, but I'm trying not to keep my hopes up.

"No, you still cheated," Mikie protests as he assembles a large hot chocolate with two shots of espresso. "You didn't know the answer to your own question yesterday."

Jim looks at Cheryl. "What was the question?"

"Who holds the world record for juggling chainsaws?" she replies, shrugging with an impish grin. "I wanted to know, so I figured I'd ask. No one else knew either."

"It's cheating," Mikie says again.

"It's not cheating. It's not like we offer a prize for the right answer," she points out, reaching for the top shelf to get at the flavored syrups. Her shirt rises, revealing a sexy back curving into well-defined hips.

God, did I ever look like that? I don't think I did. I sigh for a lost youth, then shake my head. It's easy to be jealous of Cheryl's looks. In another forty years she'll be in my position, wondering the same things about a different teenager.

Jim is back to studying the brochures again, ignoring the barely legal girl behind the counter. I smile and put his coffee on the counter. He nods at me. "Thank you."

Mikie and Cheryl are still arguing about who won and who owes five bucks. Jim clears his throat. "As the one who correctly answered today's question, I decree that the match is a draw, and no prizes will be awarded."

Mikie points at Cheryl triumphantly with a coffee mug. "Ha!"

She rolls her eyes to the ceiling. "Men always stick together."

"Get used to it, honey," I tell her as Jim meanders to the book side of the store.

I know his routine. He'll spend about three hours puttering around with the games or checking out the books, so I have some time to bag up a half-pound of my own mix that I don't brew in the store.

Cheryl follows me into the back. "Did you need something?" I ask her as I reach for a coffee bag.

For once, Cheryl looks shy. "My sister is looking for a job."

I scoop some Venezuelan beans onto a scale. "Uh-huh. And how old is she?" The beans from the scale go in the half-pound bag and I look for the Java.

"Sixteen, next week."

I raise an eyebrow at her. Cheryl blushes. It's so unlike her I can't help but laugh. "Is she actually looking or are you?" I ask her, weighing out another scoop. "It doesn't do me any good to hire someone who doesn't want to be here."

"No, she's looking," Cheryl says quickly. "It's just hard to find a job, you know?"

I nod as I take a scoop of beans from Kenya this time. It's hard to find a job these days, sure, but what I desperately want is an adult who can open or close so I don't have to keep up these hours. Trying to convince an adult to work for part-time minimum wage is something of a challenge though, so beggars can't be choosers.

"Has she filled out an application?" I ask as I drop a few more beans on the scale.

"I brought it in today. It's on your desk."

"I'll look at it," I say, not making any promises. "I just wish I didn't have to lose you."

Cheryl snorts. "You know I've been shorting the register fifty bucks a shift, right?"

"And I'm the Emperor of Siam," I say absently as I weigh out more beans. Cheryl might look like a pain in the ass, but she's one of the most honest people I know. She'd be more likely to throw in a few bucks from her own purse to make up for a short register than to steal it. The bell on the café door rings, and Cheryl leaves me for the front.

When I've done all my measuring and mixing, I emerge to see Steve behind the counter, and Cheryl having a hushed conversation with Mikie. "She's my sister," Cheryl is saying.

I look out into the café to see Cheryl's mom Maria and her sister Cheyenne, waiting for their drinks.

"I just said *hi,*" Mikie hisses, making an Italian ice.

I clear my throat and all three of my employees look at me. I crook my finger at Cheryl. "A word, please?"

She gives Mikie a meaningful glance before following me into the back room once more. I hold up a finger. "I don't want any fighting where customers can see. If you can't deal with it, you know where the door is." Cheryl blinks at me, flabbergasted that I'm taking her to task like this. It's something I rarely do to anyone, and I've never done with her. I hold up a second finger. "Next, Cheyenne is going to have to learn a few things on her own. One of those things is going to be Mikie, one way or another. Especially if she works here."

"But-"

I shake my head. "No. Look after her, and for God's sake be there for her when she needs you, but you need to let her make a few mistakes on her own while she's still safe with mom and dad. Otherwise, she won't know a big mistake when she finds it. Trust me."

Cheryl scowls at me. I shrug. "You're the one leaving for college in a few weeks," I remind her. "And Mikie isn't that much older than she is." I rest a hand on her shoulder.

"Your mom won't let anything happen to her." I smile at her. "I have a big pot of coffee waiting to spill if something does."

Cheryl grins at me. "On the crotch?"

I sigh. "Absolutely." Mikie is a sweetheart, and I honestly can't see him being at all horrid to anyone, but I've thought that before about other men.

When we come out of our little conference, Cheyenne and Maria are already leaving, with Cheyenne talking happily about something in Colorado Springs down the mountain. Cheryl smiles like a wolf at Mikie, and his eyes get big for a moment. I think that smile of hers scares him more than anything she could've said.

I leave the children to play behind the counter while I find Jim, sitting in an overstuffed chair, his long legs crossed at the ankles, sticking out like two fallen trees. He looks up from his book when he realizes I'm holding out a half-pound coffee bag. He takes it with a raised eyebrow. "Ma'am?"

"Also on the house. My own personal mix."

He studies the unmarked bag in his hand. "Dare I ask?"

"My brother once said *it's bold enough to slap your face and call you a bitch.*"

He barks out a laugh and I blush. He smiles at the bag. "Well, I can't wait to try it."

"Do you have a grinder?" I ask. "I only gave you beans."

He tilts his head side to side. "I can scare one up." His eyes glance up at me and then back to the bag. "Are you sure you don't want me to pay?"

"It's only fair for the rescue. And I was tempted to keep your blanket." Why the hell did I just admit that last bit?

He smiles, glancing at me before dropping his eyes again. He doesn't stop smiling, though. "I'd rather you didn't," he says. "My tootsies get cold on the couch."

I have no idea why I'm being so familiar with him. Maybe being a damsel in distress does this to a girl. I like his smile. I like the way his eyes sparkle when he laughs. I want to know why he's looking at my floor. I bought Java Books four years ago and I know the linoleum isn't that great, but I don't think it's bad enough to stare at.

I want ask him about that. I want to hear him laugh again or make another joke.

My shoulders stiffen. It would be lovely to have a friend, someone my age, to sit and talk with, but the potential reality is too frightening. It's far easier to banter with the children, talking about nothing, than to actually have a real conversation with an adult.

"Well, I've got to get back to work," I say, and I scuttle back to my office before I get myself in trouble.

***

My next sojourn into the night feels different, and not just because I make sure to take my keys and shoes outside with me. It's overcast, so the night is warmer than usual. My windchimes are quiet, and there doesn't seem to be anything awake right now.

A few weeks ago I startled some deer traveling through my property, and I ran back inside before I even got a foot off my back porch. Having an audience for my nightly adventures, even if it was only deer, was just too much for me. Oddly, doing it inside feels just plain wrong.

My own special blend of crazy.

I have no idea where I got this idea to scamper in the grass like a horse in heat. Maybe I had a dream or insomnia one night. Maybe I saw it in a bad movie. Maybe running my own business is nice, but still not wild enough. Not different enough from the woman I used to be.

The woman I won't be ever again, if I can help it.

I try to clear my mind, to just think about the raw sensuality, the sheer giggling insanity of getting myself off outside in my own yard.

I don't know that it's brave, seeing as how I'm quite certain no one can see me with all the trees blocking the view and the chances of anyone actually looking in my yard at three in the morning are pretty slim, but it's still in public. So maybe it's more stupid than brave.

But it doesn't matter. For almost thirty years I wouldn't breathe without someone else's approval. I'm done with that now.

"Keep telling yourself that, sweetheart."

Tonight feels different. My imagination is stronger tonight. The partner I've manufactured seems more real than ever. I can practically smell him on me.

I try to imagine the things he does, the things I want him to do. I want him to be gentle. I want him to wickedly tease me until I ache. I want him to seduce me. To want me. To need me.

I run my fingers up my chest to my throat, caressing my collarbone. The dew on the ground sends a delicious chill up my spine.

I pretend that my hands are his and I want them everywhere at once. Fingers trace my sides and belly, they swirl around my nipples in tiny teasing circles. A breeze across my chest is his breath and my back arches slightly.

I need my lover. I can almost hear him panting in my ear. He's thrusting hard and deep and I don't dare open my eyes until an electrical shudder starts deep in my pelvis and dances up my back in mindless glee.

When I do open my eyes, I see the hard dark above me,

the clouds heavy and distant in the sky. I feel like I've been cheated, somehow.

I was so close to him tonight. I could smell him on me.

I sit bolt upright and seize my robe, urgently pulling it on and running back to the house like the devil is laughing at me.

I realize that the smell I imagined was from Jim's blanket.

Chapter 3

A Leap of Faith

I wear my one sports coat to Tommy's baptism, and my boots are polished up nice and bright. These are my only concessions to the formal nature of this event, since I'm wearing jeans and a button up shirt with no tie. I can't remember exactly when it was that I had a haircut last, but I'm combed and presentable in a ponytail, at least. My son's wife calls it my "mountain man" look. If I don't get a haircut soon, she'll probably start in on how I'm getting ready to form a cult.

I shift in the pew, trying to stay focused on the ceremony at the front. I'm not comfortable in church. I never have been, and the ceremony isn't one that I approve of, really. Tommy's only just five. I don't think anyone should swear to uphold any faith when they're too young to really understand what it means, but I'm just the grandpa. That, and it's hard to throw stones at a man's faith when you have yet to find a way to vocalize your own.

I realize my left arm under my tattoo is clenched up, and I fight to relax it. I'll keep my mouth shut to keep the peace. If there's only one thing I learned in the military, it's that you can stomp all over a man's livelihood and maybe even his family, but try that with his faith, and there will be a fight. A fight in church is no way to make my grandson's special day a memorable one.

I can't focus on the ceremony, so I settle for people-watching instead. Lucas has black hair like mine used to be, and looks naturally comfortable in his suit and tie. He must've gotten that from his mom, since I remember hating my Class-A's so much Jenny always had to fuss at me to wear them.

Missy is swaying a little with Rosy in her arms, trying keep the baby happy and quiet for the duration. I swear that woman can't be more than five-foot-two at the most; she looks like a kid standing next to my son at who's six foot and some change. I don't know what possessed her to cut her hair that short, but now she looks like a little blonde pixie. I'm waiting for wings to sprout and frickin' sparkles to start flying around her, but it doesn't happen.

Bummer. It would've made church more entertaining.

There is what I suppose are the usual church attendees with the usual Sunday uniforms. Some of the men have opted for just the button-up shirt and no jacket, a few are even wearing jeans, but every single woman in that building is wearing a dress, and more than half of those are trying to make the pews look like they're infested with flowers.

Jenny hated dresses.

I smile as one of the patrons' head dips to his chest, quietly snoring. His wife elbows his side, and he jerks awake again. The poor guy looks like he didn't sleep at all, but he's of the age where I think his problem has more to do with shift-work than anything else.

I don't murmur "Amen" with the congregation. I don't know what it is I'd be "amening" to, or even what "amen" means, exactly. Even the dictionary is pretty vague about using the word "affirmation" in the definition. I only know that I have no intention of disturbing the peace. The older woman seated next to me with her too-blonde hair smiles at me. I smile back politely, and hope the service ends soon.

We go out to lunch afterward—my son and his family, and of course a few of their church friends. The lady who I'd been sitting next to in church latches on to me. It turns out she is painfully single. She tells me her name is Janice and she's not yet sixty, prattling on about how she's heard so much about me from my son's wife, Missy.

I look at Missy at the other end of the table, helping Tommy pick out something from the menu. I hear Janice say something about how Missy told her I was considering entering the dating scene. I don't know if Missy heard her, but she looks up to wink at me before turning her attention back to Tommy.

The only thing keeping my daughter-in-law alive right now is the fact that she will never know how grateful I am to her for bringing my son back to me.

Janice's hair is too blonde, and it's obvious she spent a lot of time styling it. She seems nice, but she irritates me. I can't put my finger on it on, exactly, but she feels . . . plastic. Clingy. Her nails are well-manicured and fake and I can't see her doing anything remotely close to my idea of work. She can't stop talking about the church, and she keeps inviting me to the singles group they have for people over fifty-five.

"I'm not much for church things," I tell her, hoping it'll steer her away from me. I'm trying to be polite while my left arm bunches up again.

It doesn't work. "Oh, but we do lots things that aren't at church," she says. "We just had a picnic in the park last week. Volleyball, frisbie and all that."

I can't imagine this woman hitching up her floral print skirts to spike a volleyball over the net. I try sipping at my coffee again, but it tastes awful. I've been spoiled for any other and mercilessly reminded of it when I stray from my nymph's special brew. I force myself to swallow the stuff while Janice prattles on.

"We're supposed to hike through Garden of the Gods next week," she says."Nothing strenuous, you know, but a nice walk with lunch at the end."

"I'll have to check my schedule when I get home. I think I'm supposed to paint someone's house next week." I frown in thought. "Or maybe it's tree trimming." Bald-faced lies, the pair of them, but I do not want to get stuck with this woman. She probably likes the coffee they serve here. I shiver, rolling my shoulders, hoping people will think it's just the air conditioning.

She smiles at me, touching my hand. "What a dear man you are."

I force myself to smile back at her even though all I want to do is tear my hand away from hers. Lucas smiles at me from the end of the table. *Is he in on this, too?*

Sweat beads on the back of my neck as she pulls a pad of paper out of her large purse and scribbles on it before passing it to me. "There's my number and the date for our hike. You call, and let me know."

I nod, politely put the paper in my pocket, glancing down at my watch. I pretend to be shocked before she can ask for my number in return. "Damn, I've got to go." I get up from my seat, my lunch only half eaten. Right now, I'd cut my own foot off at the ankle to get away from Janice.

Lucas looks up at me, startled. "Dad?"

I pull a few bills from my wallet and hand them to my son. "I'm sorry, son, but I promised Ms. Grayson I'd help with her car this afternoon. It's the only one she's got, and she can't afford to take it to the shop."

He glances over at Janice, now cooing in admiration at how nice it is to find a man so willing to help his neighbor. Lucas nods and takes the money. "I understand, Dad. Things happen."

I feel bad for cutting out early on Tommy's little party, but the kid is neck deep in a bowl of ice cream and doesn't even notice me scuzz his hair before I leave, so I guess he isn't too heartbroken.

It's too warm to be wearing my sports coat if I don't have to, so I strip it off as I cross the parking lot, and toss it in my truck before tearing out of the lot and away from Janice.

I have no idea who Ms. Grayson is, so I figure she won't mind if I skip looking at her car to go to the library instead. Colorado Springs has a better library system than any we have up in the mountains. It isn't that Woodland Park doesn't have one, it's that it only has one, and it's not very big. My town of Honesty doesn't even have one unless you want to count Java Books.

I browse around the books and magazines for a bit when it occurs to me that maybe what I've been seeing from my neighbor has nothing to do with sex. Maybe she's doing some new-age pagan thing in her yard. In which case, I'd feel even dirtier about getting off on watching it.

I find the religious section . . . and realize that I'm hopelessly lost. I've never actually had to research anything like this before. I pick a book at one end of the shelf and start skimming through it, trying to find a reference point to start with, but it doesn't give me much. The second one looks promising, but only says that nudity is a practitioner's choice.

Okay . . . so it's optional. *Great. What the hell does that mean?*

Over the next hour I skim through another two books, but I can't find much that's consistent. The skinny *Law Enforcement Guide to Witchcraft* at least lays things out in a form I can relate to, but doesn't shed much light on my situation. Apparently, the new-age stuff is more like thirty-one flavors with eight-hundred toppings. There are a few hard and fast rules, but not many.

I re-shelve my books and stare at them until someone clears their throat to my right. I look up to see a librarian with a cart of books she obviously wants to put away. I stand aside politely to let her pass.

"Excuse me," I say before her cart moves too far away.

She looks at me. I wave at the new age/pagan shelf. "Do you know about this stuff?"

She gets cautious. "Ummm, well that shelf is devoted to the non-Christian, New Age beliefs."

"No, no. I mean, do you know about this stuff? See, I've got a question and I don't know where to look."

She frowns for a second. "Is your question about the differences between or more of a how-to?"

I'm at a loss. "I guess it's more of a how-to," I finally say.

She bites her lip. "I'm not really allowed to answer questions like that," she finally whispers. "But there is a store a few streets down that might be able to help you. It's called *Awareness*, and it's in an old yellow house with a big pair of dragon statues in the front. I don't know the address, but you can probably find it online."

***

I do not fit in at *Awareness*. It isn't a bad place, except for the overwhelming incense weighing down the air, but it's definitely a store more geared to the crystal-crunching-hippie set than the over-fifty-and-confused crowd. Janice would probably have a seizure if she saw me in here.

That thought actually makes me smile.

I browse around upstairs, looking at the jewelry and wondering why a librarian would send me here when I find a sign "Books Downstairs" over a doorway with stairs that look more steep and claustrophobic than any I've ever seen. I'm six-foot-three, so I have to duck my head just to fit in the tiny space. It's only ten or twelve steps, but I feel like I'm trying to walk through a curved coffin. When I get to the basement it's something of a relief, even if I do feel like I'm going to slam my head on the ceiling.

There are books everywhere, and I still have no idea where to start. A lady with dyed black hair and an outfit that screams "I believe in magic" looks at me with a smile. "Can I help you?"

"Ah, well, I hope so."

She waits for me to continue. My mouth works silently for a few moments. "Is there somewhere a little more private we can talk?" I finally ask.

She nods like she's seen this before. "Michelle?" A younger woman stocking shelves looks over. "I'm going to help this gentleman for a bit, okay?" Her assistant nods, going back to fronting the books, and trying to make more room for the new stock.

The first woman takes me to a back room and closes the

door slightly. There's still a crack left so she can see out and call for help if need be, but other than that, it's about as private as I can hope for. I spill out my neighbor's performances in a rush. I gloss over the details that would make me seem more pervy than concerned, but I still feel like I need a bath after talking. "So is this some magic ritual thing she's doing or what?" I finish.

The store clerk blinks slowly at me. She looks almost as confused as I am before replying. "I'm not going to say that it *isn't* a ritual of your neighbor's design, but I will say I don't think I've heard of anything quite so . . . blatant, especially not without the other trappings."

"Like what?"

She shrugs. "Candles. Words. Maybe even a small fire. An athame at the very least."

"An athame?" I ran across that word in the library, but I don't remember what it means.

"It's a small ritual knife," she says. "More pretty than practical, usually."

The brief thought of my neighbor getting off with a knife is just as bad as the rifle. I'm retired Army, and I've seen a lot, but something like that would be just . . .

Damn. That's all I got. Just . . . damn.

The clerk shakes her head, dragging my mind away from some very disturbing visions. "But the mask really doesn't sound like anything I've ever heard of, and most nude rituals are held indoors, especially in this climate." She clasps her hands together. "If she is casting something, it sounds like she might be confused. Although based on what you've told me, I think it's more . . . ah . . . personal, if you get my meaning."

"Aha," I say, not entirely certain how I mean it. I think I'm still confused by my neighbor.

Hell, I know I'm still confused.

I rub my face with my hand as I leave the store. A wave of fresh air blows the heavy incense away from me. In my truck, I just sit for few minutes, parked in the alley behind the shop, tapping my fingers on the steering wheel.

The store clerk confirmed what I'd been thinking, and I'm happy that I'm probably right. Getting off on watching my neighbor if she'd been practicing a ritual of her faith, as ridiculous as it seems to me, would somehow be akin to pissing on St. Peter's Basilica, in my book. No, I don't believe in it, but someone does, and it's more than a little rude to disrespect it.

It's also incredibly rude to watch some lady do this kind of thing in her back yard, which doesn't help my situation at all.

I start my truck and head for home. My nymph of the woods is due back in two more days, and I still have no idea what to do about it.

Shit.

***

The day after Tommy's baptism, Simmons has me play assistant instructor to a small gun safety class. He does most of the talking, since he's a certified instructor and I'm not. There isn't much to talk about since he and a lawyer friend of his covered the legalese the day before. My assistance is only needed for today's range time, and I have to struggle not to smack the crap out of some woman who simply does not want to understand that recoil is a thing, no matter the weapon, among other problems.

This is another reason why I'm only an assistant instructor when Simmons has more than two people in his class.

Fortunately for me, the gun expends a spent shell and it hits her face, which means I don't have to. She gets ten times more frustrated than she was to begin with, and Simmons takes over while I watch over the husband and wife who complete Simmons' class. I don't have to do much with them, just remind them to keep their weight on their forward foot, and show them a few different techniques, like how you hold a gun and flashlight at the same time, things like that.

The woman who got smacked in the face gets all pissed off and stomps away when the range is called cold. Simmons just shrugs, shaking his head at me.

Once our fledglings have left for the day, I end up back at Simmons' place, cleaning guns on his dining room table. His house is lot like mine, but he's got a stable with two horses, so instead of normal books on his shelves everything is about either guns or horses.

And he likes to listen to piano music.

It's not bad, but it isn't my speed, either.

"What was the lady angry about?" I ask him as I begin disassembling my 9mm on an old towel.

Simmons snorts. "I'm not willing to sign off on her paperwork until I think she won't kill herself or some bystander." He scowls at his own gun. "I offered to spend an extra hour with her outside the class for free, but she didn't want to hear it."

I can't argue with his logic. He's got more certifications than I can think of, so if anyone can teach an incompetent how to shoot, it's Simmons. If the lady didn't take him up on the free lesson, that's her own fault.

"You realize she's probably just going to take another class in the Springs or Woodland Park to get signed off," I tell him.

He shrugs as he finishes laying out the pieces of his own weapon. "Then that will be on someone else's conscience, not mine. But I don't think she's safe, so I'm not going to sign a damned thing that says otherwise."

Cleaning a gun is a little bit mechanical and a lot zen when you're retired military. Your hands never forget the motions, and there's a process to taking a gun apart and putting it back together that leads you into a kind of rhythm where you can forget about everything for a while. It's relaxing, but I can't get my neighbor out of my mind.

I have a day and bit before my lady of the woods shows up again, and I still don't know what to do. "Are you dating?" I blurt out.

Simmons looks at me with a 9mm barrel in one of his hands and a bore-brush in the other. He blinks long and slow. "Why? Do you think I'm cute?"

I shake my head and grin. "You look like shit in heels."

"That's God's own truth," he says, returning his attention to the barrel. "Seriously, though. Why?"

I shrug. "I think my son's wife tried to set me up with a lady from their church. It just got me thinking, is all."

Simmons frowns. "I don't know any of the hotspots, if that's what you're asking. My horses take up too much time, anyway." He puts the barrel down, turning his attention to the slide. "Have you got anyone in mind?"

I pick up my bore-brush. "Maybe. She's got my attention, I'll give her that. I just don't know how to go about it, you know? It's been so frickin' long since I've even thought about dating."

Simmons starts reassembling his gun. "Tell me it isn't that girl with the hair at the coffee shop."

I nearly choke. "Oh, hell no," I laugh. "I couldn't keep

up with that even if I wanted to."

"Well, that's good. I've just noticed you spending a lot of time there, lately."

"I need a frickin' hobby," I mutter.

Simmons nods. "It might help. Find out what she's interested in and try it. Who knows? You might find a hobby of your own even if she doesn't work out for you."

I know he means something harmless like gardening, or a couples dance class. or something like that, but I don't think my lady of the woods has any other hobbies. She goes to work, she comes home, and she sometimes plays in the grass.

"What's wrong now?" he grumbles at me.

"I dunno," I admit.

"You're chicken-shit."

I think about that as a pair of pianos mock me from speakers. "Yeah."

He shakes his head. "You're still young, Beaumont. If she's here today, you have to move on it, or she'll be gone tomorrow."

***

I make a mask out of an old black flannel shirt I've got lying around. It isn't anything fancy—a bit like Zorro or the Lone Ranger, but it isn't cheap plastic and I think that's a plus.

At two in the morning my alarm goes off and I shower in a dark bathroom. My heavy metal music is playing quietly as I shave in the dark, even though it's a pain in the ass. I don't want her to see the lights on hear anything from my house. I don't want to scare her off.

Of course, she'll probably get scared off anyway.

45

I look in the mirror over the sink. The shadowy face looking back at me is less shaggy than it was the day before. I had to go to Woodland Park to find an actual barber since the one hair stylist in Honesty wants to do a lot of fancy styling that I can't make look good at home, nor do I want to. I'm a wash and go kinda guy.

The Woodland Park barber argued with me for a bit, clucking his tongue that I still looked like I was trying to be a kid with the long hair, but at least I don't look like a raggy sheepdog anymore.

Even in the night I can still see a shadow of the ink on my left shoulder from my Army days. It's too dark to read, but I don't need to see them. I know the words. "Molon labe."

Come and take it.

Those words strike me as weird, right now. For years I've always had them behind me, their defiance meaning something to me, forming a core around which I built something resembling a faith, although I wouldn't be able to tell you what it is.

Those words don't fit with what I'm doing tonight. They're not behind me. They're not in front of me. They're nowhere to be found except in meaningless ink on my arm.

My hands shake when I tie the mask on. My heart slams out of beat with my music and my ears ring, making it impossible to hear the song anyway. I slap the music off and I cannot believe I'm actually creeping quietly out my back door.

This could all go horribly, horribly wrong. *I'm sorry, officer. I've been watching her do this thing for a while now, and just thought she'd like some company.*

I wait in the scrub oak between our properties in my robe and a pair of loafers. It isn't that far from my house to her yard, but I figure it will ruin the moment if I'm cursing and hopping around because I step on a pinecone.

When I hear her door close my heart stops. Why can't I just be normal and ask her out to a movie or lunch or something? I can't recall ever doing anything this stupid. I watch her shed her robe and I time my movements the same. As she reached her hands to the sky I slip off my shoes and step out from my hiding spot.

She sees me and freezes.

Shit.

Well, what the hell did I think was going to happen? I don't want her to disappear, but somehow I know I can't speak. If I say a single word, she'll run back into her house. I raise one hand towards her, my palm to the sky.

My inner critic groans. I've watched way too many Hollyweird movies. Will the cops accept that as a defense?

She doesn't move. I can't blame her, really. If she was expecting some ripped twenty-something elf from the fairy woods, she's probably real disappointed she got Puck's dad instead.

She shifts, reaching a hand towards mine.

I move closer, and her hand shakes as I take it.

This wasn't in her script. Hell, I don't know what I was expecting, either. I think there's a "no talking" rule, but I'll be damned if I know what to do next. Hollyweird comes to mind again, and I take another step forward, raising her hand to my lips in what I hope is a sexy, yet chivalric move, in a corny sort of way.

Part of me finds it funny that I'm worried about chivalry. I'm buck-naked in my neighbor's yard, trying to seduce her while wearing a mask.

She's still shaking. I can understand that. This has got to be creepy as hell for her. I nod. I let her hand go. I turn to leave.

She touches my arm and stops me. I see a shy smile in the moonlight, and I smile back.

She guides my hands to the aspens standing nearby, so that I'm gripping a branch on either side. Every touch of hers is enough to make me jump. She's so close I can just feel her breasts against my chest. It takes every bit of willpower I have to grip the branches and let the lady take the lead.

I'm not disappointed. She lightly rakes her fingernails along my arm and down my sides, beginning to tease me. She pauses at my hips, gently tracing circles. When she drags them across my front, just below my stomach, I have to arch my back and hiss. I want her, but I keep gripping the branches as if my life depended on it.

Her fingers are still tracing patterns on my skin when her lips kiss my collarbone and begin to work down my chest. My heart is hammering now. I want to be done with the foreplay before we've even started. It's the lady's move, I keep telling myself.

When she takes me into her mouth I almost rip the branches off. Just before I break the silence to warn her, she stops. Her lips start moving back up my chest. Every move she makes rubs against my skin, and I feel like I'm going to lose it.

Just when she reaches my other collarbone I decide it's my turn. I can feel her shaking start again when my hands touch her hips. But she doesn't shy off when I trace my fingers on her skin while I kiss her neck and shoulder. It's hard on my knees to move slowly down like she did, so I sit on the ground, and pull her down to straddle me.

She hasn't seated herself like I want her to. Instead, she curls her fingers into my hair. I wrap my arms around her back. With her breasts so close I can tease them with my teeth, my tongue, my breath. She arches her back and I drop one hand to tease her. Tickling, thrusting.

Her hips start to rock; she hitches her breath. I draw my fingers along her inner thigh and my arm around her waist guides her down. A quiet moan escapes her lips when she mounts. She pushes me to the ground, her hips setting a gentle rhythm with a deep rolling lift. It isn't fast enough to my liking, but I hang on to her nipple with my teeth and let her take the lead, again.

She starts to grind down harder on me. I can see her lips moving, but there isn't a sound coming from them. Her head rolls and her hair flies like a wild mane in the wind. She gasps and writhes, panting out small sounds that would've been screams if she'd let them. What little noise there is is too much for me: I come without warning during a final whispered moan of pleasure from her.

She shivers in the dark, then slides from my hands, quickly running back to her robe and home.

I'm cold as I roll up on my elbow to watch her leave, but I say nothing to stop her.

***

I haven't spoken to my neighbor or even tried to see her for two days. To be fair I was busy—Simmons' back went out and he called me to muck his stable at oh-dear-god-it's-too-early in the morning. Then the Kerns wanted my help for a retaining wall. I could've made time to see her, maybe drop some flowers off or something, but I didn't.

I didn't realize what the "no talking" rule entailed until I ended up in Java Books without thinking about it. I'd spent the morning stacking eighty-pound landscaping bricks for the Kerns, and habit just brought me to the shop when I

49

wanted a break. The summer lunch rush with all the local kids and tourists are talking up a storm of noise you can barely hear anything over. I waited in line without a problem, but when I stepped up to place my order, I lost my voice.

She's there, working the register, and I have no idea how to talk to her.

My mouth opened and my usual order came out —"small coffee, black and bold." She rung me up and took my money without noticing me. She can't be so stupid to not realize who was in the woods with her four days before, so my one saving grace is that she didn't have time to notice me because the café is just that busy at the moment.

I somehow knew, without her telling me, that I had screwed up. I wasn't supposed to be here. Her seeing me here, like this, would somehow ruin what happened the other night.

I'm stunned that I feel like this. I'm about ready to leave when my order comes up and the kid behind the counter makes eye contact with me. If I leave without it now, I'll attract attention.

I slam the whole thing in two gulps and run before she can notice I broke the rule.

*****

I'm waiting in the bushes again, convinced she won't show, but here I am anyway. I'm almost certain she caught my mistake, and I'm going to pay for it by never seeing her again. Will she give me another chance?

When I hear the door open and shut, I relax. I've got another chance.

I just catch her smile in the moonlight when she sees

me. The relief washing over me as she begins her seduction only confirms that I am now in the weirdest relationship I've ever heard of.

Our meetings follow the schedule she had initially set for herself—one night on, eight days off. No speaking, no notes, just watch the calendar and set the alarm.

One night I pulled her to the ground before she could start and began my own persuasions. I trailed my tongue over her body—her breasts, her stomach, her thighs. I watched her hands dig into the dirt, gripping the grass in anticipation. I teased her and myself, but never delved deep. She wrapped her legs around my hips and made me take her.

Once we made love in a foggy mist.

One night the smoke from a wildfire in another part of the state had drifted in. It made the air hot and the smell of burning wood surrounded us. Our bodies were so slick with sweat we had to hold tight to each other or we'd slip away.

But we never speak. Not a single word. And we never kiss the lips.

Those seem to be the rules.

In October, I try to kiss her mouth, but she turns her head just in time. I hold her close, nuzzling her neck, taking in the smell of her hair, long and loose. I deliberately slow our pace, trying to draw the moment out as long as possible. She hasn't told me, but I know this is our last meeting of the season. The weather's turned cold, and the aspens are as naked as we are except for the wool blanket from my couch. I hold her face in my hands, caress her lips with my thumbs, my forehead resting against her own.

I want this. Why won't you give me this?

I want her to doze off in the blanket. This whole summer has felt like some bizarre badly-written fairy-tale romance. Some part of me thinks that if I can see the sunrise with her, I'll break the spell, and she'll be mine.

But my lady won't stay with me. She returns to her house, her breath steaming in the night.

Chapter 4

A Knight in the Woods

I've never understood why I raise my arms to the sky before I start rolling around in the grass. Am I asking for strength? Courage? A fairy knight from the woods?

Apparently I'm asking for all those things because tonight, someone steps out from the brush, looking for all the world like he belongs in my little fantasy. The only thing he's wearing is a mask, but it doesn't take a genius to know who the tall and lanky stranger is or why he's here.

I'm suddenly very aware that he's stronger than me. It's a terrifying moment that I simply hadn't ever thought about happening.

He doesn't rush me. He doesn't take a single step closer. All he does is raise his hand, silently asking for my own.

My stomach flips and twists into knots. *"Fucking slut,"* hisses through my memory.

The voice is enough to steel my resolve. The woman I was wouldn't frolic naked in the fields. The woman I used to be wouldn't dare consider a one-night stand even when her husband has lost track of how many affairs he's had.

I will not be that woman ever again.

My hand shakes but I put it in his. My knees want to collapse when he steps closer to kiss my hand gently. Lingeringly.

Just the way I want him to.

I can't stop shaking. I'm terrified and excited and even in the shadows I can see that he's interested, but I'm frozen. He couldn't be here to mock me, not being undressed like that, but what if the night isn't dark enough? What if he actually sees me?

I see him swallow hard, and he drops my hand without a word, turning to leave me.

No.

I will not be that woman.

Ever. Again.

I touch his arm to stop him. I smile when his eyes meet mine.

He's willing to stand and wait, to let me decide how to start and if we finish. I begin slowly, more to convince myself that I'm actually doing this. That I actually can do this.

I use my fingers first, simply running them up and down his arms and sides to see how he'll react. His breath quickens and I can see he doesn't want to wait, but he will because I want him to. My ears are ringing when I touch my lips to his collarbone. I feel light-headed and when it passes, I don't care anymore.

I can do anything. My tongue flicks out and I tease him between my kisses that travel ever downward. When I look up his face is to the sky and his lips are moving silently. I don't know what he's telling himself, but I do know that I'm going to make him focus on me.

His legs are shaking when I work my way back up to his neck.

I'm so involved in my foreplay that I'm shocked when I feel his hands on my hips. The fear returns again. Will he hurt me?

He starts tracing his fingers against my skin, kissing my neck and shoulder just the way I want him to. The stubble on his face is a little scratchy, but doesn't ruin anything. A delicious thrill travels up my spine.

He pulls me to the ground with him, making me straddle his lap. I can feel him desperately wanting me, but not forcing me.

I curl my fingers in his damp hair and bury my face in it, taking in a smell I thought I would only ever imagine. He starts kissing my breasts, and I can't stop myself from arching my back.

His fingers probe and thrust, promising more if I want it.

I can open my eyes and see he's really there—dark graying hair in my hands, a strong arm around my waist, gently convincing my body down.

The sensation is more intense than I'd imagined. I can't stop the moan. I instinctively want him on his back, even though I've never had a man like this.

Deep inside, something guides my hips. Each move produces a tingle threatening to drive me insane. I want more with each moment. I want to beg him to not stop, but I won't let the words out.

I won't beg for anything. Never again. No matter how much I want to.

The electricity is unexpected—it shoots up my back, radiating across my shoulders and down my arms. I have to toss my head or the sensation will overwhelm me. I dig my fingers into the ground, lost in my own ecstatic thrill. He forces my hips down harder on his own, clasping me to him as he thrusts deeper with a shudder that freezes his arms in place and arches his back.

I can't believe I've done it. I've had sex on my terms. Amazing, mind-altering sex.

Reality splashes cold over me.

I just had mindless animal sex with my neighbor. In the middle of the night. In my backyard. Fantastic, thrilling sex with a man I know nothing about.

He doesn't say anything when I get up. I grab my robe and flee before he might try to stop me. In my house I fall against the door, giggling hysterically and crying. I don't know if I'm excited or terrified about what I've just done.

What now? What am I supposed to do? I can't face him after this. It would be more than awkward. It would be . . . Oh, hell, I don't know. In my mind I can see his face leering at me.

But the face doesn't match what little I know about him. The man who loiters in my shop playing games and drinking coffee. The man who politely looks away from Cheryl when her waist is exposed, or keeps his eyes firmly on hers. The man who bowed so gallantly when he unlocked my door. The man who . . .

Wore a mask tonight, just like mine.

Holy shit. He knew what time and which night to be out there waiting for me. He came prepared to play on my terms tonight. He's seen me like this before. For weeks. My back slides down the door as my hands cover my mouth in shock.

He'd known. For weeks he'd seen me. Why didn't he tell me?

The possibilities spin in my head. Has he been recording

me? Am I an internet porn star, now?

Breathe. I can breathe.

Would he brag about it with his friends?

Just breathe.

Does all of Honesty know?

Breathe.

"Whoring slut."

No. No, I'm not.

Am I?

***

The bell on my shop door has been ringing nonstop today. It's driving me crazy, but I'm thankful for the work. I'm a nervous wreck, and being busy is the only thing keeping me sane. Today Cheryl and Mikie have almost drowned in customers a few times, forcing me to abandon timecards to pick up the slack. I feel like I'm back in my mother's diner after church. *Where are these people coming from?*

"Small coffee, black and bold."

The voice doesn't register in my head as I repeat the order to Mikie and ring it up. The customer pays, steps off, and I ring up a book sale after that.

"Small black coffee, up!" Mikie yells into the crowd. For a high schooler, the kid knows how to project his voice. If things weren't so busy, he'd probably be singing along with the radio. Two books, two decaf iced chai, one orange soda-

Small coffee, black and bold.

My hand shakes as I realize who I just heard. I finish the tally at the register before I look up. He's nowhere to be seen.

"Damn!" Cheryl says, staring at the door. "I don't think I've ever seen anyone slam a hot coffee that fast." She looks at me, hustling a tray of dirty dishes to the back. "Did you forget to say *to go*?"

"I-I don't think so."

"Well, Small Coffee had somewhere to be in a hurry. He just picked it up, slammed it, and walked out."

I don't have time to gossip with her as another customer steps up to the register.

***

It isn't until after I lock up for the night, in my car, that I realize what happened. Jim had a habit of lounging around my shop. I remember the time he spilled the chess game when I took his cup. He didn't strike me as a man who would be that jumpy, but if he'd been coming in because he'd seen me, then . . .

Then what? Had he been trying to work up the guts to ask me out? The possibility is ridiculous, and I laugh so hard I cry.

It was one hell of a first date, I'll give him that.

But he ran from the shop today. That isn't the act of aman who brags about his conquests. That's someone trying to save face, either his or someone else's. He must have come today out of habit, and when he realized what he'd done, he ran before I could notice him.

He didn't want to embarrass me.

The thought makes me smile and my heart skips a beat, until I wonder if he just decided not to frequent the shop of a raging slut. By the time I get home I'm so spun up, I can't sleep.

What have I done? I'm tempted to pack my bags and

disappear in the night. Just abandon the house, the business and fly to my brother's. I can sell everything remotely, change my name and start over somewhere else.

My windchimes clang and tinkle at me from all around my house, literally surrounding me in calming, disjointed music. I sit at my kitchen table with a cup of hot chocolate, reminding me why I came to Colorado in the first place.

As much as I might want to, I can't just leave. Especially if everyone else is acting as if nothing has changed. I haven't heard word one from a customer or the kids I employ. If I was now a small town porn star, I'd expect to have heard about it from someone by now. True, it was only a few nights ago with Jim, but not the first in my yard. It might have been only me, but if he'd told people or posted a video, then something would've hit me already. A joke. A knowing leer. Cheryl or her mom pulling me into my office to tell me about this thing they'd heard. Deputy Travis taking me aside to tell me that I might have a stalker. Something.

I can't leave. Everything I have is here. Unless I'm financially ruined and declare bankruptcy, there's really no way out.

I drag myself into work the next morning. I managed to finish the timecards yesterday, but I still have to finish the paychecks. Then there's the inventory, the ordering, and the new schedule. Next week Cheryl's little sister Cheyenne is supposed to be starting and I want her on a shift that isn't with her sister. I think a shipment of beans is due in today . . .

I'm working on my fourth cup of coffee when the phone rings, and Cheryl takes it while ringing up a customer.

"Is this a joke?" I hear her demand into the phone. "Because it isn't funny." She listens again, and huffs impatiently. "Fine. But if this is a joke, you'd better hope I don't find you." She scribbles down the message and hangs up. She has to help two more customers before there's a lull in the traffic so she can give it to me. I'm starting another batch of blonde when she leans against the counter, frowning at the note from her pocket.

"So this guy calls with a special blend order," she begins.

I nod. There's nothing spectacular about that. Everyone knows I sell my blends by the half-pound if anyone wants it. Not many do, because they think the grocery store sells good enough coffee, and my stuff is more of a treat. I start wiping down the counter.

"Anyway, he says he wants *one half-pound of premium bitch slap*, and he'll pick it up on Saturday. He says you know what he's talking about."

I knock over a whipped cream dispenser and the chocolate syrup, making a mess. My hands are shaking. I try to focus on cleaning so I don't worry Cheryl.

Too late—she's already looking at me with concern. "Do you know who it is? Should we call the cops or something?"

"No, no. I know who it is." A nervous laugh escapes me. "I'll have it ready for him to pick it up."

Cheryl's still looking at me.

"It's something of a joke," I try to explain.

"So, *premium bitch slap* is funny?"

God, she's such a sweet girl. I don't know what I'm going to do when she leaves for college in a few weeks. "Sort of. It's a very long story."

Another customer comes in, sparing me the embarrassment of telling a girl not yet old enough to drink a story that would require at least three whiskey sours to swallow.

Saturday. I don't work Saturday days. I open and I close, but I don't work the day. Even the boss needs a break. He knows I don't work Saturdays. My stomach clenches, and I suppress a shiver. He wants my coffee, but doesn't want to embarrass me.

Another nervous titter slips from my mouth. Cheryl looks at me, but doesn't say anything.

***

I'm shaking as I walk through the kitchen to my back door. I've showered and shaved and spent a good thirty minutes drying my hair for tonight. I thought about make-up, but I'm wearing a mask, and even if I wasn't, every woman knows what happens to make-up during sex.

Will he be here? Was it just a wham-bam-thank-you-ma'am?

I can't see him as I step out. Is he hiding behind the bushes again? I step carefully through the grass, feeling hard dirt and tiny rocks beneath my feet. After getting locked out of my house I still don't wear shoes on the way to my frolics, but leave them on the porch. It's hard to feel sexy when you're naked and wearing hiking boots.

Perhaps it's a sign I'm losing my marbles.

I try not to laugh at that thought. I'm hoping to meet my neighbor, a man I barely know, for wild and crazy woodland sex, and I'm worried that not wearing shoes is a sign of insanity.

I still can't see him. There's no breeze at all, so even the normally clapping aspens are silent. It's eerie and quiet. Will I be frightened if he comes back? Or devastated if he doesn't?

I have to take a few breaths to pull myself together and

drop my robe. I don't even lift my arms to the sky before the scrub oaks rustle and he steps out.

He silently asks for my hand again. This time I don't hesitate. The press of his lips against my knuckles sends a chill up my arm. It takes everything I have not to throw myself at him. I'm delirious that he came to me again.

He waits for me to begin, to set the tone. I ask him to hold the trees again, not from fear, but because I want him to resist his desire for as long as possible, because I want to see how far he'll let me go before he can't stop himself.

He gasps and shudders under my fingers. When he finally breaks, he's more hungry than last time. He doesn't want to let me go when we've finished. He holds me and nuzzles my neck. His body shifts, and I know he wants to say something.

I run before he speaks a word.

When I let him lead the next time, he's wicked and tender until I nearly scream. I want to beg him to take me, but I bite my lip and trap him with my legs instead, forcing him to fulfill his promise.

The next time there was a fire about a hundred miles south of us. The smoke lay heavy and thick in the early morning dark and I could barely see because my eyes were watering, but the warmth and the smell of the fire made everything more primal.

In August he once ran off without finishing, leaving me furious and desperate. I couldn't help but giggle as the desire ebbed away, and I thought of all the wretched things I'd do to my knight of the woods next time.

In the fog, I nearly froze. He couldn't have been more comfortable, but we used our robes as blankets against soft drops from the sky. He held me so tight I almost couldn't get away. I had to stand in the shower for thirty minutes to warm up before racing out the door with wet hair to open my store.

He starts to bring a blanket. My blanket. The one from his couch. As the nights have gotten colder, he's become more tender. He knows we'll have to stop soon. Unless. . .

No. Outside, in the night, I can control what I have. But inside, under a roof, we'd talk. I know we would. Words would change everything. So would lights. I couldn't bear the shame of it.

I almost break down in tears thinking about it when I'm with him. I bite my lips. and I don't let out a single peep as we finish. Then I run, because I know I can't lay there with him or I'll cry. Then he'll ask me what's wrong.

I can't let him speak. I can't let him see me as more than this. I just can't.

In my house I collapse at the kitchen table, sobbing while the voice in my head taunts me. A stupid bitch playing at being a raging slut. *"Like he gives a shit about what you think,"* Larry's hateful voice says. *"He only wants your cunt."*

I'm grouchy all the next week, thinking about that. He doesn't come to my shop except to pick up his order when I'm not around, and it makes me wonder if it's really about the unspoken rules, or if he's just being a typical guy.

Now that school's back in session, I'm the only one in the café from open until three in the afternoon. There's less help, but with the death of summer there's less tourists, so business has slowed enough that I can handle it alone most of the time during the week.

A county sheriff's car parks in front of the café. Deputy Travis. Since the beginning of summer he's come in everyday for a drink, and to talk to me for a few minutes before returning to his shift. He's nice enough, but he's so damn happy all the time. How can you be a cop and be that happy? My brother is a cop—he's sarcastic and funny as all hell, but he's not so cheerful my teeth ache.

"Hi, Beautiful," he greets me as he comes in.

"Travis," I nod. "The usual?"

He digs out his wallet. "I think I'll shake it up this time." He points to the board with my monthly special. "What's this Apple Cider Spice?"

I shrug. "Just what it says. Hot apple cider with spices. Not the premade stuff, though."

"Homemade?"

I nod.

"I'll try it," he says as if it's a big deal.

I ring him up and turn to the warmer I have dedicated for the cider. I had to clean it a million times with vinegar to get the taste of coffee out of it, but now it holds my mother special recipe, sitting innocently on the counter. Travis prattles on about some show on TV, and I make polite noises about it, but I don't have time to watch anything on the boob-tube, so I really have no idea what he's talking about.

He smiles at me as he takes his cup, his blue eyes sparkling like a little boy's at a candy store. "So, the aspens are changing," he says, sniffing the heavenly scent of apple pie steaming from the lid.

Of course they're changing. It's late September. I know what he's getting at, though. A lot of Coloradans take to the mountains when the fall colors come. They're pretty enough, but since I'm surrounded by them at home, I don't feel the need to drive an extra hundred miles out of my way to see them.

"I was wondering if you'd like to go for a drive this Saturday," he suggests.

My mind runs through a possible list of excuses before

my mouth surprises me. "Sure. Just a few hours, though. I have to close."

The smile on his face is threatening to break his head. "Great. How about I pick you up at-"

"Here," I say. Wiping down my counter. What the hell am I doing? Going on a date? Just a little while ago I was pissed because . . . well, why was I pissed? Because it seems like Jim wants to talk to me? Because he isn't trying to talk to me here?

"You never could make up your damn mind," I hear.

Maybe that's the problem. I wasn't allowed to start dating until my senior year of high school, and look where that landed me. I've never really played the field, so maybe I just don't know what I want. A day out with someone else might help me figure that out. "Is nine too early?" I ask Travis.

He shakes his head. "No. No, nine's fine." He lifts his cup and takes a sip, nearly choking on it. His eyes water. "Is this stuff legal?" he wheezes.

I nod, grinning. "My mother's own recipe."

"It's a little strong," he croaks comically.

I laugh. "You should've tried her eggnog."

***

True to his word, Travis picks me up at my café at nine in the morning on Saturday. I almost sigh in relief when we leave the parking lot. Jim hadn't yet picked up his bag order, but I was still terrified he'd just pop in for a drink to see me waiting for Travis.

Why do I feel guilty about this? It's just a drive. *"Two-timing slut,"* I hear in my mind. I grimace and look out the window of Travis' jeep as we wind east.

65

I'm not two-timing. I just need to do something new. Even my therapist has told me that more than once. I need to clear my head. My situation with Jim has me all flavors of kattywampussed right now, which is why I'm now in the vehicle of a man whom I'm not really all that attracted to in the first place.

Wow.

I'm not attracted to Travis. At all.

Why the hell am I doing this?

The trees thin out and disappear just past Honesty and we make some meaningless small talk about work and life in general. Travis pulls up a slow jazz channel, smiling at me.

Oh, dear God. I might not think of this as a serious date, but he does.

"You can call me David, you know," he says.

I nod, looking out my window. "I remember. You told me."

The forest appears in a fiery blanket of reds and golds and the road dives into them. He shakes his head, the close-cropped grey hair reflecting the autumn light coming in through the window, making him look almost blonde. "You don't make things easy," he says.

"I'm a woman," I quip. "I'm not supposed to."

He smiles at the road. "I guess that's true."

I should at least give him a chance, I admit to myself. I barely know the guy. If I can screw my neighbor stupid without knowing his favorite color, then actually talking to someone should be easy.

When the words come out, I'm not proud of myself. It's the same crap I always hide behind when I want to appear social without being social. I ask him about how long he's lived in Colorado, what he did before joining the sheriff's office, did he go to college, what kind of books does he like at make him talk about himself.

It's amazingly easy to get someone sidetracked on a subject they know well, like themselves. True to the habits of most people, Travis doesn't disappoint. But the more Travis talks, the more I'm not interested. He sounds too eager to impress me, and the things he says are all wrong. He was briefly enlisted in the Air Force as a kid just to pay for a college degree. "I majored in English," he tells me, and I straighten a little in my seat.

Maybe there's something here after all.

"One of the most worthless degrees on the planet," he continues. "I got it because it was easy, but I could've gotten a BA in Underwater Basket-Weaving and no one would care other than I have a sheepskin."

Any hope I had has died a horrible, writhing death.

I glare out the window, clamping my mouth shut. English is not an easy degree if you're serious about it. If Travis thought it was easy and worthless, then I'd hate to see a sampling of his papers. It makes me angry that he practically had an education handed to him, and he can't see the value in it, even after he got it.

He keeps talking without much prompting from me. I notice he doesn't ask me a single question. True, I'm not comfortable with the idea of talking about myself, especially not now to Deputy Travis, but it would've been nice to know that he remembered he had a passenger, and not just himself to talk to. Unfortunately, I have to pay attention, if for no other reason than the fact that it's polite.

I imagine just casually mentioning that I'm having wild and crazy porn-movie sex in my backyard with my neighbor just because I can. I envision him driving off the road, his mouth wide open in shock.

Just the thought of it makes me cringe in horror and

giggle at the same time.

He glances at me. "What?"

I shake my head. "I was just remembering your face with cider," I lie.

"It was strong stuff," he admits. "I think I'll stick to my usual from here on out."

We enter Woodland Park and turn off towards Divide, and I'm getting more and more uncomfortable in Travis' car the longer I'm with him. Even Larry could at least pretend he was a passable conversationalist if he thought it would get him laid.

Travis knows where we are and where he's planning to go —he steers us through a subdivision and before I know it, we're on a dirt road. The views are fantastic, but the ride is bouncy, sometimes even scary, as we twist through hairpin turns past other trucks and cars on a road scarcely wide enough for one vehicle. Some of the steep drops outside the jeep are both beautiful and terrifying.

Travis eventually pulls over near a large cluster of toppled boulders with a nice view of another valley, and we get out to stretch our legs. We've been driving for close to two hours now, and Travis reveals a picnic lunch and a blanket in the back of his jeep.

I smile, remembering my manners and compliment the planning he's put into this outing. As we lunch, I keep Travis talking. He likes sports and his favorite is hockey. "I never miss a game, even if I have to record it." He likes to ski, even taking all the weekend shifts he can in the department during winter so that he can hit the slopes during the week when they're less crowded.

I don't like sports much, and I hate skiing.

The tension starts rising in my shoulders when the food runs out. Travis has acquired a look that most women recognize on men—he's hoping things will turn even just a smidge romantic. I busy myself with picking up the remnants and stuffing the trash in a plastic shopping bag rather than just sitting back and enjoy the mountain view.

When I look up, he's lounging on his blanket, smiling at me. I am suddenly very creeped-out. Not even my neighbor, naked except for a mask, looks so expectant.

I can't deal with this. "We should probably start heading back," I announce cheerfully, pretending to be completely oblivious.

He looks disappointed, but he nods without argument. The road twists and turns as we wind further down the mountain and into Monument, where we pick up the interstate to Colorado Springs and then back up Highway 24 to Honesty. I'm exhausted even though I haven't done a single moment of driving. When he pulls up at Java Books, he looks at me. "I had a nice time."

"It was a pretty drive," I agree, gathering my purse and jacket, trying not to look at him.

"Maybe we could do something else soon?"

I shrug, while I cringe inside. "Maybe," I say vaguely.

He frowns at my answer but I don't give him a chance to comment. I close the passenger door, fleeing into Java Books where I can hide in my office with the door closed to have a nice little nervous breakdown.

***

Before going out to meet my knight, I stare at myself in the mirror. I can be brave. I can talk to him. I can at least kiss him. I've done almost everything else to the man. Tonight is going to be our last meeting unless I can muster the courage to speak. If my outing with Travis was a disaster, how much worse can this be?

Outside he wraps us in his blanket and takes his time, making certain I know that in every moment his thoughts are focused solely on me. He's not in a rush to leave. He has nowhere to go and nothing to do that's more important than me. It may have started as just sex, but somehow he makes every kiss, every touch, feel like he's worshiping something sacred.

For the first time, I know the difference between sex and making love.

It's something I've always wanted, something that's been denied me for my entire life. It's delicate and fragile, yet stronger than anything I've ever had.

And I am absolutely terrified of it.

He tries to kiss my mouth, and I refuse him again. I trace the tattoo on his upper arm, like I've done our past few meetings as things became less hurried and more sensual. It's only two words, faded with time. I want to ask him what it means, but that would mean speaking.

I still can't speak. I'm too afraid.

He touches my lips with his thumbs, and I can feel him begging me to kiss him. Pleading with me to at least say a single word.

My knight wants me to stay with him, but I leave when we finish, running back to my empty house.

Chapter 5

Game Changer

I drink my lady's brew every morning. It's become something of a ritual for me, and today I need that ritual more than ever. I glare at the snow in my back yard. It does this almost every Halloween, but this time it makes me angry, and my left arm aches with the tension.

The light dusting isn't enough to shovel, but it is enough to let you know that frostbite is in the air. It definitely closes the door for our meetings until it's warmer again. Who wants to explain that story in the emergency room? *Well, doc, I know it sounds strange, but it's really only kinky the first time.*

I'm lonely and frustrated as hell. I've never been to her door except the one time I failed to warn her off of her nightlife. I don't even know her name, really. She may have told me once at the mailboxes, but I can't remember. I tried looking up her address in the water district paperwork that everyone has, but all I can find is a first initial with a last name. R. Linkous. What's the "R" stand for? Rachel? Ramona? Rebecca?

Heavy metal doesn't calm my brain down—it just keeps galloping faster and faster. Rowan? Raina?

Even my books aren't even helping me.

Renee? Rhonda?

If I stay in my house, I'll go insane.

I pull on my coat, and rifle through my shed for my tools. Simmons has a few odds and ends with his property that need to be addressed. I have no idea what they are, but I know they're there. I just have to find them.

Simmons isn't home when I get there, or at least he doesn't answer the door, and that's fine. I start checking his fence line, and pushing off his mare who keeps nudging me because she thinks I might have treats for her. I nail down a few sections that are questionable, and fuss a little with the gate. The mare has decided to ignore me, but her son has taken up the task now, and is obviously looking for attention. Convincing him to go away is a touchy business. My knowledge of horses ends at "bigger than me," but I manage to get him to leave me alone after a while.

My outback hat keeps my head warm, although my ears are a little nippy as I fight with the latch on Simmons' barn. It's in desperate need of attention. For a jarhead, he really knows how to let things go until the last minute.

As I work, I don't get any less frustrated. The "no talking" rule feels like it extends to everything. I don't dare go to her house unless there's a reason other than wanting to be with her. Before our meetings, I would go to her coffee shop and lounge around, but the "no talking" rule put a stop to that.

She never actually said "don't" see her, but it feels like she'd rather not. Like if we do, it'll somehow ruin everything.

Maybe I'm wrong. Maybe she'd be happy as hell if I asked her out for lunch or something. It doesn't feel that way, though.

To not speak during our meetings was part magical, and part challenge. Once I thought I knew she wanted to use her voice, I tried everything I could think of to tease a sound out of her without using my own.

Now it's a leash that's hurting my neck.

Even with music, my house is quiet. And irritating. And more lonely than ever. And If I'm really honest about it, Simmons' place isn't much better.

As I fight with the barn latch, which somehow became so twisted it just needs to come off so I can beat it back into shape with a hammer, I realize that I don't want to be alone.

"What the hell are you doing, Beaumont?"

I look behind me to see the grumpy Santa glaring at my work. "Your latch is all twisted," I tell him. "I'm fixing it."

Simmons rolls his eyes. I beat the metal back into shape and reattach it to the door of his barn. "When did you get back?" I grunt as the screws squeak against the cold wood.

"I never left. It's called a *nap*. Maybe you should try it."

"I'm not that old."

Simmons frowns at me. "Did she dump you?"

"What?"

"The girl you were mooning over. Did she dump you?"

The latch isn't pretty, but at least it works without a fight, now. I pack my tools up. "Not exactly."

"Then what, exactly?"

"She's busy," I say. It isn't a lie. Anyone who goes into Java Books can see she's busting her ass.

Simmons sighs. "Do you want to come in?"

Translation: Do you need to talk?

I shake my head. "No. I'm all done here." I heft my tool box back to my truck, and head home. I'm not interested in talking to Simmons about the truly bizarre relationship I have with our neighbor. I just need a damn hobby.

At home, I have to stop the clock because the ticking is just too much in an empty house. The music is just as annoying, which annoys me more, because it usually isn't. I make another pot of coffee and find myself staring out random windows, fantasizing about just walking up to her house and ringing the bell. I can't bring myself to do it, though. I cross my arms over my chest and glare at nothing, letting my left flex and release because I just don't know what to do, or even how to do it.

Big tough First Sergeant can't even knock on a lady's door.

Inviting myself into her nighttime romps had been one thing, but somehow going to her house feels like an invasion of privacy. It's weird and makes no sense when I try to logic my way through it, but there it is.

It's another unspoken rule.

***

When I knock on the door of my son's house for Thanksgiving, I've got a bag of Java Books Dark Decaf under my arm. I bought it last Saturday when I picked up my normal order. I thought about bringing the custom stuff, but not many people like coffee that bold.

That and I don't want to share my lady's brew. It's mine and I have no problems admitting that I can be selfish about some things. I don't understand what we have, or even if we have anything at all, but I do know we have our shared taste in coffee, and I am not about to share that with someone else if I have a say in the matter.

When I walk in the house, Missy is trying to keep a nine month old Rosy clean in some formal baby dress of black velvet with lace everywhere. It's a battle I remember as being futile with Lucas before he was ten. Tommy runs up and seizes my legs, happy that Grandpa is here to play with him, since Mom is busy with the baby and Dad is in the kitchen.

I love my son's wife to pieces, I really do, but Missy could burn a cold sandwich, so it's best to just let my son do the cooking.

And what a surprise—Janice is there, looking delightfully floral. She smiles at me with that look guys recognize when they're being actively hunted by a member of the opposite sex. It's been four months since I saw her last. Has she really been unable to find anyone else to catch her eye?

Maybe she has, and they all did what I want to do right now—run away screaming and join a monastery. I suddenly wish I'd brought something stronger than decaf.

A lot stronger.

I square up my shoulders and march into the kitchen to busy myself with my son's coffee maker while he fusses with a can opener. I don't want to leave the safety of the kitchen for the battlefield in the living room, but there's no way around it. Tommy desperately wants someone to play with, and there just isn't enough room to help my son with anything.

I do my best to avoid Janice by playing army men with my grandson. His tactics regarding ambushes and cover fire need work, but he still wins by the sheer virtue of being "the giant that stomps on everything." It's hard to argue with that kind of firepower.

Janice and Missy are talking when Tommy goes to the bathroom, leaving me a moment to confront my son. Long legs give me the advantage of being able to rush without looking like it.

I stand at the sink filling a glass of water. "Tell me you're not trying to set me up with her," I whisper as he's struggling to get the bird out of the oven.

"I didn't find out she was coming until last night, Dad," he says with a grunt. "Missy invited her. I guess she's alone, so-" he shrugs. Then he smiles at me. "I do know she was very interested when she found out you were coming over."

I almost choke on my water. "Haven't I paid enough for my crimes?"

He slouches a little. "I'm not being mean, Dad. I was trying to make a joke."

"It isn't funny."

I want to say more, but Tommy runs into the kitchen. I herd him back out so he doesn't end up wearing a broccoli casserole before he gets to the table. Tommy wants to play cars now, but I make him clean up the army men first. He pouts about that until I rummage through his room to bring out the large dump truck I got him last Christmas, and tell him that we have to take all the army men to the hospital because the mean giant stomped on them.

Tommy immediately falls in love with this idea, and I start making wounded noises for the toys that get thrown into the truck. "Ow! Where's my insurance card? Hey! Get your foot out of my eye! Where's my boot? I can't find my boot!"

I hear polite laughter from the couch, and I look to see Janice smiling at me, her eyes sparkling in delight. Missy smiles too, despite having to dodge Rosy's hands making grabs for her earrings. "I told you he was good with Tommy," she says to Janice.

Tommy pushes the dump truck to his room, and I follow behind him, rolling my shoulders because it feels like a target's been painted on my back.

I can almost taste the bourbon.

When dinner is pronounced ready, I help Tommy wash his hands, then we make our way to the dining room. Missy has almost finished strapping Rosy into her high chair. Tommy takes his seat between Rosy and his dad at the head of the table, and Missy takes her seat at the other end. I'm seated between my son and Janice.

Hooray.

There's the obligatory holding of hands and a short prayer from my son, which I don't pay much attention to, in part because of Janice's hand. It's thin and delicate, with manicured nails and cold skin that feels like it'll break if I squeeze too hard.

I have no fear of breaking my lady of the woods. She can have a grip like iron when she wants to, and not just with her hands.

That thought banishes the desire for bourbon, bringing a goofy grin to my face. I try to drown myself in my water glass as soon as the prayer is over to hide it.

Platters and bowls get passed around. Rosy decides the mashed potatoes are better used as finger paints than as food, and that cranberries look absolutely stunning in her hair.

Tommy does better, but I can already see the shirt is going to be a lost cause, and he argues about having to eat vegetables.

"You're five years old so you have to eat five beans," I announce to end the argument. Mom and Dad both agree. I know as the Grandpa, I'm not supposed to be authoritarian, but the kid's whining is grating on my nerves, and I need to maintain some semblance of decency at my son's table. It wouldn't have been an issue for me at all if Janice hadn't been there.

Tommy isn't sympathetic to my situation. He glares at me.

Sorry, kid.

Janice clears her throat. "It's nice to see a man who's good with children."

Aw, hell. Here we go.

"I was worried when you didn't call about the hike back in August," she says.

"I'm sorry." I try to throw something that sounds sincere into my voice, but it's hard to not come off as sarcastic. "I totally forgot about it. Things just got so busy it slipped my mind." *And having a little porno-styled romp in the woods once a week takes it out of you.* I grab my water glass and start drinking again before anyone can see my smirk, only to realize my glass is empty.

I have to get up to refill it at the kitchen sink, and I'm relieved she hasn't followed me, but I can't hide in there forever. I putter around with a coffee mug. "Does anyone want coffee? It's decaf," I call out before leaving the safety of the kitchen bunker.

Tommy and Janice both say they'd like some, so I spend a few minutes making a hot chocolate for my grandson while trying to figure out if there's a way to get out of giving Janice any of my lady's coffee, even if it is just the common decaf. I can't think of a way that doesn't involve breaking the coffee maker and making a royal mess all over my son's kitchen.

Tommy's hot chocolate is done, and I bring that out first

for my grandson, then go back for Janice's coffee, but that's only a delaying tactic. With my water glass filled, and two mugs of coffee in my other hand, I don't have any more excuses to avoid rejoining the table. I screw up my courage to go back out on the front lines, taking my seat next to Janice once more.

"This coffee is wonderful," she says as she puts the cup back on the table after a dainty sip.

"I got it from the café in Honesty," I say.

She smiles at me, twirling a lock of over-blonde hair in her finger in a gesture I don't expect to see from a woman her age.

Shit.

She's trying to play the "young and fetching woman" role to catch my eye, now. "The singles group is having a Christmas party in a few weeks. Maybe you could come to that," she suggests.

I do not want to be this woman's date, implied or otherwise. "I don't know if-"

"Oh, come on, Dad. It'd be good for you to get out of the house, mingle with new people and have some fun." Missy is smiling at me, her eyes bouncing between Janice and I, totally oblivious to the fact that I want to kill her.

Which "her" is up for debate at this point.

"You were saying that you thought the loneliness was getting on your nerves," my son agrees.

What the hell? Lucas knows I don't want anything to do with Janice, and here he is throwing me at her like a steak to a starving dog. I look at him, and he's already shoved a forkful of mashed potato in his mouth, avoiding my gaze. I realize he probably didn't mean to set me up with Janice, so much as to encourage me to get out of the house.

I kick him under the table anyway. Not hard enough to

hurt, but enough to let him know I'm not happy.

I can be a vindictive bastard.

Janice is talking again, but I don't hear what she's saying. It's something about finding support in the church, and how I shouldn't hide in the mountains alone or some crap like that. When she lays her hand on mine and squeezes it, I panic.

"I have a girlfriend," I say without thinking about it.

Janice whips her hand away from mine like it's an angry snake. She looks like I just slapped her.

"Hey, that's great, Dad." Lucas is actually happy for me. "What she like?"

"Ah . . . well . . . "

Janice is watching me, not believing just yet that I actually have a girlfriend. Her eyes narrow slightly under the brows that have been plucked too thin for my taste.

To be fair, I don't know that I have one either. "She owns Java Books, up in Honesty," I say. "We actually live next door to each other." *And the sex is unbelievable, but don't ask me her name, because I still don't know it.*

"You should've brought her with you, Dad." Missy is all sorts of excited now that there's something new to talk about. She may enjoy the stay-at-home-mom thing, but she's starving for adults to talk to, and new things to talk about other than children and their antics.

"Yes, you should've," Janice agrees. "It would've been nice to meet her." She's still convinced the mystery girlfriend is a lie, but she's too polite to actually say it.

It has been way too long since I've played poker, but if I'm going to get away from this woman, I have to make her believe that I'm holding the best hand. "Well, we're still new to each other," I say. "It's a pretty recent thing, you know, and that can be awkward around the holidays, and all that.

We're just taking things slow, for now."

I cram a piece of stuffing in my mouth as the questions come, buy me time to think. *Yeah. Taking things slow. Just sex, no actual conversation or anything.*

The thought starts me laughing, and I choke on my food. It's not a sensation I enjoy, but it at least steers the conversation away from "my girlfriend" for a while.

"I'm just glad you're getting out again," Lucas says with a genuine smile once I've stopped trying to die at his table.

"So am I," I croak.

I'm not certain how I dodge the obvious questions about "my girlfriend" for the rest of the evening, but I somehow make it through Thanksgiving alive and in one piece. I would've run out just after dinner, but that would've insulted my son. The man spends a week prepping for a big holiday dinner, and even after seven years I'm still terrified that one wrong move will banish me from his life again.

The evening winds down and I help Janice into her coat, then escort her to her car because it's the polite thing to do. I'm hoping she won't try to hug me or give me peck on the cheek or something like that. She doesn't try, and I may have closed her door harder than I meant to, because she jumped in her seat, looking at me with wide eyes.

I nearly collapse in my own truck with relief. I fire it up, and get the hell out of dodge before something can block my retreat, heavy metal music slamming in the cab.

We can't get a good signal for the radio in Honesty, so most of my new music exposure in the genre happens when I'm in the Springs.

Maybe the sound of some guy growling incoherently like an ape could scare Janice off?

Probably not tonight. My windows are up, and I don't crank the volume higher than it needs to be to hear it.

My desire for bourbon fades the further away I get from Janice. My nerves are shot to hell, and a bourbon is still tempting, but I keep my eyes focused on the road, heading straight for the pass without looking for a place to stop.

I try to think about something, anything, that will take my mind off drinking, and my thoughts drift to my neighbor. Halfway up the mountain I have to turn off the radio because the signal is more static than not. In the quiet, things get interesting in my head.

The girlfriend story came so easily to me. As I said it, it didn't feel like a lie. It felt like something I really had. Something I wanted. Something worth trying for. When I pull into my driveway, it's after ten and I've made a decision. The muscles under my tattoo clench and release.

I don't like the rules.

It's time to change the game.

***

I start loitering around my lady's café again when I know she's there. I don't harass her or try to make her life hell, but I'm not going back into hiding. She sees me and gets flustered almost every time, but I stay polite and smile. How was your holiday? How's business? It's a little slow right now, how about a game of checkers? *When will you actually talk to me?*

She manages to shoot me down almost every time. Fine, thanks. Business is slow, but it always is when the tourists aren't around. I can't play right now—inventory, you understand. Maybe later.

There's a host of regulars at her store. Some hang around, and others just come in for a cup and then leave about the same time every day. There's a county deputy who always comes in around eleven in the morning, asks for "the usual" and tries to chat her up a bit before he goes back to his patrol car. He always greets her with a smile and a "Hey, Beautiful," that sounds so familiar my teeth hurt.

I don't know who he is, but I can smell the competition a mile away. I can tell by the way they talk that it's all polite surface work on her part, but the fact that she's willing to give him that much is enough to make me clench my left arm until it aches, every time.

I was here first, shit-bird.

I guess male territorial instincts don't go away with age, after all.

Once I hear him mention that they haven't gone out since they drove to see the aspens. "When are you off next?" he asks. "Maybe we could do something. Like Christmas shopping."

It takes everything I have to stay in my seat, and not insert myself in their converstaion. It hurts to know that my lady went on a date with Deputy Dawg while we were playing in the midnight woods. The fact that she hasn't gone out with him since gives me hope, though. The peak viewing season for aspens had to have been two, maybe even three months ago.

And he's offering to go Christmas shopping with her as another date.

Damn, he's desperate for another chance.

I have yet to meet a man who enjoys battling the crowds to shop for anything. I'm almost willing to go to a store between Halloween and Christmas, but it's only for the household essentials.

Then again, if she told me she needed to go gift shopping, and it sure would be helpful if someone came along, I probably would without a peep.

Stones and glass houses.

I have to struggle not to grin at my book when she shoots him down. "It was a nice drive," she tells him with an easy shrug. "But I've already done all my shopping, and I just don't have time for much else right now."

I glance up at Deputy Dawg to see him frowning at his cup. He looks like he's going to say something but decides against it, choosing instead to leave the store while she busies herself with wiping down the counter.

I see her shoulders relax as he leaves, and I duck into the pages of my book once more, hiding my grin behind my coffee.

***

There's not much to do between Thanksgiving and Christmas. I don't put up a tree because I'm the only one in my house. I don't put out lights and decorations because it's a pain in the ass, and pensions only go so far for an electrical bill. There isn't any snow on the ground this year, so I don't have any driveways to clear. My neighborhood just doesn't have much for the handyman this season. Only the Munn's hired me to hang lights this year. Last year, I almost broke my neck on their house with all the ice, but there hasn't been jack for snow this year, so it wasn't nearly as exciting.

Even television sucks, but I always thought it did, so that isn't anything new.

My music keeps the quiet at bay, but only barely.

Flipping through my books, I look for my favorite stories. Passages that can make me smile. I do the same thing at Java Books, but if I spend too much time there, my lady might try to get a restraining order, and that's a headache I just don't need.

And I'd be handing my head to Deputy Dawg on a plate. He's probably a nice enough guy, but I don't want to set him up as some kind of frickin' hero with her.

I'm bored. But it's a nervous kind of boredom. The kind that makes you feel like you should be doing something, but you're so unfocused you can't figure out what you should do, so you end up just pinging around the house and pissing yourself off.

Simmons caught me on his property again, fixing the house numbers on his entry gate. He told me that if I wasn't going to come inside and tell him what the hell my problem was, then he'd shoot me the next time I came over.

It's bullshit. I know he won't shoot me unless I actually kick in his door. But I can tell he's getting irritated with me randomly fixing up his property without him asking me to.

Banished to my house again, I end up cleaning and fixing everything that I've put off over the last few months. That only takes me a week, and I'm back to staring out windows and going nuts.

Christmas is coming up, but I'm a lazy bastard, and bought my son and his family gift cards in early November. I think Tommy's going to blow a gasket when he sees a $50 gift card just for him, but I'm the Grandpa. That means it's my job to shake the kids up like a soda, and hand them back to the parents. I do try to take that job seriously when I can.

I would get a gift for my lady, but I have no idea what she likes. It's dangerous for a man to buy gifts for a woman he doesn't know well. I sure as hell don't want to screw up like Deputy Dawg, whatever the hell it was he did.

My eyes fall on the wool blanket on my couch. *"I was tempted to keep your blanket."* It isn't much. Kind of grey.

And we were wrapped in it the last time we made love.

Digging around for a box that doesn't look like something puked in it is a bit of a challenge, but I find a paper carton with a lid holding bills that need shredding. It isn't fine art, but it will do.

I stuff the blanket in the box and dash off a quick note. Something freakishly cute. "In case your tootsies get cold."

I stare at my package. It still needs something. Something more personal. Something small enough to fit in the box with the blanket. I remember Simmons giving me some old antlers he had lying around about a year or so ago.

An idea is spawned from the corniest regions of my brain.

It's cold in my shed. My scroll saw shrieks through the antler, sending up the smell of burning hair. My drill does the same thing and for a heart-stopping moment, I think the button is too thin and the drill will break it. I manage to finish the hole without destroying the tiny disk, and I grab a rasp and a few sheets of sandpaper to take with me back inside.

It takes me two days of dedicated work to shape the ring the way I want it. I use my pinky finger to size it up, since I remember being able to do that the few times I ever bought Jenny jewelry. I'm not trained in the art of carving things, but I get the antler ring polished up nice and smooth and then leave it in the box with the blanket on her porch, topped off with wrapping paper and a ribbon.

It's romantic in a corny sort of way, but most presents men give women usually are. I just hope it's better than anything Deputy Dawg may have plans for.

Two days later I find a small gift box on my own front step. Inside is a bracelet made of colorful string and a lock of braided brown hair. The grin on my face has got to be the goofiest looking thing on the planet. I don't hesitate to put it on.

I'm still in the game.

My lady smiles shyly at me when I come into her shop next, which is a big improvement over the last few weeks. She isn't wearing the ring, and I'm disappointed, but she does work with coffee and all that, so maybe she just doesn't want to ruin it.

When there's just us in the shop, I settle in front of a checkerboard, and pat the table loud enough for her to hear. She looks up at me.

"Let's have a game," I say.

She looks around for an excuse. Her counters are clean. Her books are straight. Even the floor is tidy. Mainly because I mopped it while she cleaned her counters. She tried to protest when she saw me doing it, but I was already halfway done by then, so it was kind of pointless.

"All right," she agrees. "One game."

We set up the board and hop the checkers for a while in silence. "So what's your name?" I ask.

She jerks like she's been kicked. "What?"

"Your name," I repeat. "I'd like to know what it is."

"You've been here how many times and you've never caught my name?" she asks incredulously.

"All your employees call you *Boss*. That's it. Every time I've come in here, I can't recall a single person calling you by name."

"*What's in a name?*" she says cryptically at the board, hopping a chip and removing it from play.

Romeo and Juliet. "Is it Rose?" I ask, suddenly excited. My granddaughter's name is "Rosaline," but I wouldn't mind another "Rose."

She nods in approval. "Very good. But no, that's not my

name."

I glare at the board. "Rumplestiltskin," I mutter darkly, positioning another piece for a trap on the board.

"Excellent. Two for two."

I take in a breath through my nose, trying to banish the growing irritation. People our age are single for a reason. Most of us have battle scars, and while I'm just now starting to get an idea of what hers are, I just wish she wouldn't use them like frickin' armor.

"Will you please give me your name?" I ask softly.

She continues staring at the board, frowning like she's in a major tactical bind. "Regina."

"I'd like to talk to you, Regina," I say.

She licks her lips. "Talking used to get me into a lot of trouble." She manages to slip around my pieces and sets her chip on my line. "King me."

I do, then hop three at once. "What kind of trouble?"

The bell on the door rings. A small gaggle of high schoolers come in, babbling about Christmas Break. Regina stands to get back to work. "Game over."

I smile as I gather my coat and hat to retreat for the day.

Her name is Regina.

Chapter 6

Issues or Subscriptions?

I spend Thanksgiving alone. Which is fine. A lot better than previous years. No worrying about what will happen if the ham isn't done perfect, or if I'm out of frozen rhubarb for strawberry-rhubarb pie. Just me, a movie, and a baked pizza with my favorite toppings and ice cream that I don't have to share.

But I'm still alone.

And my knight from the woods has become my stalker. He's back to lounging around my shop for a few hours every day, thumbing through books, and taking on all comers for the games I have set out. He even spent a whole day focused on a jigsaw puzzle from start to finish.

He smiles and tries to talk to me, to get me to sit for a moment and play a game with him. It's irritating because of the weird, upside-down relationship we have. I feel exposed, more so than I ever did in my back yard.

On the other hand, Deputy Travis irritated me because

he kept talking at me, not with me, on our one and only date.

"I knew you were just a slut."

Today, I actually play several games with Jim because the store is just that dead for customers, and if I cleaned my counters any more the steel finish would wear off.

And it helps silence the hateful voice in my head.

"King me," I say. Again.

Jim does with a smirk. "She speaks."

I look at the board, waiting for his next move, in every sense. He likes to sit backwards in the chairs pulled up to the tables when he plays or reads. Which is weird, but in a charming sort of way.

He hops a chip, and I look at one of the clocks I have scattered all over the store. It's two-thirty on Tuesday, and the lunch rush is gone, not that there was much of one. The chances of anyone coming through that door between now and four-thirty is pretty low because there's a screaming, freezing wind howling through, scaring off even the bravest of regulars.

Except Jim. Who has a bag of my own blend somewhere in his pantry, making the entire visit a social one. He drums his fingers on the back of his chair, waiting for my next move, in more ways than one.

"Are you always this annoying?" I ask before I think about it. I'm shocked I said that to him, and keep my face studiously on the board. Sure, I talk like that to my employees, but I'm something like thirty-five years older than they are, so things are different.

He raises an eyebrow. "If being annoying is what it will take to get you to talk to me, then yes, Regina, I am."

The comment irritates me. The casual use of my name makes me feel like he's got one up on me. His desire for more than what I've already given is frustrating. He's a guy; they're only supposed to want sex. The fact that I can't seem to make myself talk to him is even more irritating. I lean back in my chair with my arms folded across my chest. "So you're playing with me? How many points for when I get pissed?"

It's all a show of bravado on my part. I'm terrified of what he'll do now that I've shown something of a spine. A flicker of worry dashes across his eyes. He folds his hands over the top of the chair, his gaze never leaving mine. Instinct tells me to drop my eyes, but I force myself to at least focus on his eyebrows. When he speaks, my mouth drops at the natural cadence and feeling he pours into his words.

"If we shadows have offended, think but this, and all is mended." He doesn't finish the quote. He doesn't need to. Now his eyes are dancing at me.

I can't help but smile. "A Midsummer Night's Dream," I say.

He straightens. "I can't remember the rest," he admits. That easy grin on his face is disarming, and I feel safe for a moment.

"I would've thought you more of a Richard the Third kind of guy," I say.

"A horse, a horse?" He shakes his head. "I don't like the propaganda crap, I never did."

I gape at him. "Are you a professor in hiding or something?"

He shakes his head again with a smile, tapping out a cadence on the table with his hands. "Career Army enlisted. Technically, I was a mechanic. I retired about thirteen years ago."

The bell on my door rings, and a wall of freezing air

blows Deputy Travis in for the second time today, bundled in his uniform coat and hat. "Damn, it is cold out there!" he declares as if it were a news flash. He smiles at me, seated with Jim in front of the checkerboard. "Hey, Beautiful! I'm glad to see you actually sitting for once."

I stand, moving for my counter. "The usual, Travis?" I ask. He's told me several times to call him *David*, but I stick with the Travis embroidered on the uniform patch to keep him at arm's length.

Especially after our first and only date.

Travis sniffs with a nod. "With as cold as it is, hell, yes."

He talks about nothing in particular while I assemble his drink. I glance behind him to look at Jim. For less than half a second, the gaze he levels at Travis' back is pure murder. Travis catches the direction of my eyes and turns, only to see Jim sweeping his short canvas coat onto his arms with a graceful swirl.

He's leaving.

I don't want him to leave me alone with Travis. I don't think Travis would hurt me, it's just . . .

It's just what?

I realize that I like him more than Travis. A lot more.

"Where are you going?" I manage to ask before Jim fights the door open. His mouth quirks, and he sweeps the beat-up outback hat from his head to his chest, once more feeding me lines with a depth of feeling I haven't ever heard in them, even when my own professor read them aloud in class.

"*The weight of this sad time we must obey, to speak what we feel, not what we ought to say.*"

King Lear.

And with that, he was gone.

Travis frowns and hooks a gloved thumb over his shoulder at the door. "What was that all about?"

I want to cry, and for more than one reason.

***

My therapist is in Colorado Springs; I meet her on Thursday evenings. It's only December fifth, but it's our last meeting until after the new year, and I can't keep it all buttoned up any longer. I spill the whole story, from beginning to end. My personal time in the yard, Jim joining in, my date with Travis, everything. I don't get into the pornographic details, but by the time I'm done, all she can do is stare at me.

It's horrible. She sits across from me in a chair that makes the space feel more like a living room than a doctor's office, her slacks neat and tidy with her business conservative blouse and wide brown eyes that can't stop staring at me.

I hide behind my hands, wretchedly ashamed at everything I've done. *"Fucking slut."*

She rubs her face and tucks a graying lock of short hair behind her ear. "Well. That's quite an adventure."

I can't help but to laugh. It's too ridiculous, too incredible, not to.

Dr. Beas readjusts herself in her chair, crossing and re-crossing her legs, her grey pants loudly rustling in the sudden quiet. I can tell she's never come across something quite like this. "Were you worried about mentioning any of this before?" she asks.

I frown, looking out the huge window she has on her north wall. It's night, and I can't see anything other than my own reflection in the glass, but it's better than looking at her.

I swallow. "I'm a slut, aren't I?"

"No. I don't think so."

"Let's be honest—that's what women are called who act like this, right?"

"Words can mean a lot of different things, depending on who says them and why."

"I'm a slut," I mutter.

"Your husband used words to hurt you, among other things," she says. "But I do not think you're a slut, by any stretch of the imagination."

I sigh. *"Slut."* The voice in my head is just hateful, with a touch of smugness.

"Let's start from the beginning," she says. "Why, exactly, did you start?"

"I don't know," I say. "I guess I felt like I needed to do something completely different than what the old me would do." I flop backwards on the couch. "You told me to do something exciting to break things up."

She raises her finger in protest. "I meant something like skydiving, or zip-lining, or maybe even a tattoo. I did not mean for you to put yourself into an illegal and potentially dangerous situation."

"Illegal? It was in my yard, surrounded by trees, where almost no one could see."

"But someone did see, and he could've called the police and filed charges for indecent exposure if he were so inclined," she points out.

The thought of Deputy Travis coming to my house to lead me away in a pair of handcuffs because I was frolicking naked in my backyard is mortifying, to say the least. "Well, it's done now, and I don't know what to do next."

My therapist bites her lip in thought, templing her fingers together in front of her face. "Well, that's true—the past can't be undone." She frowns for a moment. "I'd like to ask you some questions, and I hope you feel comfortable enough to be honest with me. You know that nothing leaves this room, but if it gets uncomfortable, I want you to let me know."

I swallow hard, suddenly feeling very small. "Okay."

"At any time, when you were with your partner, did he make you feel uncomfortable?"

"No."

"How did he make you feel?"

I look for the words. The voice in my head comes up with some real winners, but I kick them to the side. "Special. Like I was the only important thing in the world."

"You said he was loitering at your work. Is he threatening you?"

"No."

"Do you ever feel unsafe when he's around?"

"Awkward, but not unsafe."

"Do you think he will threaten you in some fashion?"

"No."

"Did he ever force you to have sex? Coerce you somehow?"

"No."

"Did it ever feel like you were forcing him?"

"No."

"Did you use protection?"

I blink at her. I'd had my tubes tied years ago at my husband's insistence. I'm fifty-three years old. Protection had never occurred to me. "No."

Dr. Beas doesn't say anything negative about it, but I do see a tiny flicker of concern in her eyes. "Have you been tested for disease?"

I squirm on the couch. I feel like I'm being scolded by

my mother again, which is funny in a bizarre sort of way because Beas can't be much older than me. "Not recently. Not since the divorce."

"Have you shown any symptoms of disease?"

"Not that I've noticed."

She looks at me for a moment. "I think you should get a panel just to be on the safe side. Other than that, I think you're incredibly lucky."

"So what should I do?"

"Well, you said he's trying to talk to you, and you don't feel threatened by him, so perhaps talking to him isn't a bad idea?"

I feel very cold. "I can't do that."

She taps her mouth with her fingers. "The woman who first walked through my door three years ago wasn't nearly as bold as you are now. But it isn't uncommon for women such as yourself to develop problems with intimacy."

"I've had some of the wildest sex imaginable, and you think I have intimacy issues?" I can't help but laugh.

She smiles lightly. "I think the years you were abused have crossed some wires. Intimacy isn't just sex. It's talking with your partner. Trusting them. Letting them in to see who you really are."

Just the thought of actually saying something of value to Jim is enough to make my stomach flip.

"The fact that you tried to go out on a normal date with another man is commendable, and I'm proud of you for that. But you said he spent the whole time talking at you, not with you, and that's why you wrote him off, right?"

"Yeah," I admit. There's a little more to why I'm not thrilled with the idea of giving Travis a second chance, but that was a big part of it.

"And this—Jim?"

I nod.

"Jim is now trying to do just what you said you wanted, and you feel an attraction of some kind to him, so I think it might be beneficial if you talk to him. If he's hanging around and he isn't threatening you in any way, then maybe you should try. In public. Get to know each other."

I'm bouncing a leg, looking out the window. Just thinking about saying anything of importance to Jim is terrifying.

She tilts her head to the side, regarding my jittery leg. "I sense a problem with that idea."

"It's against the rules," I say before I even think about how ridiculous it sounds.

"So the two of you discussed rules of engagement before everything started?"

"Well, no. We never actually talked. It's more implied."

She leans back in her chair. "What are these rules?"

I squirm some more. "No kissing the lips. No talking."

"Is that it?"

"The no talking rule kind of extended to meeting each other in public."

The clock on her shelf ticks away the time. "So you never actually discussed these rules. Neither of you actually said yes, this is how we're going to do things. Am I correct?"

Sometimes I really hate my therapist. I slump. "Yes."

"So you want to keep the rules. You want him at arms length, to keep the sex casual."

"Yes."

"And it sounds to me like he's not interested in the rules anymore."

I nod again.

She leans forward, resting her elbows on her knees. "I

want you to be very careful, Regina. I want you to be safe. As long as you feel safe with this man, you need to talk to him. You need to either clearly vocalize new rules or clearly break everything off. If he really is trying to talk to you, those are your only options."

"I could run." It's a lame joke. I've invested everything I have here. I can't just pick up and leave.

"You could," she agrees. "And it might solve the immediate problem, but I don't think it will take you to the root of it all."

"I guess ignoring him until he goes away won't work either?" It was a rhetorical question, but she answered it.

"Probably not."

"I suppose I could ask about the tattoo." I mutter.

It wasn't something I'd intended for her to hear, but she's a therapist, so she's probably used to listening for the things people barely say. "Tattoo?"

I look away, blushing. "He has a tattoo on his arm," I say as I place my right hand over my left arm, just below the shoulder. "It's just two words, but I don't know what they mean."

She cocks her head to the side. "What are the words?"

I frown in thought. I got a good view of them one night when the moon was full. I blush at the memory of what we were doing, and try to focus on the words. "*Mole Label*?"

Her brown eyes look thoughtful. "*Molon labe*?" she offers after a moment

"Yeah, that's it."

She leans back into her chair again. "It's Greek. From the battle of Thermopylae."

I shake my head. She continues. "A small garrison of Spartans took on an entire army of Persians. Of course the Spartans lost, but legend has it that the King of Sparta was old to surrender and throw down his arms. Instead, he said *Molon labe.* It means *come and take it.*"

My stomach tightens. Some men get tattoos just because. I don't think that was Jim's logic. *Come and take it* strikes me as something that means a great deal to him.

But do I really want to find out what that is?

***

Cheryl's mom Maria is a trip. When Cheryl went to college, she asked her mom to keep an eye on me. I know this because that's exactly what Maria told me. Now that Cheryl's back from college for the break, she'll be working my counters again, starting tomorrow, but Maria still comes by every day by like a gossipy fairy godmother, regardless of whether her daughter is back.

"You are way too uptight, honey. You need a girls night out," Maria says to me as I wipe down a table. She's sitting at another table with a spiced hot chocolate after coming in to show off her newly dyed hair. I don't think there's anything wrong with going grey gracefully, but other women disagree with me. And Maria has decided to take a page from Cheryl's book with vibrant purple streaks breaking up the monotony of a standard dye and highlight.

I'm in a good mood tonight. Jim had been in earlier, and I'm proud of myself that I actually started a conversation with him.

About teenagers and how they drive us crazy. It isn't deep, but it is talking, so it counts. I start to clean my counters. "What did you have in mind?"

"You should come over to my house tomorrow. The housebeast is taking the boys skiing so I'm throwing a ladies only party." She giggles. "Just in time for Christmas."

I look at her from the corner of my eye. "Do I have a choice in the matter?"

"No. No, you don't. Especially since I know that Cheryl and Cheyenne are going to be here working." She scribbles her address on a napkin and hands it to me. "Eleven o'clock. Bring a snack to share."

***

I show up at Maria's house with a vegetable tray. I'm not sure I want to be here, but I'm going to try and have a good time. I do crave friends my own age, even if I have no idea how to relate to them.

I'm the last guest to arrive and things are already swinging. Someone puts a wine cooler in my hand almost before I've shed my coat. I don't know how many other women are here but there is a lot of laughter so it's easy to smile.

I flutter around the kitchen and dining room, listening in on the typical complaining that women do about their husbands—he can't find anything in fridge because he won't move the milk. He never notices the trash is spilling over and needs to be taken out. God forbid you try taking the remote from his hand.

These women have no idea how easy they've got it. Try making an anniversary dinner, and your husband doesn't show up until after midnight because he was out with some tramp whose name he can't remember.

Again.

Maria claps her hands to get everyone's attention. "Okay, ladies, let's go to the living room!" We allow ourselves to be herded into Maria's living room and once we get settled in, I realize what's going on.

Maria is hosting a sex-toy party.

The *consultant* is a woman named Amy who would fit in anywhere—a bank, a salon, a real estate agency. She starts in with her pre-packaged spiel. There's laughter and off-color jokes from the assembled ladies as the products are pointed out and explained. Amy is perfectly comfortable with talking about sex, toys, bath products, everything. There's no comment that can budge her off her game, and she freely laughs with everyone.

Massage lotions get passed around and tried on hands. Books get flipped through. Lingerie is shown and we're told most sets come in "real woman sizes." Vibrators are turned on and playfully jabbed into waists.

I immediately fall behind my social camouflage. I laugh, dabbing some lavender massage oil on someone's nose. The books are frank, with illustrations leaving nothing to the imagination.

I dramatically turn one book upside down. "What is this?" I quip. "The Kama Sutra?" Wild giggling surrounds me. "You do know that page forty-nine was translated wrong? It's supposed to be the right foot, not the left. If you do it wrong, you'll end up in the hospital."

Maria jabs me in the waist with a vibrator. "Feel the rubbery goodness," she says with a wicked laugh. I giggle because I'm supposed to, but I'm not terribly interested in toys.

There is a frank discussion about what the menfolk do right and the things they need to work on. "Communication is an important aspect of sex," Amy says sagely. "If he's not doing something right, you really need to tell him what you want."

"Oh, like he'll listen!" some lady pipes up. I think she works at the bank, and I know she's on her fourth drink.

She gestures to her generous bust line. "I've told him they're boobs, not bread dough!"

Cackling and pants-wetting laughter explodes in the room. I laugh along with everyone else and sip at my drink. Amy starts in with how to talk to one's partner about sex, gesturing at the book. "He's not psychic, you know," she says.

With Jim I'd never said a word. I never felt the need to. He seemed to know what I wanted every step of the way. The stories I could tell these ladies would make them think we're professional porn stars.

If we didn't need to talk before, then what the hell is the big deal now?

Someone, I don't know who, interrupts my thoughts. ". . . if all he wants is sex, tell him to get lost," she's telling a younger woman. "A relationship is about a lot more than the bedroom." Other women hold up their wine coolers and toast the declaration.

Ah. Well. If it's put that way . . .

"Fucking whore."

I snatch up an article of lingerie from the table to distract myself. If I don't focus on something, right now, I'll cry.

I thoughtfully consider the sexy thigh highs with the garter belt in my hand when someone else pokes me with a vibrator. "You don't need that," the bank teller says to me, at least halfway to being blitzed. "You have to have a man first."

The words sting. Amy swoops in to the rescue. "What's wrong with being prepared?" she asks. "Besides, a little bait on the hook never hurts!" More laughter.

The party finally winds down around four, and I'm glad to leave. I'm certain I've been labeled as a prude by the women at Maria's party because I didn't place any orders, but my problem has nothing to do with prudery.

It's that batteries can't hold you. I had almost thirty years of that shit with a living man. I don't need a vibrator to remind me of what I walked away from, thank you very much. Toys don't caress your skin or kiss your shoulder, or ask you how your day went.

Sure, some women use them with their partners, but after this past summer, I can't imagine that it's anywhere close to having the real thing.

Do I even have "a real thing?"

"They act like ladies when they're out and about, but they're all just whores when they close their doors," I hear my ex-husband's voice recite from the vaults of my mind. I can't remember how many times I heard him say that while he got spruced up for an evening out, whether or not I was coming with him.

I cringe, sobbing as I drive. Without thinking, I head for home rather than work. I sit in the car long after I've pulled into my driveway, bent over the steering wheel, screaming and crying hysterically until I'm numb.

I have to get to work. I have to show Cheryl how to close a few times before I leave her on her own. She jumped at the idea of being queen of the castle while I'm gone back east, but it isn't nearly as easy as she seems to think it is.

I see my face in the mirror and decide Cheryl can wait another hour while I pull myself together.

When I leave my car, I notice a large box on my porch, tied with a bright ribbon. I stump inside, carting the box with me and dropping it on my kitchen table until I can put my coat away.

It takes me a while to work up the courage to open it. I should have taken some of Maria's wine coolers with me when she offered them. Maybe getting good and blitzed would make it easier for me to open my mystery present. I finally just tear off the wrapping paper and open the carton.

Jim's blanket is inside with a note. *In case your tootsies get cold.* There's a smaller box with it and my hands shake while I try to open that one.

There's a bit of tissue and a ring that looks like it's been carved from a bone or an antler or something. It isn't anything fancy and it's a touch too big for my finger, but it's a lovely present, all the same.

You're going to have to talk to him.

I lift his blanket to my nose so I can smell it. Smell him.

So I can believe that I'm not a whore.

Chapter 7

One Step Forward

I haven't been to the Munn's Christmas party in years. They hold one every year for the neighborhood with enough lights on their property to act as a beacon from space. I know this personally because it takes me two whole days to hang them all. My pension check tries to hide under the bed every time I think about what their holiday electrical bill must look like.

I'm always invited to the party, but I've rarely gone. It always seems like too much of a bother to kibbitz with people about nothing. I went once, after I sobered up, because Simmons wouldn't leave me alone until I did.

On the up side, that was where the unofficial handyman gig first started. It isn't much money, but anything to supplement a pension, and keep me at least a little active is a good thing. On the down side, all the introductions and the stories and men with their wives made it hard for me to want to stay sober the last time I went. I managed to hold myself together and was a grumpy bastard for the rest of the season, but that year was still a rough party.

It was my first sober Christmas after Jenny died. I haven't been back in nearly eight.

I decide to go this year before Simmons even has a chance to badger me about it again. Maybe Regina will be there. And if she's not, it beats sitting around the house. Of course, if she isn't there, I'll probably be back home in an hour, shedding my boots and coat to cozy up with a book.

Do I even have a plan if I see her there? *Hi! So I was thinking we could talk. No? Would you feel more comfortable if we just found an empty room and got kinky? Do you think we could fit in your car like horny teenagers?*

I have no idea what the hell I'm going to do. All I do know is that I have to talk to her. I'm making progress at her work, but it feels like I'm trying to hump it uphill with a hundred pounds of gear on my back.

I hope different terrain will make things easier.

I brush my teeth before leaving. As I meet my own eyes in the mirror, I have a pang of guilt as I remember what day it is: the fourteenth.

Jenny died on December fourteenth.

I've thought about Jenny less and less over the years. Almost not at all in recent months. They say that's a good thing. That it's a sign you're moving on, and healing and all that.

But I suddenly feel like a shit who's about to deliberately cheat on his wife.

I can almost hear phantom laughter coming from my bedroom.mpty.

It is, but I can still imagine feeling a pillow being thrown at my head. *"It's time to be practical,"* the ghost whispers in my ear. *"If she can't see you as a good catch, then she's dumber than she looks."*

Jenny was an Army wife, from start to finish. I wipe a tear from my eye as I grab my sports coat and leave the room.

She's right, even if she is just in my head. It's okay to move on.

It's about time I did.

***

Simmons meets me at my door. I offered to drive to the party since we're both going, and he lives just down the road from me. True, the Munn's don't live that far away, but on a winter night one mile feels like ten, and no one likes that idea.

He pulls himself into my truck and draws the seat belt across his chest. "So how have things been?"

I've steered clear of him ever since he threatened to shoot me. He's only come over for one inspection since then, and we didn't talk much. I was laying on my couch with a library book while he snooped through my house, before leaving in a huff. I'm pretty sure it was because he found the empty donut box I "hid" under the bed a week earlier.

Simmons is diabetic.

I remember one year buying a bunch of apple cider that looked like wine bottles and hiding them all over my house. He made me carry a back pack filled with canned food and water bottles on a forced march through the neighborhood, while he rode along with his horse. I didn't think the cider bottles were a big deal until he threatened to never talk to me if I did it again.

So now I use junk food to taunt him instead.

I back out of my driveway and Simmons clears his

throat. "Beaumont? How have things been?" he asks me again, a little more intently than I like. I realize that's because I didn't answer him the first time.

I shrug. "They've been."

He looks at me.

"I haven't been drinking," I huff. "I was just thinking about the donuts."

He scowls at me. "You're a cruel bastard, do you know that?"

"I'm Army, you're Marines. We're supposed to have a hate-hate relationship."

Simmons snorts and looks out the window at all pine trees and naked aspens in the failing light. "Your son?"

"He's fine."

"Is it the neighbor lady?"

I almost drive into the drainage ditch on the side of the road. "What?" I told him that I was going to the party because for the last three years I acted as a kind of taxi service for those who drank too much, so it just seemed more efficient to already be present than to wait by the phone again. Which wasn't a lie, exactly.

"She's cute, single, you've been mooning over some woman, and you're going to the Munn's Christmas party without me saying a word, so something is going on."

I think of Simmons as a cross between my own personal savior and a drill instructor. I imagine he sometimes still thinks of me as that idiot blubbering on his couch, begging for help to dry out. I swear he took sadistic pleasure in physically dragging me out of bed to muck his stables at four in the morning, every morning, for a year as I clawed my way back to the world of sobriety. I later found out that he'd been a Marine drill instructor in a past life, so sadism comes naturally to him.

Sadistic or not, when a man helps you fight your way back to the land of the living, you tend to trust him. That doesn't mean we gossip about intimate life details, but I'm willing to talk to about Regina. "I'm not sure what we've got," I finally admit.

He nods. "A couple of dates, then a cold shoulder?"

"Something like that." The road twists and curves up and down. The land is nothing like what you would imagine for a mountain Christmas. Everything is brown without a speck of snow anywhere. It's only snowed once since the Halloween dusting, and that melted off in less than a week. The dead brown around us is unbelievably depressing.

"What did you do?"

"Damned if I know. I thought women liked it when men tried to talk to them."

His eyebrows crawl up his forehead. "What did you say?"

I shrug. *"Hi. How are you?"*

Simmons frowns under his beard. "Does she play for the other team?"

"Nope." Of that I'm very sure.

Well, I'm pretty sure.

He looks at me but doesn't say anything. He doesn't have to, because even with the failing light he can see me blushing like some kid caught with condoms in his pocket by his mom. He directs his gaze out the window again. "Probably a rough divorce."

"I don't think it was a pretty marriage," I agree as we pull up to the blinding lights surrounding the Munn's house. I find a place to park along the road that won't get me boxed in later, and unbuckle my seat belt.

"Beaumont," Simmons says before I can open the door. I stop and look at him. "Women are weird. They can take things without a blink that would make a man cry, but their scars run deeper, especially if it was a bad one. Go easy on her."

"I'm trying," I tell him. I pull my coat sleeve up to show him the bracelet. "She gave this to me for Christmas." I shake my head. "She smiles at me, but it's almost like she's afraid to talk to me, even about the weather." I can't tell him that I gave her a ring. Rings mean things to men, especially when they give them to women, and I don't want him jumping to the wrong conclusions.

He narrows his eyes at me. "You been drinking at all?"

I shake my head. "No," I tell him again.

"Good. If she sees you with so much as a beer in your hand, you'll probably scare her off for good."

"Was I that bad?"

He shrugs. "You weren't great, but it isn't you that hurt her the first time."

"You've talked to her?"

"No, I'm saying seen this stuff before. I was assigned to Family Services after being a DI."

I blow air from my mouth, long and heavy like a sigh. If Simmons had spent time in Family Services while he'd been active duty, then he probably knew what he was talking about. "Any advice?"

His eyes go distant, like he's trying to sort through everything he's ever had to deal with. "It's kind of like combat," he says after a moment of thought. "You never know how, when or why someone's going to crack. You just know that it will happen, sooner or later."

I wait for him to say more. He doesn't.

"I don't know how helpful that is, Simmons."

He shrugs. "It's the best I got."

"Shit," I mutter.

"Pretty much."

***

"Damn, Jim. It's good to see you!" Gordon Munn says as he ushers us in from the cold. He gives us the basic directions of what is where in the house, and I take Simmons' coat and shed mine with everyone else's in a guest room and mill about.

The Munn's house is one of the largest in the ShadowPines neighborhood. I think "McMansion" is what the media calls the style these days. I'm not sure I can see Gordon having the golden arches embossed on the custom stucco and flagstone, but it is a damn sight bigger than my single level double-wide.

Gordon notices my bracelet as he offers me a beer. "Are you having some kind of mid-life crisis, there?" he asks, pointing at it with a black finger. "Isn't that something the kids wear around?"

"What?" I look at the band around my wrist. I feel proud and even lucky to be wearing it. I only take it off to shower. I wave the beer off, taking a can of soda from the counter. "I like it. It's my lucky charm."

He nods, Letting the subject drop before taking me through his house and introducing me around, which seems a little redundant since most everyone knows me as the neighborhood handyman. Then she turns and I see her. My neighbor. My lady of the woods.

Regina.

The slacks and turtleneck she's wearing flatter her figure, and she looks way more hot now than in a thin robe or nothing at all. Her hair's out of the braid she always wears at work and is pulled over a shoulder, framing the face

I'm not allowed to kiss.

"So I'm certain you two have at least seen each other since you live next door," Gordon says, totally oblivious to the red flush that springs up from Regina's turtleneck to her cheeks at his choice of words.

Why, yes, Gordon, we have seen each other. I try to hide my own blush and smile behind my soda. *Although I couldn't tell you her favorite color if my life depended on it.*

"Well, maybe not," he continues. "Anyway, Jim, this is Regina. Regina, Jim."

Regina sticks out a hand to shake. I almost raise it to my lips but catch myself, opting instead for the polite squeeze and pump that's expected of me. My ring is on the middle finger of her right hand and just that she's wearing it at all is enough to make me happy. She smiles when she catches sight of her bracelet on my wrist again. We chat with Gordon for a bit, talking about the lack of snow concerning us all and what not.

Regina manages to slip away after only a few moments.

It takes most of the evening to chase her down to a quiet corner so I can talk to her. The house is huge, so part of the chase just involves getting past the neighbors who all want to chat about something or other. The other difficulty lies in the terrain—I can't seem to be on the same floor at the same time she is. I start to wonder if she isn't just a figment of my imagination when I hear her voice behind me.

". . . from my mother."

I spin and see my target. She's boxed herself into a corner with Simmons. I have no doubt that he planned it that way once he figured out I was looking for her.

Who says Army and Marines don't work well together?

I tap him on the shoulder, my eyes flicking at Regina. He smiles, and makes some excuse about finding Gordon's wife since she mentioned she was interested in getting a horse herself.

"So where do you think she'll put her new pony?" I ask, stepping into the space Simmons left behind. "In the garage next to the Beemer?"

Regina leans her back against the wall, shaking her head, but it doesn't quite feel casual to me. "Guest room. That way it can have breakfast in bed and a skinny latte before a morning ride."

I move back half a step as I laugh. I don't want her to feel threatened, but I also don't want her to run away, either. She smiles around her drink, her eyes briefly twinkling with mischief. The moment is followed by an awkward silence.

I cough politely. "Do you like your ring?" If she didn't like it, I don't think she'd be wearing it, but it's a place to start.

She looks at it and blushes. "Yes. Thank you."

I nod. "I'm glad. It took me two days to shape it." I smile at her. "It's the first time I've ever done anything like that."

She looks at her ring again with something approaching awe. I don't think I would've gotten that reaction from her even if it had been a frickin' diamond.

Maybe she thinks it's too much, now that she knows I made it myself. "My bracelet was a nice present, too," I hurry to tell her. "I almost never take it off."

Alarm dances in her eyes. What the hell? She's seen me wear it the last few days at her store. She blushes, casting her gaze around the room, deliberating avoiding me before managing to smile at the floor. "I wasn't sure you would. It's kind of cheesy."

"I don't think it's cheesy. I sure as hell wouldn't want it on a pizza."

She laughs a little, but she's trying to hide behind her cup of whatever, trying to shrink away from me into the wall. Trying to find a way out. *Come on, Regina. Throw me a bone, here.*

"Do you just want to go somewhere?" I blurt out.

"What?" Her eyes are filled with terror.

"I think Midnight Mountain in Woodland Park is open all night," I suggest. "We could maybe get a booth, and make fun of the weak stuff they pass off as coffee. You know, act totally crazy."

She shakes her head. "Liquor license. They have to close no later than two."

I check my watch and then catch her eyes again. "Really? It's only just eight. If we left now, we'd get there before nine and there wouldn't even be a line to get in. Is that the best you can do?"

She opens her mouth and closes it again. I look at my soda, trying to stop my frustration from exploding. What the hell do I have to do just to-

"Shakespeare?" she asks, her voice a little hysterical.

The name is so sudden it feels like a punch to my chest, and I almost take another step back. "You're surprised a grease monkey reads something other than comic books, huh?"

"The collection in your house is scary," she says, with something that would be admiration if it didn't feel like she was flogging herself to say it.

"I should probably thin it out soon. I don't think I've picked up some of those books in forever."

"Well, you can always bring them to the store."

"Aha! Someone's under the mistletoe!" Gordon's wife calls out, pointing at us.

Regina and I both look up to see how we've been

trapped.

She shakes her head with a smile, but I peck her cheek before she can step away. She's flustered and steps away from me, getting lost in the neighborhood crowd.

When no one's looking, I yank the fake mistletoe from the ceiling and stuff it in my pocket, ribbon and all. Rude, I guess, but it isn't like those things are expensive.

I almost kissed Regina under that mistletoe. So now it's mine.

***

Regina manages to dodge me after the party. The girl running Java Books with the purple hair says something about a vacation over Christmas to her brother's place in North Carolina. I still come by every day to pass the time, but even the coffee doesn't taste as good when she's not there.

Christmas at my son's house is nice and understated. There's no church service I'm asked to attend, and I show up around lunch for presents. Thankfully, Janice is nowhere to be seen. Everyone is in the living room, and the smell of turkey coming from the kitchen makes my stomach growl.

My son and his wife cheated this year, giving me a generic gift card that can be used anywhere. I don't mind because it's hard to shop for the hermit of the mountains who says he doesn't need anything. And technically, I cheated too, but I also remember getting duplicate gifts for Lucas when he was young from well-meaning relatives, when what we really needed was more breathing room in our budget.

Rosy is surrounded by her toys and clothes, but she's more enthralled with the shiny ribbons that wrapped her packages than anything else. She crawls across the floor to pile them on my boots with the serious deliberateness that can only be found in a small child.

I smile and shake my foot, and the shiny streamers fall to the floor. She giggles and starts piling them up again while Tommy bounces on the couch with his gift card, declaring that he's going to buy a car or a motorcycle, having cartoon inspired visions of tearing up the highway in his new hot rod.

Missy takes a picture of her daughter decorating my foot before picking her up and settling Rosy in her lap. My granddaughter's attention has suddenly been taken up by her own gift card lying on her pile of Christmas loot and grabs it. I don't know what Rosy plans to do with it, beyond gumming it to death, but it's her first experience with money, so there's probably a mother-daughter shopping day in the near future.

"How's your girlfriend, Dad?" Lucas asks as he lifts Tommy off the couch. "We do not jump on the furniture," he tells his son, depositing him on the floor near his toys. Tommy finds another truck and starts pushing it around on the floor, using the wadded up wrapping papers as boulders to destroy the vehicle in a cataclysmic avalanche.

I try not to smirk at Lucas, remembering a similar scene when he was that age. "Visiting family," I say, frowning at the coffee in my cup. It's the weak, nasty brew that passes for coffee at the grocery store.

I'm officially a coffee snob.

I take it to the kitchen and dump it in the sink, coming back with a glass of water.

Missy looks at me from the floor as I settle back on the couch. "Is this like the girlfriend we never see because she supposedly lives in Canada?" She tosses her head to flip her blonde hair out of her face. She's letting it grow out again and it's reached the annoying stage—too short to do anything with, but too long to be anything other than a nuisance.

"No. Regina really does exist, thank you."

"Janice was shattered after Thanksgiving," she says. "She still won't talk to me."

"Well, when she does, you can tell her she's been spared a lot of grief. About the only things I know how to do well is curse and fix engines."

"Will Regina be back for New Year's?" Lucas asks.

"She's supposed to be."

"We'd like to meet her," he says. "The church is holding an adults only party. Maybe you could bring her to that."

I roll my eyes to the ceiling. "Yes, Dad. I'll see what she wants to do."

"Oh, come on, now," Missy says, pulling the card from Rosy's grip, replacing it with one of those chew-toy things they've got for babies these days.

"Do you have to give the girl a dog-toy?" I ask.

Missy tries to hit my leg, but I manage to move it in time. "You were slick at Thanksgiving," she playfully glares at me, "but you're not getting away that easy this time. We want to know what she's like."

"She's busy, for starters," I say, trying to get out of the conversation. "She's got her own business."

"And?"

"And what?" I'm getting irritated. "Regina's got brown hair, brown eyes, her last name is *Linkous* and she owns Java Books." I don't know what else to say because I don't know the woman that well myself, and being pushed about it just frustrates me. I don't want to rip Missy's head off, but if she keeps pushing that's what will happen.

"Dad will bring her around when she's ready, Missy," Lucas says, seeing the warning signs, and trying to save the day. "I didn't bring you around until we were engaged."

The silence is awkward. We all know why he didn't bring her around. Lucas had just turned fourteen when Jenny died. I'd only been six months out of the Army and suddenly the anchor for my entire world had been ripped away. I honestly don't remember much for the five years after. A few memories jump out at me with horrifying clarity, but I don't always know where they fit in the calendar.

My son has assured me that I didn't beat him, but he won't tell me what I did do. I can only assume that I said a lot of nasty shit, and ignored a lot of important moments when he needed or wanted me to be there. I remember being shocked when he was leaving for college because he didn't tell me until the day he left.

I remember the phone call before Thanksgiving his first year away when he said he wasn't ever coming home again, but everything else is a shady blur at best.

He and I got past the dark times, each in our own way, but there had been a lot of pain on both sides. It took a lot for Lucas to overcome it and be willing to invite me back into his life. I don't know if he doesn't talk about those years because he doesn't want to make me feel bad, or if he just doesn't want to dwell on them.

Bitterness doesn't just ruin coffee.

The silence in Lucas' living room is deafening. Missy and Lucas are trying to find a way through the morass. I nod my head and step through the moment. "It was a good thing he didn't bring you by earlier," I say to Missy, putting my glass on an end table. I hold out my arms to my granddaughter. She leaves her mom's lap and crawls to me.

"It gave me time to clean my house," I say as I lift the baby to my lap.

"I don't think your house has ever been dirty," Missy says, thankful that I'm not going to dwell on the past.

"Not true. I distinctly remember leaving my dishes in the sink before I left," I say.

"The sink was full of soapy water, wasn't it?" Lucas asks.

I shrug. "I'm lazy, and it gets the job done."

"You can at least tell us about her," Missy says.

"No."

"She's not real," she says glumly. It's a little dramatized, and I raise an eyebrow at her, but I don't walk into the obvious trap she's set for me. Missy blushes.

Rosy has noticed my bracelet on my left and begins to tug at it. "Oh, no, no, no," I tell her gently, pulling my left arm out of her grip so I can try to get it off before she ruins it. "She's real enough," I tell Missy as I fumble with the clip. *But I'll be damned if I know why she doesn't want to be.*

Lucas looks at my arm as Rosy screams in outrage that I've taken the pretty bracelet out of her chubby reach and stuffed it into a pants pocket. "What's that, Dad?" he asks. "Some cheap friendship bracelet thing?"

"That is my Christmas present from Regina," I tell him as I tickle my granddaughter to take her mind off my bracelet. "And I don't think it's cheap at all."

Missy holds out her hand. "I want to see it."

"No. It's mine," I say, shaking my head at my granddaughter. Rosy squeals with laughter.

"If the mystery woman gave you a present, it's my job to make sure it's an acceptable one," Missy says.

"It's got a lock of her hair in it, and it's mine. Period," I say.

Missy and Lucas both blink in shock. "Her hair?" Missy asks, her jaw almost touching the floor.

"Ewwwwwwww," Tommy says.

Missy shushes him with a quick wave of her hand. "You're not allowed to get any more serious with this woman until we've met her," she tells me.

Rosy is squealing under my fingers again, her laughter tripping over itself. "Yes, Ma'am," I say.

I'm not lying, and even if I was, it isn't like Regina's making it easy for me anyway.

Chapter 8

A Shoulder to Lean On

"I'm glad you came out, sis," Will says as we watch his kids play in the snow. We've just finished shoveling his walk and driveway. He's got his VT Hokies hat on, and his breath steams in the cold.

This is the first time I've seen him and his family since I left for Colorado. His youngest is now six and still hasn't warmed up to me yet. The other kids are nice enough, but they keep their distance. Will's wife Erin offered to take me shopping with her today, but given my finances, that would mean me following her around all day and possibly even carrying some of her bags than actually shopping, which is entirely too depressing.

"I hear UNC won the last game," I say, looking pointedly at his hat. My low back aches from shoveling and I try to stretch it out.

"Shut up." He pulls the snow shovel from my hand to place it with his on the porch. "I'm still in mourning."

"You've lived in North Carolina for almost twenty years, Will. It's time to accept them as the home team."

"Never. I will defy the nay-sayers until the end of time."

I sigh. "You're worse than a Broncos fan."

"At least I'm not a sell-out."

"True."

He has no idea the plans I've made for stealing his cherished Hokies hat and replacing it with an Air Force Falcon's one the day I leave. I smile at his kids playing in the piles of snow we created while shoveling to hide my devious smirk.

I'm his big sister. I'm supposed to be evil.

"How's Colorado treating you?" he asks. We haven't really had the chance to talk more than an hour at a time since I came out two days ago, what with his work schedule and all, but now he's off today and tomorrow, so we can actually talk.

Yay.

I shrug, kicking at some snow at the edge of the walk. "Okay." I really shouldn't not want to talk to my own brother, especially after everything he's done for me, but I don't want him to know how kattywampussed I've gotten in the last few months.

"If you need some money-"

"I'm fine, Will," I say with a huff. He knows I didn't want to come back, and he can see I'm still wearing the same winter coat I had when I left. "Things are tight, but nothing worth a charity case." My breath steams in the cold, and my sunglasses almost aren't enough to block the glare from all the snow. Eight inches of the stuff, at least. "It's so brown in Colorado," I murmur.

Will snorts. "I'll trade you. You can have back problems from shoveling, and I'll sit in shorts year round." The kids

The kids seize the shovels to make snow forts for an impending battle.

"It's still cold, dufus," I tell him. "There's just no snow."

Will smiles, looking at his kids. There's some serious snowball stockpiling going on between the three of them, along with frantic shoveling and packing of snow walls. The eldest, Dakota, surrenders her shovel to the youngest now that she's done making a mound of snow for her defensive wall. Will stuffs his gloved hands in his jacket pockets. "So, is he treating you right?"

The question came from nowhere, and my mouth drops open. My little brother gives me a sidelong glance under his sunglasses. "I'm a cop, Reggie." He nods at my gloved hands. "You always hated wearing rings, and here you show up wearing a homemade one out of antler that I have yet to see you take off, except to help with the chores."

"People change. Maybe I bought it."

"Then you got ripped off. Even the junk coming out of Asia is made better than that piece of shit."

I glare at him, hate rising in my chest. "You take that back. Right now."

Will doesn't even look at me, watching over his children and the street beyond. "Is he treating you right?"

"You suck," I grumble at him.

He waits for an answer.

"He tries," I finally admit.

Will nods. "You're not making it easy for him."

I sigh. "It's hard."

Snowballs fly through the air. Shrieking laughter follows. A truce is declared and immediately violated by the eldest girl, the only one strong enough to use a shovel as a catapult with a load of snow. "Dakota!" her father snaps. "Take it easy on your brothers."

He turns his attention back to me. "If you need more closure, I can arrange something," he suggests. "It'll be the worst case of suicide by decapitation that anyone in law enforcement has ever seen."

I laugh. "You're a bad man."

He nods his head from side to side. "That's probably why I'm a cop," he agrees.

The snowball fight dies because the ammunition has run out. There's a flurry of activity to make more. I never had kids. I wanted them once, when I was in high school.

But then I got married.

Will clears his throat. "Seriously. Is he a good guy?"

I know what he means, and I try to dodge the question. "I think he is."

He spins to look at me. "You don't know?" he asks incredulously.

"I-" I don't know what to say. Somehow my little brother has always been able to sucker punch me even when I'm expecting it.

"It's cheap to run a basic background check on the internet!"

The truth is that running a check never occurred to me. Having a playmate join me for my midnight romps hadn't occurred to me, either. Things just happened. Nothing's happening much now, but-

"How long have you been dating this cat?" he demands.

"Off and on since summer." It isn't exactly a lie. I hope it's good enough to slide past him.

It isn't. Will stares at me before slipping a hand under his sunglasses to rub his eyes. "Jesus Christ. You're sleeping with a guy you don't even know?"

"I never said I was sleeping-"

"Cop," he reminds me.

If there was only one thing Will was ever good at it was reading people. When he was in high school, he was so good at it he used to scam the girls into dates by pretending he had "psychic powers." His grades never reflected those mystic abilities, but he managed to scrape them into graduating shape by the end of his senior year.

"It isn't like that, Will. He's-" I stop myself. He's what? Incredible in the sack? Persistent as hell? "He's trying. He really is."

"Is he a drunk?"

"No."

"Is he married?"

"No!"

Will takes his sunglasses off to pinch the bridge of his nose. "You had a fling, and now you won't talk to him, is that it?"

"I came out to visit, Will, not get interrogated."

"Reggie, just tell me."

"Why are you being such a turd all of a sudden?"

"Because you're my sister, and I don't want you hurt again!" he shouts.

The kids freeze in the yard, staring at us. I glare at him. "You may be a cop, but you're still a little shit," I say before stomping inside.

I strip off my boots in the foyer, and head straight to the guest room, slamming the door. It's childish, but I have nowhere else to go. I throw my coat to the floor and flop on the bed, scowling at my socks. I can't stand more than a few moments of silence, so I yank out my phone and call my store.

"Java Books," a hurried voice says into the phone. I can hear the busy clatter in the background.

"Hey, Steve, it's the boss." I lie down, pinching the

bridge of my nose. Will and I both got the habit from Mom.

"Oh, hey, Boss," he says. "Did you need Cheryl?"

"Sure."

There's some muffled shouting and Cheryl's voice comes on the line. "Hey, Boss."

Jim's right. All the kids do call me "Boss." The thought of Jim brings up my brother and I blink back tears. "How's the store?" I ask, trying to keep my voice level. I dig my free hand into my jeans pocket, searching for his ring.

"I hate you," she says just as I find it.

"It isn't as easy as you thought, is it?" I chuckle at her, playing with the ring.

"You could've warned me," she half-whines into the phone. "Mikie got sick so I had to juggle schedules on the fly."

"That's the joy of being in charge. I did try to warn you, but you were so starry-eyed at the thought of playing the boss you didn't listen."

There's a muffled conversation on the other end and the phone gets passed to someone else. "Hi, Beautiful! Merry Christmas!"

Deputy Travis. Hearing his voice is something of a disappointment. "Merry Christmas, Travis," I return politely.

"You'll be back for the New Year's party, right?"

"That's the plan." I suddenly hope a freak snowstorm lands on North Carolina, trapping me here until after Valentines' Day.

"Okay! You save me a dance!"

"Sure," I agree without enthusiasm. Travis doesn't hear it because he's already passing the phone back to Cheryl. "So, five more days?" she asks hopefully. The bell on the door is ringing non-stop in the background. The girl has got to be frazzled.

"If I don't get snowed in by the gods of good fortune, I'll pick up my keys with my mail on the twenty-eighth."

"You don't have to go," she tells me. "It isn't like it's a red carpet deal or anything."

"I'm a business owner in Honesty," I sigh. "The New Year's party is a red carpet deal. If I don't go it'll look bad."

"Seriously? You're kidding me, right?"

"No."

"You could always say you're sick and not go," she tells me. "There's a wicked stomach bug going around right now. I'm hoping to catch it so I can drop the freshman fifteen."

"Oh, please," I snort. "Like you need to lose weight."

"My mom says the same thing." I hear her tell Cheyenne there's more chocolate in the back behind the caramel and that she's actually going to have to move things around to find it. The noise in the background lowers, and I know Cheryl's moved into the office and closed the door as much as she can. "And you're going with Deputy Travis?" she asks, her voice low and serious.

"No. I just said I'd save him a dance. That's it." I fit the ring back on my right hand, but I keep fidgeting with it, rubbing and spinning it with my thumb.

"Mom told you about him, right?"

Maria had indeed told me about Deputy Travis after our drive through a beautifully scenic hell. He'd just gotten out of marriage number three, which made me that much more not interested in giving him another chance. "Yes. I've been warned."

"Good. Oh, and that other guy has been moping around here, too," she says.

I stop playing with my ring, sitting up slowly. "Other

guy?"

"*Small coffee, black and bold*," she reports. "Should I tell him about your hot date?"

My stomach flips. The ring feels heavy on my finger. "Why would you do that?"

"It's obvious *small coffee* likes you," Cheryl says. "I just figured you were giving him the brush off, too. If we play it right, we can get the message through to both that you're not interested."

Jim's been moping? "No," I tell her. "Jim's a . . . a different situation," I stammer into the phone.

"Oh. My. God!" she squeals delightedly.

"It isn't like that," I rush to say, my finger with the ring on it starting to itch. She's going to tell her mom, I just know it. And then it'll be all over Honesty in two days, and in China via the internet before five.

"Whatever you say, Boss," she agrees. "Was there anything else?"

I want to tell her everything. I want to unload my soul on someone, anyone, even if it is a first-semester college student. "Merry Christmas, Cheryl," I say instead.

"Merry Christmas!"

I hang up before she can say anything else, and drop my phone into my purse on the floor next to the bed. Jim's been moping at the shop? I pull a fancy throw pillow into my lap, plucking at the fringe for a few minutes before I stop. I take the ring off my finger, andturn it in my hands for the thousandth time. I can make out the lines from the sandpaper on the surface of the antler. He took the time to shape the inner ring with a soft curve so that it would be comfortable to wear. It isn't a perfect circle, but he made it himself.

He made it just for me.

What the hell is wrong with me? I was so proud of myself when I made that bracelet for him. I thought I could finally, actually be an adult and talk to him, but the minute I saw him wearing it, I was terrified of it. Terrified that I'd given him something I'd regret. How is that different than the woman I used to be? How can I say that I will never be that woman again when I can't even talk about the weather to a man who I have literally fucked stupid in my backyard, multiple times?

Jim seems like a nice guy, and I can tell he's trying, but I'm too afraid to let him in. Tears burn in my eyes. Things were supposed to get better. It wasn't supposed to be like this. Why does my happily ever after have to be so hard to come by? Everyone else has them so easy. Why can't I?

Someone knocks and the door opens. Will pokes his head in, his brown hair thin on top. "Reggie?" he asks quietly.

I sniff and he comes in, sitting next to me on the bed. "I'm sorry," he says after a moment, clasping his hands between his knees. "You're right. I shouldn't be drilling you. Especially not for Christmas." He takes my hand. "I'm just worried about you, Regina. I saw you hurt, and-" he cuts himself off.

I know it's hard for him. He feels like he should've seen the signs, and still blames himself. He thinks he abandoned me when he moved to North Carolina after college. He wonders if he'd stayed in Virginia, he would've been able to see what was really going on, and maybe stop it years before I did.

Erin told me he still has nightmares about it. That he's scared now that Dakota has started high school and is taking a serious interest in boys. He's making her take martial arts lessons at his gym twice a week even though she doesn't want to.

The thought that I hurt my baby brother creates a knot in my chest.

"It would kill me to see it start all over again," he finally says.

I lean on his shoulder and he wraps an arm around me. My little brother. My protector.

"I'm sorry I cursed in front of the kids," I say.

I feel him shrug. "They hear worse at school, probably."

They probably do, but that doesn't make it right.

"Mom's doing okay," he says after a few moments. "But I don't think you should see her."

I screw my face up to keep from crying. We've managed to avoid the subject of Mom until now, but it had to come out sooner or later. If Will thinks I shouldn't see her at the nursing home, then that means she's said some things recently. Things like why haven't I given her grandchildren, yet? Or where is that handsome man of mine, Larry? *"Treat him right, sweetpea. He's a good catch."*

She was already starting to slip before I left Larry. The news of my divorce sent her over the edge, somehow. Maybe she couldn't handle the fact that she hadn't seen the signs for all those years. Maybe she felt like she'd failed to protect her daughter. Maybe she felt that she'd somehow made me stay longer with him than helping me leave a bad situation.

Maybe she couldn't accept that her daughter, raised upright in God's ways, got a divorce.

I stare at the floor. Mom had been the pillar of the family, running her own business and raising two children after her husband died. To my knowledge, she never went on a date or skipped out on a single Sunday sunrise service. Not once.

If she knew what I had done in the last few months, she'd probably up and die because I'm such a disappointment.

The only one I have left is Will. He squeezes my shoulder reassuringly, resting his head on mine.

I realize I don't want Will holding me. I want Jim. I want him here. I want to see him drive everyone nuts by turning a dining room chair backward to sit in. I want to see his long legs sticking out in front of him while he sits in the overstuffed chair in the guest room. I want him to badger me into playing a game of checkers, or irritate me to the point of wanting to scream because he keeps trying to get me to talk.

"He wants to talk to me, but . . . "

"But you're afraid of what he'll say? Of what will happen next?"

I nod.

Will nods too. "Sadly, I see this kind of thing a lot."

We sit on the bed without talking for a while, with me trying to stifle my sniffling nose. He pulls the ring from my grip to look at it. "Was this a Christmas present?"

I can only nod.

"He made it himself, huh?"

"That what he said."

He turns the ring in his hand, inspecting Jim's workmanship. "You do know that rings are important to guys, right?"

"This isn't high school, Will."

He shakes his head. "It doesn't matter. It's a ring. Even if he didn't propose, it's still important to him. Men can give women jewelry all day long unless it's a ring. I still sweat anytime I buy a ring for Erin."

"I gave him a bracelet."

He tries not to laugh. "A bracelet? What is this guy, a Rocky Mountain Rapper?"

I snort as I envision Jim decked out in gold chains. "No. I made it." I pull at my braid. "I braided a lock of my hair with some string."

Will freezes. "You used your hair?"

"Yes."

"Oh, shit," he sighs.

"Don't be like Mom," I beg him. Mom may have been a good Christian woman, but she was superstitious as all hell. Right before I left, she still insisted on having a glass pickle jar sitting on her window, filled with salt to foil evil spirits. "It's just hair."

"It's your hair," he corrects. "That's a big deal for a guy."

Will isn't thinking of superstitions. He's thinking I've told Jim one thing, but then confused him by doing something else. I don't know what to say. I knew it would be important when I made it, but I don't know how to make much else that's crafty and fast and the ring demanded a return present of equal value.

"I don't mean to confuse him," I sniff. "I just can't make my head work right." I take the ring back from Will, and slide it on my middle finger again. I don't regret giving Jim my hair. I was happy when I saw him wearing it. Happy and horrified all at once.

"What's his name?" Will asks.

"Jim."

My brother waits. I can feel him trying to not tense, trying not to rip me a new ass because I didn't give the last name. I wipe my nose on my sleeve, giving up. "Beaumont. He lives next door."

"That's how you met him?"

"He's the neighborhood handyman." I laugh. "I got locked out of my house." What a story that would make if I told Will all of it. He'd probably die of a heart attack right next to Mom.

"And you think he's okay?" There's no accusation. There's only the question.

I wipe at my eyes. "I think so."

He swallows. "Do you want me to look him up?"

"Nice abuse of power," I joke.

He shrugs. "I haven't bullied anyone for a week. If I don't do something at least vaguely criminal, I'll lose my mind."

"If you want to."

"Do you want me to tell you what I find?"

"Aren't you going to anyway?"

He sighs. "You think he's a good guy, right?"

"Right."

"Then unless something pops that I don't like, no."

"Why?"

"Because if he is a good guy, then you need to talk to him, and if I tell you what I find, you won't have anything to talk about."

"You suck."

He squeezes my shoulder again. "Most people aren't like Larry. If you want to fly, you've got to step off the cliff."

I wipe the tears from my eyes. "I fell last time."

"I know, Reg. I know. And it took a while, but eventually you got back up." He takes a deep breath. "Relationships aren't easy, but if this guy really is worth crying over, then you've got to meet him halfway." He tilts his head down to look me in the eye. "It's the only way you're going to find out."

Chapter 9

Pop

Honesty has a little New Year's Eve party in the community center every year. I haven't been. Ever. But I notice the signs posted around town and decide to go this year. Especially after the girl running Java Books slips me the tip that Regina is planning to be there, but so is Deputy Dawg and Regina isn't so thrilled about that idea. Cheryl's a nice kid and she means well, so I didn't lecture her about sticking her nose in other people's business.

I did ask her why she dyed her hair like a frickin' peacock, though. She just smiled at me with those bright eyes. "It matches my tat. Maybe you should come around after work, and I'll show you."

She'd laughed when I shuddered visibly. If I'd had coffee in my mouth, she'd have been wearing it. I'd noticed her even when I hadn't wanted to. She's an attractive kid and her curves are in all the right places, but to me she's still just a kid. Don't get me wrong, she's an attractive little jaw-dropper, but I'm not interested in a kid. I want a real woman.

"Relax, I wasn't serious," she'd said, trying to get her giggles under control. Once she'd pulled herself together, she gave me an obvious once over, not because she was interested, but because she cared about Regina.

Men know when they've passed the friend test. It's been years since I've ever had to take such an exam, but apparently Cheryl felt I'd passed hers.

This kid's got nothing. Jenny's friends ran me through the ringer, and still didn't like me.

"You're a nice guy," Cheryl told me. "Treat her right, okay?"

I was a little irritated, and I threatened to tell her father about her antics if I caught her pulling that *wanna see my naughty tat shit* again. She'd just laughed again.

It was something of an empty threat. Her Dad's probably trying very hard to not think about the things he knows his little girl is doing while she's away at school. And realistically, what's he going to do even if he does find out? Ground her?

The community center for Honesty is actually pretty nice, given how small the town is. It isn't large, but it hosts club meetings and dance recitals and a mess of other things throughout the year, so the town actually takes some pride in keeping it up.

The New Year's party isn't half-bad. There's a DJ on a stage and a mirrored ball, streamers hanging everywhere, and a huge net over the dance floor, filled with balloons and just waiting for midnight. There isn't a kid in sight. An overpriced bar next to a small buffet line covered in appetizers is pushed up against the wall. Every beat-up table the center owns is out on the floor with nice tablecloths, surrounded by chairs. The tablecloths don't match and the chairs are the crappy folding metal kind, but if that's the worst this party has to offer, I can live with it.

I chat with some people—mostly meaningless crap about the dry winter, or politics. I ask around about Deputy Travis and even manage to look sympathetic when I hear he's sick with a stomach bug, and probably won't be making it tonight.

Oh, darn. What a shame.

Of course, any conversation with alcohol involved inevitably wanders around to the *no shit, there I was* stories. Most are funny, some are lost on me, and they all pale in comparison to mine, but I'm not about to try and one-up anyone. A gentleman doesn't reveal those details.

A gentleman also doesn't screw a lady stupid in her own yard, neither.

I can only handle the mindless blather about the latest television show for so long before I sequester myself against a wall, watching people and wishing I could give serious thought to the bar when I see her.

I drop my punch in the trash, and work my way across the crowd. She's smiling and talking to a small group, and I manage to squeeze in before she realizes it. She's not wearing some Hollyweird dress that only a woman with a lot of plastic surgery and an iron girdle could fit into, but it is nice. Black with short sleeves and some flowers stitched around the bottom. I really don't care what she's wearing. I ask politely if she would like to dance, then take her hand to lead her to the floor when she hesitates.

It's a slow number—that means I can hold her with my hand on her low back. She's graceful about it, dropping an arm on my shoulder while I hold her other hand. Just holding her is a bit of a thrill for me.

"What are you doing?" Regina asks.

I smile at her. "Well, I'm dancing with a beautiful lady. Although, if they play anything faster, it might look like I'm having a seizure."

She laughs, but her body feels tense under my hand, like she's ready to run with a moment's notice.

"Do I smell that bad?" I ask. "I don't normally wear aftershave but I thought I'd fit in better if I did."

"What?" The topic change has her confused. I can't say that I'm not. I have no idea how to talk to a woman who would rather have sex than talk about anything, even the weather.

"It feels like you're about to run," I say.

"Sorry." She looks around. At the DJ behind his table, the people milling about, the dance floor, even the ceiling tricked out with the net and balloons, but not at me.

I tap her hand in mine with a finger. "Hey. Over here. The guy trying to look suave and sophisticated."

She tries to look at me and even smiles, but she can only manage a few seconds.

"So I'm planning a New Year's resolution," I say, trying to get her focus back.

"What?"

I don't think she meant to ask what I was planning, but I still take the ball and run with it. "I've decided that if you won't talk to me by July, then I'm done." My left arm tenses and relaxes again. I've said it. Now I just hope she understands I meant it.

She looks like I've slapped her face. When Janice looked like that it was funny. With Regina, I want to curl up in a corner with some bourbon.

"I'm sorry," I tell her, shaking my head. "I just can't keep doing this. You have to talk to me or I'm just not going to bother trying, anymore."

She presses her lips into a tight line, but she nods. The song ends, but she doesn't try to run away like I expect her to. A new song starts and she straightens her shoulders. Her grip on my hand feels more secure for a moment. We start dancing again. She looks like she wants to say something, but doesn't know how to begin.

"So, I'll start," I say, coming to her rescue. "I'm Jim Beaumont. People call me *Jim*, but I prefer *James* if they're close. I like the color blue, hiking, and steak. I don't do church, and I'm retired Army. Your turn."

She smiles, laughing nervously. "I'm Regina Linkous, and I own a bookstore and coffee shop that just stays in the black."

I smile at her. "Where are you from, Regina?"

"Virginia, originally."

"And what brought you to Colorado?"

She forces herself to stand taller and swallows hard, looking past my shoulder. "I divorced."

I figured that much.

She clears her throat. "So why does a mechanic quote Shakespeare?"

It's a diversion. She knows I know it. I can see it in her face but she's talking, dammit. I can't force the subject back or she might shut down.

"Once upon a time," I say, "the military encouraged NCO's to get an education. The more education you had, the better your chances of making rank."

"You majored in literature?" She looks amused by the idea.

I shake my head. "History."

"That explains some of your collection," she agrees with a nod, still amused by the idea of a nerdy grease monkey.

"Some of them date to my graduate courses," I admit.

Her eyes round a bit in awe. "Graduate?"

"Master's degree." I shrug and grin at her. "Not much use when you're working on an engine block, but it looks pretty on a résumé."

She drops her gaze to my chin. I can barely hear her. "I only just got my Bachelor's a few years ago."

"Good for you."

She presses her lips tight together and looks away.

"Hey," I say, bringing my face down and over so she has to see me. "I really mean that."

She blinks a lot as she nods. Shit. I just made her cry. I pull her in closer. "Shhhh. It's okay." I kiss her head, taking in the smell of her hair. "It's okay."

To someone glancing at the dance floor, we probably just look like we're dancing really close together, but it feels to me like Simmons was right and she's about to crack. She clings to my shoulder and hand, unable to say a word, using everything she has to keep herself under control. I don't need her to tell me what happened, but I can't stop myself. "He didn't let you, did he?"

She shakes her head, a tiny, vicious movement of hair and pain. "He would let me sign up for a class if he was in a good mood, but-" She takes a deep breath. It feels like she's hanging on to me to keep from drowning. "I didn't finish until after I'd left. He wouldn't let me." She's breathing fast, shaking like an abused dog.

You don't make it to First Sergeant without having seen something like this at least once. I now have a good idea about how bad her marriage was. Being angry about it is normal, but I'm not angry.

I'm pissed.

I am raging. Livid. Pissed. I want this guy's name. I

on the floor, not dancing so much as swaying now.

"Regina?" I say into her hair. "Regina, I want you to promise me something." I drop my head so I can speak directly into her ear. "I want you to promise me that if I ever hurt you, ever, that you're going to tell me. You promise me that you'll let me know so I can fix it."

She nods into my chest.

Nodding isn't enough. "No. You say the words."

I hear a voice like a mouse tiptoeing into my ear. "I promise."

"What do you promise?"

She takes a shuddering breath. "I promise to tell you if you hurt me."

I can barely hear her and I swear she's going to fall. I hustle her over to an empty table and seat her in a chair before running to the bar for water.

***

Jim sits me down in a chair and holds my face, forcing me to look at him. "I'll get some water. I'll be right back. I promise."

As soon as he turns his back, I'm up and running for the ladies bathroom. I bang open the door and fall into the first open stall, slamming it shut and leaning against the door.

I can't stop shaking.

"Promise you won't ever do that again, baby." The voice in my head is hateful and twisted and not Jim's at all, but the words are still the same.

"Promise me."

Someone knocks on the stall door. "Regina?" Maria. She must've seen me rush in here because she sounds concerned. "Regina, honey, are you okay?"

I try to keep my voice level and calm. "Yes."

Maria doesn't buy it. "Did he hurt you, honey?"

Did he hurt me? Yes, he did. For nearly thirty years. "No. No, I'm just . . . It's been a heavy day."

"If he hurt you, you just tell me. I have a truck, and I'm not afraid to use it." It isn't hard to see where Cheryl gets her attitude from. I laugh hysterically, and slap a hand over my mouth.

"Regina?"

"Thanks, Maria," I manage to say. "But Jim's not the problem."

"Okay." She doesn't sound so sure. "You've got my number, right, honey?"

"Yes. I'm fine. Thank you."

I hear her huff, then leave, her heels clicking on the floor like a woman who is about to tear someone a new ass. I get the feeling she's gunning for Jim. I want to stop her, but I can't.

I can't stop shaking. My ears are ringing so loud I can't hear anything. My knees are about to slide out from under me.

I just have to breathe. I've been through this before. I can breathe, dammit.

Spots swim across my vision. I brace myself between the stall walls, locking my arms to help me stand. The cold metal under my hands shocks me for a moment. It's smooth. Chill, but starting to warm. There's a rough spot under my first finger that I keep rubbing, feeling the difference between it and the rest of the surface.

I am not going to pass out. I will not be that woman. I can breathe. Slowly. Calmly.

Breathe.

Tears burn my eyes. Shit, no. Not now. I don't have a

way to fix my mascara, and I don't want everyone staring at the blotchy-faced me that emerges from the bathroom after an incredible crying jag and a face scrubbed clean in the sink.

"Don't fight it when it comes," I hear my therapist say. *"Your frustration, your anger, all of that will make it worse. Feel something with your hands. Pay attention to the smells around you. Breathe. That's all you need to worry about. You have all the time you want, all the air you need. Just breathe."*

The make-up doesn't matter.

Just breathe.

Jim will understand when I see him again.

Just breathe.

Larry isn't here and he never will be.

Just breathe.

I don't know how long it takes to pull myself together again, but my arms feel numb, and my fingers are cold and tingly when I finally drop my arms from the stall walls. When I step out, I feel oddly detached, almost like I'm floating somewhere just above my head.

I didn't bring a purse with me tonight, just my phone, license, some cash and a credit card stuffed into my bra, so I have to make do with the paper towels at the sink to straighten my face.

Maria appears behind me, looking into the mirror with kind eyes. She lays a hand on my shoulder. "He's still out there waiting for you, honey."

I nod and lick the folded corner of the paper in my hands to sharpen the eyeliner that smeared during my panic attack, but I don't say anything.

"He's lucky he's a thinker, or he'd be dead by now," she tells me.

I laugh. "Did you hit him with your truck?"

"I tried," she says. "But he managed to straighten things out before it got ugly."

They'd been talking about me while I hid in the bathroom. My shoulders tighten. I force myself to breathe, trying to make my shoulders drop once more.

"Cheryl told me about him," she says. "Any man his age who can shudder when she makes an offer has got to be halfway decent."

My hands shake and I pull the paper towel away from my face to refold it, even though it doesn't need it. "She did what?"

"Cheryl was trying to be grown up, and she made him an offer. She wasn't serious, she just wanted to see how he'd react when you weren't around." Maria smiled. "On the one hand she was glad he didn't try to take her up on it, but the first thing she asked me when she got home was if she'd really gotten that fat. Once she told me the whole story, I lectured her for an hour about how dangerous it was."

I snort a laugh, trying not to cry. Cheryl was looking out for me. A kid not even old enough to drink was trying to make sure I didn't get stuck with the wrong guy.

"He threatened to tell Chuck if she did it again, so that's got to be worth something."

I sniff. Jim had even tried to take Cheryl to task for acting like a little tart, when another man probably would've just leered at her. My paper towel is now useless so I throw it away and pull another out of the dispenser.

She smiles at me in the mirror, and squeezes my shoulder before leaving me alone to fuss with my face.

I eventually realize that straightening the make-up is just a lost cause, so I wash it off, leaving my face just as blotchy and wretched as I imagined it would be.

Where's my mask when I need it the most?

I have to take a few more deep breaths before I'm ready to step out into the open again. The ladies room is well lit with fluorescent lights, but the main room in the community center has been dimmed to provide atmosphere, so at least there's something to hide some of the horror that's my face right now.

I scan the room, finding Jim at the same table where I left him, methodically folding a napkin. There's a small pile of mangled napkins on the table in front of him, like rejects from an origami zoo.

I clear my throat behind him and he shoots up from his chair like a rocket. "I'm sorry," I say. "Some things are harder than they should be, sometimes."

His eyes get wide looking at my face, so I guess the lights aren't dim enough. He looks like he wants say something, but he snaps his mouth shut and silently offers me his hand instead. I let him take me out to the dance floor once again for something slow. I'm too exhausted to think about appearances or personal space. I let myself melt into him, resting my head against his shoulder and letting my eyes drift past his neck.

After a few moments of silence, he clears his throat. "So what's your favorite color?"

I let out a small laugh. "Red."

"I've got a son and two grandkids. You?"

Everything feels so distant. "No." I close my eyes, a part of me wishing he would just be quiet.

After a few moments of blessed silence between us, he says, "You can ask me questions, you know."

I don't want to talk. I just want to be. "What's the tattoo about?" It's a dodge, just like what I did to Travis in September. Though I am curious, even if only distantly, at the moment.

I feel him nod. "It means elf for a while. My mom tried to keep me going to church and all that, but it backfired. After high school, I joined the Army."

I'm listening to his story, envisioning an angry young man with a mane of tangled black hair, rebelling against everything and everyone just to get away.

"Anyway, over the years, I sort of cobbled together something ethics or faith-wise that seemed to work for me, but I don't know that I could explain it so that it makes sense." He shrugs a little. "When I ran across the story of Thermopylae, the words seemed to fit the attitude. So I had the ink done when I turned thirty." I can feel him smile and huff a small laugh. "Jenny gave me a lot of shit for having a mid-life crisis when I came home with it."

The name is like cold water trickling down my back. "Jenny?" Was every single man my age divorced? Are they all just racking up the points on the board?

"My wife. She died thirteen years ago. Car wreck down the pass."

"I'm sorry." And I am. I was ready to assume the worst before I even knew what the worst could be.

He shakes his head. "You didn't know. It was a long time ago."

The song ends, and something fast takes its place. We leave the floor for a table as the crowd starts to get wild. He holds a chair for me to sit before pulling another one close for himself. I can't help but smile as he turns the chair backwards and sits, obviously wanting to continue talking. I don't want to talk. All I can think about is how I would like to slip into bed, and feel the weight of my blankets around me.

"So, maybe we could try something really kinky—like

dinner and a movie?" he suggests.

I shake my head slowly, the movement threatening to make the world spin in my head. "I don't know if I feel comfortable with that, just yet."

He blinks slow. "So let me get this straight. Everything that happened last summer you're perfectly okay with, but dinner and a movie is a total turn off?"

I open my mouth to say something, only to realize that I don't know what to say.

"Help me out, here," he asks me.

I sigh because I'm tired. "I'd like to," I say, I'm too tired to come up with another dodge. "I just don't know that I can go that far, just yet."

Jim looks at me like I've just shown him indisputable proof that I'm an alien from another planet. "I'll admit most movies are crap, but where I come from, things usually work a little different," he says. "The talking comes first and then-" He swirls his hand suggestively in the air between us. "The rest is considered *going further*."

Women trash-talk men a lot when we're with each other. Stories abound about the lazy, helpless, stubborn male who's only real interest is sex, not the work involved to keep the woman happy and interested in a relationship.

Jim isn't playing to type.

So why the hell aren't I? I should be looking to snap Jim up and shut him away in my closet so no one else can steal him from me. Why the hell am I not trying to keep him?

He's still waiting for me to explain. Something my mother said comes to mind. The words flip themselves in my head and leave my mouth before I even think about what I'm saying. "If you're getting the milk for free, then why do you need the cow?"

His left hand takes mine, the bracelet I made for him

clashing with his coat. Several lines of macrame knots in embroidery floss surround the tiny lock of hair. "Maybe I like to know she's well cared for." His smile is tired, and even a little sad. "But I will say she doesn't look like a cow from here."

He's so sweet. It takes everything I have to smile at him. The music of Auld Lang Syne starts. I didn't realize it was so late. How long was I kattywampussed in the bathroom?

He takes me out to the dance floor once again, holding me close as we sway. A few people have gotten seriously blitzed because they're trying to sing words they obviously don't know, loud and off-key. It's funny, and I would laugh except that I'm so tired.

I can feel Jim's lips near my ear. "I don't know what happened in your past," he breathes, "but I do know what I would like to happen in the future."

If I look at him, I'll start crying again, so I stare at the crowd past his shoulder instead.

"I want to get to know you, Regina." He holds me tighter as the balloons begin to fall. "But you're going to have to trust me, at least a little bit."

"Trust me." How many times have I heard that before?

Someone stomps on a balloon and I jump, the sound snapping me out of my daze. Jim smiles at me before I peel myself away from him. "I have to be work in a few hours."

He looks like I just told him I killed his dog. I don't want him to feel that way, but I have to leave. My nerves are strung so tight I can barely see, and there's a ringing in my ears that didn't come from the balloon. "Thanks for the evening," I say as I squeeze his hand.

Another balloon pops.

I have to leave before I do.

Chapter 10

An Ass of U and Me

Fortunately Cheryl still hadn't gone back to school yet, so she was able to cover for me.

New Year's Eve took it out of me in spades. I was so exhausted I could barely get out of bed for three days. I wasn't hung over or suffering from a cold—I was emotionally wrung out. She told me the rest of my employees were glad for the extra hours, since they know what's coming with the passing of the holidays. I suspect Mikie was more interested in Cheyenne, who probably knows more about running the counter from her sister than he does, but she doesn't seem to mind the extra attention.

Kids. Life is so much easier at that age.

When I come back to work, the party stops. I have to slash the hours to make up for the fall in business after the holidays, which means I also have to pick up a truly vicious schedule myself to keep things moving.

Jim shows up in my shop every day for his usual coffee

and loafing. Once he sees how much more I'm working, he starts doing the odd things. He'll snatch a washrag to wipe down tables, or mop the floor if he thinks it's dirty rather than let me do it. He polices the shop for trash and stray dishes. Once I even caught him in the back, loading the dishwasher.

When February comes, business is still dead, which is my only saving grace when my main sink drain behind the counter stops. Jim decided to be especially heroic and was gone and back with his tools before I could turn around twice. He probably already had them in his truck from whatever work he'd been doing before he came by, but I feel bad because when I offered to pay him he just smiled at me as he stripped off his watch and bracelet, tucking them into a jeans pocket. "Knights in rusted armor don't take advantage of ladies in distress."

Just looking at how I'm running my business has got to tell him money is an issue for me right now, dammit. Visiting my brother hit my savings harder than I thought it would. Now I've got my persistent suitor sprawled under my sink, moving his lanky legs out of my way every time I have to get something, making a necessary repair for free.

I don't like debts hanging over my head. I barely use the one credit card I have.

I have to pay this off, somehow. What would he accept? A conversation?

My stomach flips as I realize that, yes, he would be ecstatic if I paid him by talking. I look over my café and see a ghost town. Not even the card guys are there. Deputy Travis has already come and gone, and the lunch rush was anything but a rush. Jim's coat and over-shirt are draped on a chair, and his hat is resting on the table, but there's no need to move them, since there are no customers to speak of. My counters are clean and everything has been stocked.

There are no excuses for me to hide behind. I bite my lip, considering the beaten boots and well-worn jeans sticking out from under the sink. His t-shirt is black today with a well-known and wrinkled face painted white with black paint surrounding the eyes and drawn done the cheeks like running mascara. I never thought of Jim as a heavy metal fan.

It should not be this hard. The man has seen my tonsils through my vagina, for God's sake. My throat is dry.

I don't let myself think—I just kick his foot and he moves, thinking I need to get around him. I kick at his foot again. "Heavy Metal?" I ask.

"Everyone has a vice," he says from under the sink. "I don't smoke, I don't drink, I don't even watch TV that much. If I don't have something a little deviant, then I'd probably have to rob a bank or something."

I laugh at the thought of Jim trying to do anything criminal. "But metal?"

"Is this thing soldered on?" he mutters before answering me. "Well, what's your dirty secret? Rap?"

I shake my head with an embarrassed smile. "Jovi."

"Hah!" One of his hands comes out from under the sink, a finger pointing in my general direction. "I knew it!"

"Skydiving?" I ask as the hand disappears again.

"Oh, hell, no." He grunts muted curses as he fights with getting the trap off. "I was Army for a reason. I like my feet on the ground." More cursing. A clang. "Son of a bitch!"

"Everything okay down there?"

"Yeah, just clipped my knuckles. What about you? Have you ever jumped out of a perfectly good plane?"

I shake my head even though I know he can't see it. "Thought about it."

"Skiing?"

"Blacked my eye."

He tilts his head out from under the sink, looking at me as if I were insane. "What?"

"I swear that tree jumped in front of me on purpose."

He laughs, and goes back under the sink. "Did midget sadists install this thing?" he complains. "I can barely get my hand in here."

"It was here when I bought the business." Java Books had been in the red almost every month for a year when I bought it. The woman who owned it didn't know what she had in inventory, how old it was, or even what it took to make decent coffee. Turning the business around had been a struggle in the first year, but I was in the black by the end of my first month of ownership, so it gave me enough hope to keep going. It's more successful now, but it's still a slow slog. "I'm hoping in another few years I'll be able to afford another loan to make renovations," I tell Jim.

"You need a fireplace," he says.

"It would be nice atmosphere," I agree. "I'll put it on the list after a bigger back room, larger counter area and new linoleum."

"Good," he grunts. Another clang. "Shit!"

"I can call a plumber," I tell him. "It's okay. Really."

"No, no. He'd have the same problems. It's tight, and I can't see a damn thing." A hand emerges from under the sink, waving me over. "I need you to hold a light right here," he says, gesturing to some spot I can't see.

I get his flashlight, and try to maneuver around him to get the light where he needs it. It isn't easy; I practically have to lay on top of him to get the light in the right spot because there just isn't any room behind the counter for a plumber and his assistant.

I can see his face when the trap unexpectedly falls off and slams into his nose. He shouts a litany of curses as dirty water pours from the sink above and he shimmies out of the way as best he can with me on top of him. By the time I get the bucket under the sink it's a futile gesture, and I'm straddled across Jim's lap while he's holding his nose, blinking through the pain.

I gently pull his hands away to look. His hair and shirt are soaked in rinse water and coffee grounds and there's a bruise already forming on the bridge of his nose. "Well, you might have a shiner when the bruising is done, but it doesn't look bad," I say. "I'll get some ice."

His hands seize my hips, keeping me in his lap. We're both wearing jeans but only now am I aware of how hard he is against me.

It's been months for both of us. Desire claws at my stomach, but it feels wrong. It isn't dark and there are no masks. We were talking and . . . things felt like they might be okay.

Things might actually be okay. For a few moments, I actually felt safe just talking to him.

He doesn't seem too interested in talking right now. One of his hands slides up my back, pulling me closer. "Business is slow," he murmurs. "You could knock off early for the day. Maybe a movie." He shifts his hips to sit straighter. The side effect is a small grind against me, and I take in a quick breath. On impulse I grind achingly slow against him, making both of us gasp.

I haven't made out like this since high school. I'd forgotten how wickedly frustrating it was. I want him. Here, right now.

"Well, we could do that, too," he says with a playful smirk. "But I'm good for just a movie." His hand drifts from shoulder to my head, pulling me in for the kiss I know he wants. A kiss I'm terrified of.

"I thought you wanted to talk," I manage to say. "Get to know each other."

"Talking is good," he says, his lips brushing against mine. "I like talking."

I'm ready to do whatever he wants.

"Ahem," a customer clears her throat. I leap to my feet before I can even register the shock and terror coursing through my veins. On the other side of my counter is a woman about my age with very blonde hair and perfectly drawn eyebrows. Behind her is a small group of people milling about the shop, stretching their legs, browsing through books, reading the menu.

Maybe even checking out the interrupted porno behind the counter.

If I'm lucky, Ms. Manners will be the only one who saw anything. A quick glance behind her and I see a chauffeur's van with the words Green Valley Fellowship on the side.

A church van.

I was so horny a van full of churchies came into my shop, and I didn't hear a single ring of the bell on my door.

I look down at my apron, dirty sink water splashed all over it. "We're having some problems with the sink," I explain. Over-plucked brows rise up in response. "Let me change, and wash up and I will be right back," I say.

Jim stands up from the floor and if looks could kill, Ms. Manners would be six months dead already. Her eyes get wide, and her mouth opens slightly in shock. "Jim?"

My blood runs cold. Ms. Manners knows Jim? My Jim?

"Oh, hey," he says, snatching a towel from the counter to mop his face. "Jeannette, isn't?"

"Janice," she corrects him, her voice icy.

My fists clench. I struggle to not explode right there. It's like I'm seeing the same movie all over again. *He can't even remember her fucking name.*

He shrugs, pulling the towel around the back of his neck. "Janet, Jeannette. I got the J right."

I'm too shocked to react when he plants a kiss on the side of my head before strolling into the back office as if he owns the place.

Ms. Manners pinches her lips tight in suppressed fury. "Don't worry about the coffee," she says to me while glaring at his back. "I'll wait until Cripple Creek."

***

The other members of Ms. Manners' church group didn't get quite the show she did, so for about twenty minutes I hustle drinks and books almost non-stop. When their van pulls away, I storm into my office to see Jim doodling on a pad with his chin in his hand.

"What the hell was that all about?" I demand, waving my hand towards the front of my store. I'm angry. I'm hurt. I've seen this crap before. I've been made to feel like the cheap slut when the other woman showed up at my door, looking for her boyfriend. My husband.

I am not doing it again. I won't. I don't give a damn if he does hit me. Better to get it over with now.

He tries to look past me into the café. "She's gone, then?"

"Of course she's gone!" I shout. "Would I be acting like this for a fucking audience?"

He sighs and leans back in my chair. My. Chair. He tugs on the towel around his neck. "The first time I met Janice it was at my grandson's baptism in July. She tried to hook me, I got away. At Thanksgiving, my daughter-in-law tried to set me up with her again and . . . " He pauses.

I've been through this before. My vision narrows to a tunnel. I cross my arms over my chest. "Did you sleep with her?"

I'm prepared for his confession. *"Of course I did. You didn't think I'd let a piece of ass go by without at least trying it, did you? Stop being so greedy, sweetheart."*

I am not putting up with this crap again. I won't. I'm so angry I'm glaring right into his eyes. I'm ready for him to stand and take a swing at me. There's a half-full urn of hot coffee just behind me. All I have to do is take three steps back and-

He shudders dramatically. "Uuuaahhll. Hell, no. I told her you were my girlfriend."

My arms fall. I didn't expect that kind of a confession. "You did what?"

"I told her you were my girlfriend."

I point behind me into the empty shop. "So what was she all pissed about?"

He sighs. "I'm guessing my daughter-in-law had built her up to think that I might be interested in her. Janice scared the hell out of me at Thanksgiving, and I panicked. I don't think anyone really believed the girlfriend story except me."

I have no idea what to say. Thanksgiving? He'd been thinking of me as his girlfriend since Thanksgiving? Should I be offended or flattered?

Come to think of it, it was right after Thanksgiving that he started showing up again, badgering me to talk to him.

He pushes away from the desk, crossing my tiny office in single step before I can scoot back. His hands hold my shoulders gently. No painful grip, no digging fingers. One of his thumbs caresses my shoulder. "It kind of slipped out before I really thought about it, but it didn't feel like a lie."

All I can do is blink.

"I know you're probably not thinking about me that way, but-"

"I need you to finish the sink and go." My knees feel weak.

"But-"

"Please." I shrug out of his hands and leave my office. "I can't do this right now."

***

Did I wrong Jenny during our marriage and just not realize it? Is that why I keep screwing things up with Regina? Some kind of ghostly revenge?

My imagination produces phantom laughter from my kitchen as I lay on the couch with a tiny black eye and a headache. *"Of course, Shit-wit,"* I hear. *"Because I have nothing better to do than to haunt you. It isn't like I have grandchildren to look after or anything."*

It's been two days since Janice ruined a perfect opportunity. Regina won't even acknowledge my existence in her store beyond filling an order for coffee.

"No good deed goes unpunished," I mutter to myself. I want my headache to go away. I want to know what I did wrong, again. My cell phone rings. I pull it from my shirt pocket to take the call.

It's my son.

"So I hear you were having sex in full view of the public with some raging slut," Lucas says. I can hear the grin on his face. The little shit thinks it's funny.

156

I wonder where he gets his sick sense of humor from.

"The rumors are sadly mistaken." I pinch the bridge of my nose. The pressure feels good, pushing back against the pain. "And you can tell Janice if I hear her call Regina a slut ever again, she and I are going to have many unpleasant words."

"I figured things were a little overstated, but I thought I'd check and be on the safe side. Missy's over the moon about it though."

"Janice must have added a few chapters I wasn't there for," I comment. "As I recall, I'd just had a sink trap smack me in the face behind a very crowded counter." There was a little more to it than that, and maybe there would've been even more if the Laughing God Murphy hadn't taken a hand in things, but I'm certainly not going to tell my son that.

I don't give a damn if he is married. He's not old enough to hear my stories.

"For Missy it's more about having an eyewitness to the mystery girlfriend." I hear Missy shouting something in the background. "She says you have to bring her over to meet the family," my son dutifully repeats.

"I'm working on it."

"That doesn't sound very promising."

"Things take time."

The sounds from my son's house go quiet, and I know he's in another room now. "Dad? Seriously. You've been dodging this girlfriend thing for months. What's going on?"

I frown at my ceiling. "We've both got battle-scars," I sigh. "And some hurt more than others."

"Divorce?"

"Yup."

"Bad?"

"I'm pretty sure he was an abusive son of a bitch."

I hear Lucas blow air from his mouth. "Be careful, Dad," he finally says. "Some divorced ladies can be pretty damn bitter. Janice is one of them." My son doesn't curse. Ever. So I know he's worried.

"I'm not worried about Miss Priss Janice," I say.

"Neither am I," my son agrees. "It's your girlfriend I'm worried about."

"This isn't Hollyweird, son. She's not going to turn into an axe-murderer."

"That's not what I'm getting at," he says. "I'll bet your girlfriend is still hurting. Just talking to Janice about the weather is like walking on eggshells. If you're a man, she assumes everything without getting her facts straight first."

"Well, Regina isn't much better. She was under the impression that Janice and I had something going on the side."

"Say what?" My son is shocked. I have my faults, many of them, but he knows infidelity is not one.

"You heard me."

"You told her how things really were, though, right? You got it straightened out?"

"Eggshells, son. Eggshells." I sigh and stare at my ceiling. "I was being an asshole," I admit.

I can imagine Lucas rubbing at his forehead like his mom used to do. "What did you do?" He's even got her tone.

It's enough to make me want to cry.

"Oh, for God's sake, James. Do I have to beat you over the head with it?" I look over at the kitchen table to make sure it's empty before I let my head fall back on the pillow with a sigh. "Janice had this high and mighty attitude with Regina. I couldn't help myself." I was also pissed she ruined a perfect moment for me. "I called her Janet. On purpose."

My son snorts, trying to suppress his laughter. "Do you enjoy shooting yourself in the foot?"

"Not really, but that's why Regina thought I had a thing with Janice."

"Wow. Talk about timing. Valentines is this coming week."

"Really?" I'd honestly forgotten about that.

"Yup. Maybe you should do something above and beyond flowers and candy," he suggests.

"What are you and Missy doing?"

"I've got Tommy set up with a weekend sleepover at a friend's house and Eddie's parents said they'd take Rosy, too. I'll probably have to pay up on their anniversary, but I think it'll be worth it to take Missy to Estes Park."

"Slick."

"No," he says. "Slick is Valentines' Day. The day before, I'm taking the day off work and cleaning the house. I've got some of her friends taking her to Denver after Tommy goes to school."

I can definitely hear him grinning ear to ear. "You've gained in wisdom, my son," I intone seriously. "You've got a hotel lined up for Saturday?"

"A gentleman does not reveal such details," he says. I can still hear him grinning.

I'm glad for him. I really am. And I'm jealous as hell.

"Maybe you should try something like that," he says.

"I don't have a key to her house, son. We're not that close, yet."

"You've got picks, Dad."

"I also have competition from a county deputy," I grumble.

"Oh. Okay, maybe cleaning her house isn't such a good idea," he backtracks quickly. "Is there anything else you can do?"

"I'm working on it," I tell him, an idea forming in my head. My wife's memory mocks me. *"Really, James? That's what you're going to do? A huge bouquet and an apology for all the world to see?"* I can almost see her leaning against my bookshelf with her arms crossed over her chest. *"Do you not remember how many times I told you you'd be a damn sight more sexy if you'd scrub a toilet? At least Lucas listened to me."*

I sit up, resting my elbows on my knees, suddenly uncomfortable. I rub the back of my neck. "Are you okay with this?" I ask.

"Ah, okay with what?"

"Me dating. Are you—do you think-" I can't even finish.

"Dad?"

I take a deep breath, but words fail me. I honestly don't know what to say.

"Dad, listen to me." Lucas' voice is drowning in concern. "I miss her, too. I-" He takes a moment before continuing. "I didn't understand when I was younger the way I do now."

I can feel the tears form. I don't know how many times I failed him, I just know I did it for five years straight. "I'm sorry, Lucas. I am so, so, sorry."

"Yeah, well, that was then." His voice is trembling. "Things are different now." He sniffs, and huffs a tiny laugh. "I don't think Mom would want you to be alone. When you weren't around, she'd sometimes call you *helpless*."

I didn't know that. "That sounds about right," I say. "I proved it more than once."

"I don't think you're helpless, Dad. You might need help, sometimes, but you're not helpless."

I don't know what to say.

"Dad?"

"You're the postman's kid," I say. "No kid of mine would be this forgiving."

Lucas laughs.

Chapter 11

Breakthrough

I won't decorate Java Books with queasy hearts or offer Valentines specials because I hate Valentine's Day. I really do. It isn't that I want to spoil it for other people, or I'm "rebelling against the establishment" as Steve likes to say, but it is a personal thing. Valentines has been a miserable time of year for most of my life. So when Jim shows up with his healing shiner and a single rose at Java Books on Valentine's Day, I'm all out of sorts. He waits until there's a lull in the traffic, then traps me in my closet of an office.

"Did you really think I slept with her?" he asks.

My eyes dart to the storefront, worried someone will hear us. I don't want to have this conversation here. But I didn't answer my door at home when he knocked, and I've done my best to steer clear of him for the past week and a bit, so I guess it is my fault.

I turn to my computer and start working on . . . something. He's waiting for an answer. I sigh. "After you

you explained things, no."

"But he would've?"

Jim doesn't know who "he" is beyond the concept that "he" existed, but the assumption is accurate.

My vision blurs, and I blink to clear it. "She has a pulse," I manage to say.

I'm angry. At Jim for not giving me a good reason to be angry. At Ms. Manners for just breathing. But mostly at myself for not clearing the air between Jim and I. My shoulders slump and I close my eyes. "I'm sorry."

Jim leans down, resting one hand on the top of my chair, and the other on my desk, holding his rose. He touches his lips against my hair. "I'm a lot more picky than that," he says. "Happy Valentine's Day." He leaves my office and the flower on my desk without another word.

I hear the ringing bell from my door, and dash the tears away before rushing out to the front again. I take care of the line of customers that have formed in the brief two minutes I was gone, make another mental note to hire someone older than high school to at least help with the days during the school year, and then look up to see Jim, seated backwards on a chair at a tiny table, his reading glasses perched on his nose, already engrossed in some swords and sorcery novel.

I actually prefer to see that than the rose he gave me.

Jim brings me a sandwich from the deli next door that I barely have time to enjoy before the Valentines lunch rush hits. I don't know why I wasn't expecting it—it's Friday. People are leaving work early to get all spruced up and ready for their night with a special someone.

I hate Valentine's Day.

In one moment I'm slamming out order after order and in the next, everything is quiet. I start another three batches of coffee to brew, and take a moment to breathe. I look up

I look up to see my tables and chairs are straight and clean, wiped spotless by an invisible busboy. A noise in the back room draws my attention, and I realize the dishwasher has been set to run. Out in the café there's serious a game of bridge in the far corner, so I know none of those guys had anything to do with helping me. The building could be on fire, and they wouldn't notice unless their table was burning.

It takes my eyes a few moments to find Jim, settled in the overstuffed chair bordering the café and the bookstore, looking for all the world like he's hardly moved. He looks at me over his glasses, and winks.

It's enough to make a working girl swoon.

An hour later Deputy Travis walks in, carrying a mixed flower bouquet and a smile. He must be off work, because he isn't in uniform and his ski jacket is bright and colorful. "Hi, Beautiful!" he says, handing me the flowers.

The bridge game broke up about ten minutes earlier, leaving the store ghost-town empty except for Jim. His over-shirt is nearly the same green as the upholstery on the chair, making for perfect camouflage if he doesn't move. He looks up at Travis' back, his expression flat and calm, but I see the murder in his eyes before he drops his face to his book again.

The other day I'd been ready to believe Jim had fucked Ms. Manners. I can only hope he won't jump to the same conclusions about me and Travis.

"I saw the way you looked at him," I hear from my past. I smile, taking the flowers to cover my nerves, wondering if there's a diplomatic way out of this situation. How many hints that I'm not interested do I have to give this guy before I have to get outright rude?

I guess I could say that this is the one way Jim is typically male—he doesn't back off either.

"I've decided that if you won't talk to me by July, then I'm done." That was Jim's New Year's resolution. I can either tell him to go away forever, or run out the clock, but there's a deadline and once it passes, I know there won't be an extension.

That bothers me. Not his deadline or his persistence, but somehow knowing that when he's done, he'll be done. No more trying.

"The usual?" I ask, depositing the flowers in my office, forcing my voice to be light and casual.

"Well, sure," Deputy Travis agrees.

Jim turns a page in his book. I don't believe he's reading a single word right now.

I begin to mix up Travis' favorite concoction, some sugary excuse for coffee involving chocolate, caramel and whipped cream. I want to throw up every time I make this thing. Who would do this to good coffee? A serial killer? What does it say about me that I put this shit on my menu, and know how to make it?

I guess it means I'm desperate for money.

I purposely make it in a to-go cup with the lid snapped firmly down, hoping he'll take the hint as I hand it to him.

He doesn't. He takes a long sip, closing his eyes as if it were ambrosia. I suppress a shudder. When his eyes open again, he smiles at me. "I still feel bad about New Year's-"

"Don't," I interrupt while shaking my head with a smile. I was actually relieved he'd been too sick to be at Honesty's community center party. The last thing I needed that night was to watch Travis and Jim go at it in some bizarrely civilized alpha-male smackdown. "I found another dance partner."

Travis blinks, and adjusts his footing. "Well, I'm glad, but I still think I should make it up to you," he continues.

"It's bad manners to stand up your date."

Dammit, this guy is just not catching the hint.

"I was thinking I should take you out tonight," he says. "Midnight Mountain?"

I grab a towel and move around to the front, wiping down already clean tables. Ordinarily, I'd keep the counter between us, but there's nothing to do back there and he can see that. Out front, I can at least pretend that the feng is not shui for how my chairs are placed or something, to avoid looking at him.

I would love to be the cruel bitch who can heartlessly crush a person's hopes, but I'm not. I'm still trying to be polite, and tell this guy to bug off without hurting his feelings in the process, despite the obvious set-up.

How stupid does Travis think I am? Midnight Mountain is hard to get into for dinner on a regular Friday night. It would be impossible for a Friday night Valentines unless you have a friend in the manager's office, which means that Travis probably does.

Or he has a backup plan. Like the date whose car mysteriously breaks down in the middle of nowhere. I can tell he's carefully thought this out, unlike the last man who asked me to Midnight Mountain.

Jim had just wanted to go somewhere we could talk back in December. He probably would've gone for a gas station food lounge if I'd suggested it as a counter-offer. I know that. I knew that when he'd asked, I was just kattywampussed.

Much like I always am.

Jim turns another page in his book. My knight in rusted armor is leaving me to my own devices. He has no intention of interfering with me and Travis.

Why don't men ever do what you want them to do,

when you want them to do it?

"Thank you, Travis, but I already have plans," I say.

I can see Jim relax, and he smiles, turning another page.

Travis looks crestfallen. "Oh. I didn't realize." He plays with his cup. "Who's the lucky guy?"

"That would be me," Jim says without looking up.

Travis spins, startled that there's someone else in the store. I suck in my lips to not laugh at him. Jim was easy to miss, but Travis is a cop, so he must have been so keyed up to ask me out, he didn't notice he had an audience.

Travis sizes him up. Jim barely raises his head enough to look at him over his glasses. The differences between the two men are staggering, even with Jim sitting down. They might be the same age, but that's where the similarities stop. Travis can't be more than five foot nine, and his grey hair is close-cropped. Jim is over six foot and lanky, his hair more salt and pepper and kind of shaggy. Even their coats clash, with Travis' bright colored ski jacket complete with lift tickets on the zipper looking somehow like a child's against Jim's beaten canvas coat draped on the back of the armchair.

"Nice eye," Travis says to him.

Jim nods his head to the side. The shiner isn't so bad— just a small line more than anything, but it's still noticeable. "I got it fixing a sink. Trap fell."

There's some mysterious man-thing happening silently in front of me, despite the words. I know they're saying something, but I have no idea what. It makes me nervous.

"So what are the plans?" Travis finally asks, looking at both of us, trying to call my bluff.

"I haven't told her yet," Jim says without missing a beat. He smiles. Friendly. Devious. Wicked.

It melts my knees.

"I want it to be a surprise," he adds.

Travis nods, his face a neutral mask. He smiles, lifting his cup at me as he leaves. "Well, then. Have fun, you two."

Jim waits until Travis' jeep pulls away. "Did I do that right?" he asks.

I suddenly realize he still isn't sure where he stands with me. He's worried that I want to play the field, that his little alpha-male challenge with Travis might have been too possessive, too presumptive. He's worried I'll tell him to go away and never come back, because that's exactly what he would do if I asked him to.

"Yes. Yes, you did," I say with a relieved sigh.

"This isn't the first time he's asked you out, is it?"

My mouth quirks. Jim has been in the café so much over the past few months that he's had to have put two and two together to get four by now. "No," I say reluctantly. "But one date was enough. I'm not interested."

I retreat to my office to toss the flowers in the trash. Part of me feels bad about doing that. The guy had probably spent weeks planning a romantic Valentines, only to get shot down in under five minutes. "I don't think he's a bad guy," I say cautiously, trying to avoid sounding like a gossip. "But there are too many things that are too different about us to make me even want to go for round two."

Jim's eyebrows rise as he looks at me, waiting for an explanation. I feel more than a little awkward right now, seeing as how Jim's willing to hear me out before coming to a conclusion, whereas I had practically attacked him without getting my facts straight.

On the other hand—"We're just too different. I don't know how else to explain it. He kinda creeped me out a little bit."

Jim shorts a laugh. "He creeps you out but I don't? How

does that work?"

Oh, God, I wish I knew.

"Cheryl's mom told me he's got a few divorces under his belt already. When a woman hears that, it makes her wonder." It's a lame excuse.

On the other hand, when a man shows up unannounced and naked in a woman's backyard, shouldn't that make her wonder? *Like, a lot?*

Maybe my therapist is right—maybe my wires did get hopelessly crossed. Now I wonder if Jim is someone I'm interested in, or if I'm just using him as some kind of bizarre revenge-fuck.

My nose twitches—does it smell more intense in here than it did before Travis came in? I swear my sinuses are suddenly drowning in chocolate and bitters, the perfume of the flowers stabs up into my brain, the pastries in the tiny display are overwhelming and-

"Being a cop can't be easy," Jim says, looking back down at his book. "It's probably hard to find a woman willing to put up with that."

Jim's voice has shattered the moment. Things smell normal again. The flowers in my wastebasket look at me reproachfully. Travis might just be a nice guy with a run of bad luck with women. Now I feel bad for even suggesting around the edges that there might be another reason for why he's single. "The sage voice of experience?" I ask, trying to hide my confusion and embarrassment and make a joke of it.

What the hell was that with my nose?

Jim gets a weird expression on his face and closes his book.

"I saw the way you looked at him. The way he looked at you." It's a playful, sinister voice. Not Jim's, but still just as

real.

Jim takes a deep breath. "Jenny wasn't my first wife," he says.

I'm shocked.

"My first wife," he frowns in thought. "Shit. I was barely twenty. We were young and stupid, and didn't understand what having a spouse in the Army meant. We got married, I deployed a month or two later and when I came back, she was knocked up with my best friend's kid."

"What happened?" I can only imagine what Larry would have done.

"I got a divorce, and later thanked my lucky stars we hadn't been married more than a year and a half." He looks at me. "I should've told you, but I don't really count that one."

The confession has him worried again. I shrug. "I couldn't date Travis even if I wanted to anyway," I say quickly, wiping down a clean counter. "His usual is the *Cloud Nine*."

Jim frowns at me. I point to the menu above my head and he and looks for the name. His lips move slightly as he reads. "Does that come with ice cream and a cherry on top?" he says after a moment.

I shake my head with a giggle. "I just hope his mom doesn't find out. She'd ground him for ruining his dinner."

Jim laughs, and a load lifts from my shoulders.

Sometime after the evening rush we get involved in a strange game involving authors and adjectives. I don't know how it started, but it banters back and forth, each of us trying to trip the other up.

"Heinlein," I say.

"Philosopher," he replies without missing a beat. "King."

"Repetitive. Rice."

He tosses the day's newspaper in the trash. "Ugh. Rand."

"*Ugh* isn't an adjective."

"It is now. Rand."

Mikie has his coat on when he emerges from the tiny area in the back that serves as coat locker, break room and pantry. He's been listening to this game for the last hour. "Who's Rand?" he asks, making his way to the door.

"A migraine," a customer says as I hand him his decaf coffee.

"No comments from the peanut gallery," Jim quips, re-shelving the stray books.

"Actually, I'm going to go with that one," I say, pointing at the man who offered it. The customer laughs and leaves.

"Howard," I say, following Mikie to the door, and flip the lock after him.

Jim spreads his hands as if it were the most obvious answer. "Conan."

I laugh and turn the sign from "open" to "closed" before returning to the counter. "Two in a row. *Conan* isn't an adjective. Two in a row. You lose." I have no idea if that was a rule for this game, but it is now, because I said so.

Jim starts flipping the chairs off the floor onto tabletops to mop. "No, I don't. I'm a guy. *Conan* is a noun, verb, and adjective to us."

I shake my head, smiling. "That is so cheating."

"*Cheating*?" he demands playfully. "*Cheating*?" He takes the mop handle and wheels its bucket out to the tables where he poses dramatically, his hand on his chest. "I would have you know, dear lady, that your coffee has ruined me for all others. I haven't been able to drink anything other than your brew for months, now. I don't even try, anymore."

"Good." I zee-out the credit cards, and tally the register while he mops and takes care of the trash. I'm only off by fifty-seven cents after counting twice. Jim has replaced the chairs on the floor, and is wiping down the tables and seats while I count a third time to be safe.

I bag the profits, reset the cash drawer, and turn my attention to the counter, topping off my syrups and stocking my little fridges underneath. Jim has already capped the bucket of used grounds and kicked it to a back corner, waiting for Mr. Ellis to make his daily compost pickup tomorrow evening.

I don't know how that man does it, but Mikies' dad manages to have the most productive garden I have ever seen, and the dirt here is crap for growing anything. It isn't even soil. What's on the ground is just dried out, crushed granite. Most gardeners here tell me that even composting in Colorado is nearly impossible because of how dry the climate is.

I hear Jim washing the excess dishes in the sink by hand as I rummage in my large refrigerator. Something shatters on the floor.

"Job opening!" I yell at him while carting milk from the back to the little fridges in front.

"It figures," he says, grabbing a broom.

In my office, I go through my closing checklist. If Jim hadn't stayed to help, I'd have been here until after eleven. As it is, it's after ten and I closed at eight. I rub my eyes. I have got to hire someone other than teenagers so I can actually sleep every once in a while, but how do you convince an adult to work for part-time minimum wage?

Jim leans against the doorframe to my office. "All done?"

I stretch and yawn. "I just have to do the drop at the bank, and then it's back to the grind at five tomorrow."

"I thought you didn't work Saturdays."

I sink back into my chair. "Even if I don't work, I still open and close."

"Java Books was open while you were gone."

I smile. He still came even when he knew I was gone. The thought sends a thrill down my back. "Cheryl was back from college for break. She was all excited when I gave her the keys. When she gave them back all she would say is *never again*."

Jim laughs.

I swing my chair from side to side. The armrest either hits the desk on one side or the wall on the other. "All I can get to work here are teenagers and, well . . . "

Jim nods. "They're teenagers."

I shrug. "They're good kids, but things tend to go wrong at opening and closing." I close my eyes. I made a mistake sitting down, because now I don't want to get back up.

"Anything else to be done?" he asks.

"Just crazy Valentine's sex," I joke, my eyes still closed.

"Ah."

I hear several clicks and the lights are out. I sit up with my eyes wide, but I can't see a thing, which means my door is also closed. "Why is it dark in here?" My hand fumbles the power button on my computer monitor just so I can have something to see by to find my flashlight. Ghostly blue light filters through the room.

"Turn that off," Jim grumbles at me.

"But it's dark," I say. "Why is the door closed?"

"I'm finishing the last item on the to-do list, unless you

don't want me to."

The last-?

Oh.

He waits for me, the computer screen still glowing.

I turn off my monitor, and we're drowning in darkness once again. He pulls me up from my chair, groping for the tail end of my braid, pulling the band out and combing my hair loose with his fingers. He's not saying anything in the pitch black, his lips more interested in my neck.

I have to smile. There aren't any masks but it's dark enough to compensate for that, and everything else. I'm tired, but when his lips find a particular spot on my neck I don't care anymore.

I pull both his shirts over his head, dropping them somewhere on the floor. I can feel him moving under my hands, but I don't know what he's doing until he suddenly shrinks in height with a soft clattering of boots.

My eyes have adjusted, and enough light is trickling in from under the door that I can see his outline. My shirt gets tugged loose and his hands stroke my stomach and back before working the clasps on my bra.

I hook one of my legs over his hip as the last catch is undone, and I suddenly feel like I have an uncomfortable rope hanging limply around my shoulders. He holds my leg on his hip, running his hand up and under as I try to reach my foot. It smacks against the edge of the desk a few times and we fight each other before he stops, pulling back slightly.

"What's wrong?" He sounds concerned, like he's crossed a line he didn't realize I'd put down.

The words are like a blow to my chest. He spoke. He's asking me what I want. He's nearly frozen in place, waiting for me to tell him to stop. To leave. To stand on his head.

Yes, he's been irritatingly persistent, but I realize he'll do just about anything I say, I just have to tell him. That was always his rule: I can choose how everything goes, I just have to use my words. *Get lost. Come here. Mop the floor. Bang me in my office.*

I've never had that kind of power over anyone before.

The blatant reality of it all swirls in my head. A hysterical giggle trips out of my mouth. "I'm wearing hiking boots."

He's still frozen. "Really?"

I nod, the power of speech making my head feel light. "I can't reach them like this."

He lowers my leg so both feet are on the floor again. My shirt and bra get pulled over my head and tossed somewhere in the tiny room. His movements are awkward, and I can feel him digging in one of his pockets as he starts kissing my chest, slowly kneeling in front of me with a small grunt. He undoes the button and zipper of my jeans, but doesn't try to pull them off. Instead, he kisses my stomach, running a teasing finger under the waistline of my panties.

I press my back against the wall, reveling in the sensation until I remember the underwear I'm wearing— basic cotton granny panties.

Not sexy at all.

Jim's whisper banishes my mortification, his breath on my skin sending a delicious sensation through my body. "Don't," he kisses my stomach again. "Move." I get the feeling that he's grinning.

I hear a small click and there's a thin pressure on the top of one boot before a series of tearing pops rise from my foot. Another three pops and he draws my foot out.

He cut my shoelaces with a knife from his pocket. If

this were a movie, I'd say it was a lame addition to a sex scene. But because it's Jim with my boot, it is undeniably hot.

He makes quick work of the other boot and there's a click of the knife closing shut while he pulls off my boot with one hand. He glides his hands up my legs to my waist before pulling my jeans off with agonizing slowness. As soon as he has them off my feet, I start to join him on the floor but he stops me with firm hands on my hips, guiding me to my office chair and making me sit on the very edge. He shifts his shoulders under my legs and a moment later I lose my mind.

When he finally pulls away, I'm gasping. My tiny office has gotten warm and musky with the door closed. I hear him shedding his pants, but it doesn't register until he pulls me up to my feet again.

I start shuffling around so he can sit, but he pushes me against the wall instead, pinning his arm between it and my waist. There's a loud clatter from my chair being kicked away and slamming against the desk. He brings my leg to his hip, trailing his fingers down to my foot and guiding it to the edge of my desk. I realize what he's doing and I shove my heel against the lip of the desk, pushing at it for all I'm worth.

My arms hang on to his shoulders as he positions my other leg the same way and comes in closer. The shifting of positions gave me a moment to breathe, a moment for my muscles to go from wobbly to stable again. That changes in an instant.

His first thrust is slow, and he moves his feet to get more leverage but it does the trick. I gasp, and my arms are frantic to find a way to hold him close without falling. He manages to wriggle his other arm between my back and the wall, grabbing my right shoulder and pushing me down to meet him as he rises up.

Each time, I feel my stomach tie itself into a tighter knot. Tiny explosions rocket up my spine, and I can't stop myself from begging James not to stop, don't stop, don't ever sto-

A scream tears itself from my lips and he stiffens under me, his arms pulling me down on him even harder than before.

His head drops to my shoulder, nuzzling my neck. I hear him chuckle and the sound shivers down my spine.

"Wha-What's so funny?" I am mortified. Why is he laughing at me?

He pulls in ragged breaths and kisses my neck. "You called me James before you screamed," he says, his chest heaving. "And I have no idea why, but I think you just did something more important than a run-of-the-mill orgasm."

"I'm sorry." It's an automatic response and I want to find a hole in the earth and hide for saying it.

James shakes his head. "No," he gasps. "Don't apologize. I liked it." He kisses my neck again, his lips just under my ear. I can feel him grinning. "I liked it a lot."

Talking like this is making my head buzz like I'm on my way to getting blitzed. "It was a very nice surprise." I start giggling, and I bury my face in his shoulder while he laughs, helping me bring my shaking legs back to the floor again.

Maybe Valentines isn't so awful after all.

Chapter 12

Knocked Down

I don't go to Java Books on Saturday because Louis Harrison needs my help. The starter in his car died, and what should've been no more than three hours, if you include a trip to the parts store, turned into seven hours, and ended with frozen fingers.

Who the hell designs an engine that requires a midget contortionist with six hands to change a frickin' starter?

Sunday morning I'm up and puttering around my house, taking in the heavenly scent of Regina's coffee brewing in my kitchen, nodding my head in time to some newer metal coming through the speakers of my stereo. It's still dead brown outside, but even with the cold and yesterday's irritations, I'm still feeling good about Friday. Regina enjoyed herself. She enjoyed me as much as I did her.

Afterward was a little strange since she kept her back against the wall, and wouldn't let me turn on the light to find our clothes. She'd finally relented and let me turn on the computer monitor, but she absolutely wouldn't move away from the wall until she'd pulled her shirt on faster than a guilty teenager.

It's weird, but I guess most women are in some way. I'm wondering if I'll be able to get her out for an actual date—dinner, maybe a nice conversation about books—as I sift through the news when I see a headline that freezes my blood.

"Armed robbery at Java Books."

I spill my coffee, staring at the article in horror.

"Yesterday, police report that Regina Linkous, the owner of Java Books in Honesty, CO was held up at gunpoint when-"

I don't finish. I don't clean up the mess or put on my coat. I just run out the door and hotfoot it to Regina's house. Her car is in her driveway under the carport shelter and I run past it, down the rough stone steps to her porch, and pound on her door.

She doesn't answer. My arms and hands are aching from the cold, but I don't care. I hit the door again. "Regina! Regina, it's James! Open up!"

Maybe she's still in bed. I glance at my watch to see it's just after nine. She gets up to be at work by five every morning. There's no way she's still in bed.

I pound the door even harder, turning the handle, desperate to get in. "Regina! I will break down this door if I have to!"

The locks click. The door opens.

I feel like I've been punched in the stomach. She has a black eye and a swollen lip. The air nearly whooshes out of my lungs when I see her.

I push my way inside without being invited, cupping her face in my hands like it's a soap bubble ready to burst.

"What happened?"

The bubble bursts.

She sags against me, curling her arms into her chest and sobbing, hiding her face in her hands. The story comes out in a hiccupping rush. He must have been waiting for her, because she hadn't even unlocked the door before there was a gun in her back. He wore a ski mask. He hustled her in; had her open the safe under her desk. Then he hit her with his gun, and ran.

Everyone can agree she was lucky that was all he did.

We're sitting on the floor of her foyer as I try to comfort her, but if she feels violated, I feel like a helpless failure.

"Things tend to go wrong at opening and closing," I remember her saying. The perfect time to hit the store would be right as she opens, or just as she leaves. When she's alone. Observe the target, note the routine, attack at the best anticipated moment. I know that. It's basic tactical doctrine.

Fucking basic tactics.

And I let her get hurt because I wasn't thinking. She shouldn't be there alone. If Jenny had owned Java Books, then I sure as hell would've opened and closed the store with her every day. I would've hung around until I saw her employees show up, so she wouldn't be alone. I would've waited until the store was too busy for someone to just walk in like that. I would've been there.

I should've been there.

But I wasn't, and Regina got hurt.

She's curled up around her legs and I can't even get an arm through to go around her waist. She tugs at her hair and mutters something, but I can't hear it.

I lean in closer. "What?"

"Stupid fucking bitch!" she shrieks at me. She drops her

face to her knees and covers her head with her arms. "I'm just a stupid, little bitch!" she sobs.

I know where those words came from, and they're not hers.

I grab her shoulders. "Look at me." My voice doesn't give her room to argue. She uncurls slightly, looking at a point on my face somewhere between my nose and eyes. I give her a small shake. "No. You look at me."

She's trying to suck up the sobbing, trying to hide the sounds and pinch her mouth shut so her lips don't shake. I realize fucktard may have said and done the exact same thing I'm doing right now, but I can't let that stop me. She has to hear me. She has to hear my words. Not his.

"You. Are. Not. NOT. A stupid. Fucking. Bitch." I say. "You are not a slut, or a whore, or any other fucking name that asshole pinned on you."

She starts to collapse on herself again and I pull her shoulders back up. "You are not any of those things," I say even louder. I'm about ready to fall into a parade ground bark if she doesn't start listening. "You are a strong, intelligent woman. You are bold, and passionate, and you make the best damn coffee I've ever had."

That last startles a laugh out of her. I haul her to her feet, pulling her deeper into her house. I have no idea what the floor plan looks like, but the kitchen isn't far off from the front door, so I manage to settle her into one of the chairs around her tiny table, and turn back to fill a glass with water.

I open one cupboard after another to find a glass. She's sitting at her table, looking at her hands. She looks at the glass when I set it in front of her, but doesn't touch it.

"I'm sorry," I mumble. "I should've been there."

"Did you know it was going to happen?"

I shake my head. "No. But you're alone in the mornings

and at night. It's the perfect time for something like that."

"Then it isn't your fault, is it?"

I sigh. "It doesn't feel that way."

She lifts the water to her lips, taking a tiny, tiny sip. I'm not even sure any water has left the glass. "It's not feeling. It's fact," she says, trying to make me feel better.

I frown at her and grip the counter behind me "I'm supposed to be the knight coming to the rescue, not you." I want to kick myself as the words come out, because I'm too late to rescue anybody right now.

She smiles slightly with a small shrug, trying so hard to show me a brave face. "A damsel's gotta do what a damsel's gotta do."

I smile back. Maybe she's already shaking off her breakdown in the foyer. Maybe she just needed to vent for a while before feeling better. "And what is my noble lady of the woods going to do now?"

She pauses and takes a drink. "What do you mean?"

"I'm assuming the shop is closed today?"

"Obviously."

"And tomorrow?"

Fear dances in her eyes. "I hadn't thought about it." She's drooping again.

How the hell did this woman romp around naked in her yard last summer? The answer comes to me almost as soon as I'm done asking myself the question: *Defiance.*

She was lonely. She was scared. So she made herself do the craziest thing she could imagine to prove to herself and the world that she was not going to just sit and accept it. *Molon labe.*

My left arm flexes and releases again.

"Why do you do that?" she asks, pointing at my arm, trying to dodge the subject of her store.

I'm wearing a T-shirt with paint splatters and holes all over it. I didn't take the time to spruce myself up before coming over, because I was worried about other things. I pull up my sleeve for her to see my tattoo, this time in the full light. "Call it a nervous tick."

She swallows hard, and looks at her drink. I pull out a chair from the table and sit next to her. Her black eye looks horrible. She turns her head to the side so I can't see it. So she doesn't have to see me.

"Look at me."

She closes her eyes. I can see her trying to shut down again. Trying to shut me out again.

I move to her side and kneel on the floor next her. "Regina, you have to look at me."

"I'm tired-"

"You have to go back tomorrow."

Her hands tighten on the glass, her knuckles turning white.

"I'll be with you," I tell her. "But you have to go back. You have to. Or. He. Wins," I snarl the last words and she her eyes flicker with fear before darting away again.

No, dammit. I can feel every bit of ground I've gained with her in the last few weeks slipping away from me. My left arm is so tight it's aching. I don't want to lose her. Not like this. My knuckles are white on my left fist as I watch her wilt ever so slightly. Her pulling away like this hurts me more than her black eye.

She stares at me, her mouth open in shock.

I feel hope. Not because I've hurt her, but because she cares enough about me that my opinions matter. I still matter. I've got her attention. Now I've got to keep it. "Just wrap it all up, and send him a card saying he was right all along," I say viciously. I don't want to hurt her, but I want her to react. To feel. To come back to me.

She slaps me. It's a real ringer, too.

Her hands clap over her mouth and her eyes are wide in fear.

The skin on my face tingles and burns. I bring my gaze back to her eyes, holding them in mine with every ounce of will I have. "Did you ever do that to him?"

She shakes her head slowly, terrified about what's going to happen next.

"Then you're learning," I say with a nod of approval. "I said some mean shit. That being said, you need to listen, so I don't have to say that crap again. I don't like being hit, and where I come from, being slapped in the face is fightin' words."

She nods, small and slow, her hands still over her mouth.

"We are going back tomorrow," I say, leaving no room for argument. "We are not going to let that son of a bitch ruin everything you've built. Are we?" It doesn't matter which son of a bitch I'm talking about. They both hurt her. They both took something from her, and I'll be damned if I let her give up now.

She shakes her head silently, not daring to take her eyes off me. I'm afraid to touch her. I'm afraid to wrap my arms around her and hold her. I'm afraid she doesn't understand what I've just done or why. To her, I must look like fucktard right now. I sigh and drop my eyes to her feet. I'm afraid I've scared the hell out of her. That I've stepped across too many lines.

I've hurt her.

Promise or not, fear can shut anyone down, and words can hurt more than a fist.

But I had to, dammit. I need her back. I have to give

her a reason to defy again.

I can only look at her chin. I slowly reach out and take one of her hands from her mouth and guide to my tattoo. "What does that mean," I ask, not daring to look in her eyes.

It takes her a few moments to push the words out. "Come and take it."

"Do you understand now?"

"Yes," she whispers.

***

As promised, I follow her to work and help her open. She's a little unnerved by the fact that I'm now openly carrying a gun on my hip, but she doesn't argue about it. Legally, she can't. She doesn't have a sign posted on her door saying weapons aren't allowed on the premises, and Colorado is an open-carry state.

I'm pretty sure she's not thinking about the legal aspects of things right now, though.

It's like a frickin' field day when word gets around that the store is open today. I'm glad, though. Everyone coming by to offer their support has got to be worth something to her. Knowing that I'm not the only one who cares has got to boost her morale even just a little.

Her customers ask her if she's okay, and a few nod approvingly at me, hanging around in the cafe and armed as I am. Deputy Travis doesn't seem to like it when he stops by. I let him have his whispered conference with Regina in her office, with him playing on being worried that I'm threatening her somehow. He didn't seem to like the answers she gave him, but he left without hassling me.

He did throw me one hell of an "eat shit and die" look,

though.

I'm there from open to close for about a week, and she won't look me in the eye, she won't talk to me, and she sure as hell won't say my name. I'm back to square one.

Shit.

I'm frustrated. I'm angry. I want to find the asshole who hurt her, and beat the shit out of him with my bare hands.

But I can't.

The next week I back off. I take her to work, help her open, and wait until about nine or ten before leaving; come back before seven, help her close, and escort her home. I hope the space will at least get me a smile when I walk through her door in the evenings, but all I can get is a barely murmured "Thank you," when I close her car door for her. She's withdrawing into herself, and I can't figure out if it was the robbery or me that did the most damage.

I don't want to lose her. I can't lose her. Not like this.

After two more weeks, I'm too frustrated to wait it out any longer. When I drive to Java Books that evening, I bring a duffle bag I've stuffed as tight as I can with every towel and sheet I could get in it, and then used an entire roll of duct-tape to wrap it closed.

She locks the door and tidies up the counter. I stick to my usual routine of re-stacking books and mopping the floor, quietly waiting for the chores to get finished. She comes out of her office bundled in her coat and ready to go, only to find me sitting backwards in a chair, blocking the door. I've moved the other tables and chairs off to the sides to clear a small space. My socks and boots are off, my holster and gun are on a nearby table, and the duffle bag is at my feet.

She frowns at me. "That's a health code violation," she says, nodding at my feet.

"Sue me. Take off the coat."

She huffs. "It's been a long day-"

"I don't give a damn. Lose the coat and the shoes."

She crosses her arms. "No."

"We're not leaving until we do this."

"Do what?"

I stand and my leg easily clears the top of the chair. Java Books is not so big that she can get away from me after two of my steps. I seize her arm and point at the door. "It happened right here," I say. "Right here is where you gave up."

"He had a gun!"

"I'm not talking about the damn gun. I'm talking about you. You gave up. You gave up everything you built. Everything we had because it was easier."

"I did not!"

"Then why won't you look at me? Why won't you talk to me? Or even smile? Is it because I wasn't here? Is that it? You blame me?"

"No."

"Then what? Was I too mean at your table?"

Her mouth works silently for a few moments before she finally stops trying to talk all together. I let go of her arm and step back to the door. "Lose the coat and shoes," I say again.

She obediently sheds her coat. She double-knots her hiking boots, so untying the shiny new laces takes some time, but she's finally barefoot and glaring at my chin.

"Show me how you make a fist," I say.

She brings her hands up and loosely balls her fingers, keeping the thumbs out of her grip. "My brother is a cop," she says, still not meeting my eyes.

"Good. Then this should be easy." I pick up the duffle

bag, fighting with the weight and the handles that aren't meant for this kind of treatment. I finally get it positioned solidly in front of my chest. "Hit the bag."

She does, but she put no heart in the strike.

I glare at her. "I said hit the bag."

"I did."

"We're not leaving until I can feel the hit."

She puts more force into the next one.

It's not enough. I look at her, summoning the expression of disgust I'd used so many times against the soldiers under me when they were slacking off. "Really? Is that the best you can do?"

She gets mad and throws everything she has at the bag. "Ow!" She massages her right wrist sullenly. "Are you happy now?"

"No. Your brother may have taught you to not break your thumb, but he didn't teach you shit about form." I toss the bag to the floor, and stand behind her, pulling her hands apart. The tension is flowing off her body like a hot flame. I try to avoid touching her any more than I need to. "Make another fist."

"I'm tired," she complains through clenched teeth.

"Before I came along, you probably weren't getting to bed before midnight, so suck it up," I say mercilessly. *You want me to ride herd like you're a Private? Fine. I can play this game.* "Make another fist."

She huffs, but does as she's told.

"Punch."

She strikes at the air in front of her, then grunts in pain. When she brings back her fist, she rubs at her elbow this time.

"Lesson one:" I say. "Power doesn't come from the shoulder. It comes from the hips." I nudge her left foot forward with my own. "Try to keep your shoulders in line with your hips through the whole move," I tell her. Without anything even resembling seduction I grab her hips and jerk-twist her right hip forward and back. "Can you feel that?" I say.

"Yes."

"Good. Remember it. Lesson two: don't twist your arm during a punch. It's a style you haven't trained in, so you'll jerk out your elbow, and fuck up your wrist."

"It's a punch," she says, irritated with me.

"No. It's a style of punch, and it's one I can't teach, so we're sticking with basic brawling. You punch straight out with your thumb to the sky and bring it back in again." I grab her hand shoulder, guiding her body through the motions a few times. "Got it?"

"Yeah. I got it. Are we done?"

She's pissed. At me. At her ex. At her brother. At the dipshit who held her up, but mostly just at me.

Because I'm here. Because it's easy. Because I'm not letting her crawl into a hole and die like she wants to.

"No," I say, coming out from behind her and picking up the duffle bag again. "Hit the bag."

The expression on her face is a cross between irritation and rage. It's too funny not to laugh at, so of course I do.

That really gets her pissed. She starts pounding on the bag, throwing everything she has into it, trying to punch through it to get to me. I let her attack slowly move me back towards the door, and when my foot touches the chair, I start pushing the bag at her, using it to drive her back towards the counter even as she keeps hitting it.

With a hard shove, I knock her off balance, making her fall on her ass. She glares at me as I toss the bag towards the door. "Now we're done. Tomorrow we'll talk about your footwork," I tell her.

"Tomorrow?" she demands. "What the hell-"

"Every time you close this shop, we are going to work on something," I say, walking towards my boots.

"Excuse me?"

I spin on her, rage filling my chest. "I am not giving up without a fight," I say. "And I'm not going to let you do it either."

Chapter 13

Two Steps Back

"How's the sparring going?" Will asks over the phone.

"He's a fucking asshole," I say bitterly, slamming my teapot on my stove. I want hot chocolate, but I'm too angry to make it the good way by slow-stirring the milk as it heats, adding just the right amount of vanilla to the chocolate chips, so I'm settling for tea. It isn't what I want, but since no one else seems to care about what I want, why should I?

"Good."

"How'd the background check go?" My stomach drops after I ask. What should I do if he did find something? I'm supposed to go back to close in two hours. I suppose I could call Travis. He gave me his card with his personal number on the back when Jim first started playing bodyguard. "*If he so much as blinks in some way you don't like, you call me,*" he'd said.

The thought of calling Travis doesn't make me feel good at all. It makes me feel helpless. I don't even want to think about how it would make him feel. Probably like some dashing hero riding in to save the day in a bad movie. I feel nauseous when I think about gazing up into his eyes with gratitude and longing.

Maybe I could call Maria and borrow her husband? I don't want to do that, either, but if Jim has a history-

"Nothing I'm going to tell you," Will says cheerfully.

My brother is a fucking asshole. I want to throw the phone across the room. Of course he hasn't found anything worrisome on Jim. If he had, he would've told me long before now. It doesn't take two months to run a background check. But he's still an asshole because I can hear him grinning. "If you're not going to even try to make me feel better, you can hang the fuck up."

He chuckles, which only makes me even more furious, but I can't hang up. There's something rude about hanging up on someone that I can't shove aside, at least not with my own brother on the line. Will sobers up quickly. "There's nothing worth talking about. If he's a shithead, then it hasn't popped in the legal system. The only things that did come up was a prior divorce thirty odd years ago, and his second wife's accident."

"What happened?" I shouldn't be asking about it. Jim already told me. I shouldn't be gossiping about a dead woman and her husband behind his back. It isn't fair to him.

I want to hate him.

I can envision my brother standing in his living room, looking out his front window, aware of the traffic and tells from the people he can see on his street in the growing dark. "The divorce is pretty clean cut," he says. "They were kids, and all that's on the record is *no fault* after seventeen months of marriage. Number two was black ice and a three car pile-up against a mountain wall. She was one of two least it was quick."

I can't hate him. My eyes blur with tears.

"Reggie?"

"Why can't I make this work?" I sob. More words come out before I can stop them. "It's not fair. Why is he pushing me so hard? Why am I so angry? Why do I hate him?"

"Regina? Listen to me." It's my brother on the line, but it's also the cop. "It's normal, okay? Nightmares, depression, acting out of character, it's all normal after something like this. You. Were. Mugged. Your life was threatened. What's happening to you now is normal. Everybody goes through it. It's different for everybody, but everybody goes through it. You're going to be hit especially hard because of Larry. It's okay. It's normal."

"You sound like my therapist."

"Then you need to listen to him."

"She's a woman, dufus."

"Great. Listen to her, too."

"How do I get him to stop with this sparring crap?" I grumble. I know exactly how to do it—just tell him to go away and never come back because I'm not interested in anything anymore.

But it would be a lie.

I don't want him here.

I don't want him to leave.

What the hell is my problem?

The tears are hot against my hand when I brush them away. God, I am so tired. I've lost track of how many panic attacks I've had. I can't take the meds during the day because they make me dopey, and that's no way to run a business. The night Jim was late to Java Books was the worst. I broke dishes and knocked over my two of my urns before he came rushing through the door.

Simmons' back had gone out, and Jim had to drive him to the Woodland Park medical center earlier in the day.

I was so angry with both of them for . . . I don't know. I was just angry. I thought my obvious shakes would be enough to make Jim relent and just forget about the stupid bag for one night, but he didn't. He was just as ruthless as ever.

Heartless bastard.

Will still hasn't said anything.

"What the hell am I supposed to do if someone else holds me up at gunpoint? Use my awesome kung-fu skills?" I ask sarcastically. My brother is a cop. He knows the odds when one guy has a gun and the other doesn't.

He sighs. "I don't want him to stop teaching you," he admits. "You need this, Reggie."

"There was a gun, Will."

"What Jim's doing isn't about the gun," he says patiently. "It's about you. And maybe even about him, too."

I feel betrayed. Bitterness rises in the back of my throat. Why is everyone pushing me? Haven't I been through enough? Will was all set to hate him around Christmas. Now it's April and he's singing a different tune. He's even using Jim's name like he knows the guy.

"He's right," my brother is saying from eighteen-hundred miles away. "You gave up something from inside you when you got robbed. You have to take that back. Even if Jim doesn't stay in your life, he's still right about that."

I don't want to hear this. Not from my brother. "I have to go," I say, hanging up on him before he can get in another word.

***

"So they caught the guy?" my therapist asks as she closes the door behind me.

I nod. "It was one of Mikie's friends."

She frowns. "And Mikie is?"

"One of my employees."

"Was he a part of it?"

I shake my head and settle on the couch, clutching my coat in my lap like it's a magic talisman. The memory of Mikie's face when he came into work the other day after school had said it all. The cops had arrested his friend the night before, and the story had run in the news that morning. Mikie had been devastated. The poor kid even offered to quit. "He'd been talking about his job, and mentioned that I always open by myself."

I look at the tiny decorative water fountain Dr. Beas has on her windowsill, the water burbling cheerfully over the polished rocks. "It never occurred to him that one of his friends would do anything like that."

"Where did his friend get the gun?"

I'm still looking at the fountain. She must have hard-water in her office tap—the water in the fountain has left ugly, chunky white lines all over the smooth stones. "Does it matter?"

I feel ugly. I feel hateful and ugly. Even with Larry I'd never felt like this. Helpless, weak, numb and stupid, but never like this. Never ugly.

She looks like she's about to say something but decides not to. "I guess not. He could've used a kitchen knife, and it still would've been dangerous."

I nod.

"Is Mikie still in your employ?"

"Yes. I think he's looking for another job, but he's still with me at the moment." My lips move indecisively.

She waits for me, calmly poised

"When—when Jim found out he-"

She leans forward, concerned. "Did he threaten Mikie?"

I shake my head, pulling my coat tighter into my chest. "I don't think so."

Silence. The clock ticks. The water trickles. The air crushes my shoulders.

"What did he do?" she finally asks.

Mikie had been in bad shape. He dropped things, he wouldn't sing along with the radio, he could barely call out orders. When the kid's shift was over, Jim was already there waiting for me to close, and watching him like a hawk. It had been a few minutes before I realized Jim left when Mikie did.

I'd been terrified. I remember gripping the counters until my hands ached, telling myself to pull it together. I thought I was going to pass out. It was dark outside with another hour to go until closing, and then Jim saunters back in as if nothing happened.

I wasn't worried about Mikie. I was terrified about what would happen to me.

When did I get this selfish and ugly?

"I think Jim just talked to him," I say.

"About what?"

"He wouldn't say, but whatever it was, I think it made Mikie feel better." Mikie is still quieter than usual, but he seems to have gotten a grip on himself. He even smiles at Jim when he won't at me.

That hurts. It also hurts to remember that I hadn't been thinking at all about Mikie, about what Jim would do to him, could do to him.

I'd only been worried about me if Jim didn't come back.

How did I become so ugly?

Dr. Beas nods. "Well, I suppose that's a good thing." She crosses her legs. "Are you going to get a gun?"

The question returns me to the store after I'd closed the same night Jim talked to Mikie. I was angry at Jim for being a prick about the punching and the kicking. I was angry because I wasn't doing it right. I was angry because I was tired, because I still feel violated, and I just want to curl up and hide from the world in a hole somewhere.

I was angry because for a terrifying moment I thought I was alone again. I was angry because I realized I had become the woman I used to be again.

"*Why don't I just get a gun?*" I'd suggested.

Fifteen minutes at the most. That's all Jim goes for with the sparring after hours. I've watched the clock. Sometimes it's as little as five minutes, but he never goes over fifteen.

But I wanted it over and done with, and a gun seemed like an easy way out. Jim stopped and blinked at me. "*I already own a rifle,*" I reminded him. I sounded more catty than I meant to be, but I was so angry with everything.

Angry with me. With everything I'm doing wrong. I'm angry with the lessons, with Larry who taught me to be helpless, with myself for spending most of my life just laying down and taking it.

And I want it to be all Jim's fault.

Angry because I know it isn't his fault. It's mine, but I want someone to blame.

Jim dropped his duffle bag, and went to his gun. I saw him pull out the magazine, and remove all the bullets. He cleared the top chamber with an easy slide, and slapped the empty magazine back into the gun.

He put the gun in my hand, and stopped. His hands held mine, the unfamiliar weight of the weapon awkward in my grip. "*The safety's off,*" he'd said, looking at our hands. "*It's not loaded."*

"What am I supposed to do with it?" I asked him. He had a weird expression on his face. Tired. Ragged. Worried.

Haunted.

"You're going to pull the trigger."

I blinked at him. *"When am I supposed to do that?"*

He swallowed. *"You'll know."* He walked to the door, and stared out the window with his back to me. He tilted his head, rolling his shoulders a few times.

I heard him take a deep breath. I knew he was going to rush me, but when he turned, the look on his face was pure rage. He was on me before I even realized he'd crossed the room. His voice was huge and frightening and I have no idea what he said but when he raised his hand to slap me I dropped the gun.

The slap never came. Instead, his arms were around me, holding me up because my knees gave out. *"I'm sorry, Regina,"* he'd said, his voice cracking. *"I'm so sorry, but you needed to see that. That's what it's like. I want you to be safe, but you just gave him the gun. I'm sorry. I'm so sorry."*

"Regina?" Dr. Beas asks, pulling me out of the memory.

"I'm not ready for a gun," I say. "I don't know if I can shoot anyone with it. Even if my life did depend on it. If I want to, he said he'll help me find one and get lessons, but not right now."

"He?"

"Jim."

"Did he say you weren't ready?"

"We both agreed on it. He . . . showed me a few things. About what it's like to use one." I shake my head. "I'm not ready. I don't think I can pull the trigger."

She nods. "It's good you recognize that in yourself. A

lot of people don't think about that before diving into it. It's only in the moment, when it happens, that they realize the responsibilities inherent in carrying a gun. And sadly, often it's too late."

Without a shadow of a doubt, I know that Jim has been in that moment.

I know he's killed people.

Of course I knew it was possible that he had when he was in the Army, but somehow it didn't feel real until I saw him like that. It wasn't something I'd ever thought about. It's something I know he'll never talk about, but it's a shadow I can now see lurking behind him.

I'm not sure how Larry would carry a shadow like that, but I do know he never would've hidden it from me. He'd have used it, without hesitation.

Jim had to summon it, to bring up when he didn't want to, just to show me a taste of it. Then he shoved it back into a box, locking it in the closet again quick to hide it from me. From himself.

Does Jim have nightmares? Are they like mine? How can he not see me as some weak, pathetic thing when he's seen and done so much?

"How are the self-defense lessons going?" she asks. Her voice startles me. Should I ask her about Jim? She said she's treated former military-

"I don't know that I would call them actual lessons," I say instead.

She raises her eyebrows. "At our last meeting you said he was trying to teach you how to fight. Has that changed?"

"No."

She frowns at me. I know it's something in my voice that set off her therapist radar.

I huff. "He's angry at me," I say.

"Why?"

"He says I gave up."

"There was as gun in your face," she protests. "What did he want you to do?"

I shake my head. "He says it isn't about the gun. It's-" I don't want to say it. I force myself to say it and I almost choke on the words. "He says I gave up on us." I look at the floor. "Even my brother agrees with him."

Beas squints her eyes. "How did you give up?"

"I don't know!" I howl before collapsing into my lap. "I can't talk to him anymore! I can't even look at him!" I can't stop the tears. I'd spent so many years stifling them so as not to anger Larry. I know all the tricks there are to crush my need to cry until I'm alone.

My tricks are worthless now.

I cry until I ache. I just can't stop. All the helpless rage comes out in choking screams and a river of tears and snot. At some point in my hysteria, Beas left her chair to sit next to me, holding a box of tissues in her lap. She has a neutral mask on her face, but I can see it's taken quite a bit of her own willpower to not touch me, to not invade my space.

When I'm calm enough to be somewhat coherent, she hands me the box. "You were actually talking to him before," she says.

"I was, and things were getting easier and then the-that-the-"

"The robbery happened?"

I nod, holding my arms to my stomach.

"Did he say the robbery was your fault?"

"No." I sniffle and wipe at my eyes.

"But you stopped talking to him?"

I can't even look at her.

She waits for me to say something, anything. The clock

keeps ticking. "The robbery traumatized you again," she says. "It's very common. It's normal. But the fact that you're not talking to him anymore, has maybe hurt him in some way."

No. Jim can't be hurt. It's not possible. He's stronger than I am. I can't imagine him being hurt. I don't want to. I can't. Despite everything, I can't believe I hurt him.

I'd just die if I believed that.

I know I hurt him.

My therapist continues. "And if I'm understanding what you've told me correctly, I wouldn't be surprised to discover he might also blaming himself for the robbery."

I shake my head. "It wasn't his fault."

"I've worked with a lot of different people over the years," she says. "And Jim sounds like he's a nice guy, but he's also sounds very . . . male, in that he wants to protect who he cares for. I'm not saying he thinks he owns you, but men like Jim tend to be . . . " she's trying to find a word that fits.

"Territorial?" I offer, remembering the silent exchange between Jim and Travis.

"I'm leaning more towards the word protective. And you told me he was retired military. Do you know if he saw combat?"

I know he's seen combat. "He hasn't told me," I sniff.

She nods. "He might not ever tell you if he has. You were traumatized by your previous marriage, and then re-traumatized by the robbery, by an actual gun in your face. And it sounds to me like he's been traumatized by the fact that he somehow feels he allowed it to happen, especially if he's a combat veteran. I'm not saying what he experienced from this is more than what you're going through, but he's probably hurting a little, too."

I glare at the trees outside her window, clenching the tissues in my hand. I don't want to admit that he's hurt. That he can be hurt.

That I can hurt him.

"Does he know about your ex-husband?" Beas asks.

The question catches me off guard. "He knows I have one. He knows—knows . . . "

"About the abuse?"

I can't look at her. I focus on the damp tissue in my hands, trying to smooth out the wrinkles. I can't even nod.

"Regina?"

"I think he knows it happened."

"Not the details, though."

I shake my head. He never asked for specifics, and I never told him, but he's smart, so I find it hard to believe that he can't put two and two together to get something reasonably close to four.

"The robber took more than your money, Regina. He took your peace of mind, your sense of safety. He violated your sense of self. He made you feel weak, and small, and helpless all over again, and it's normal to pull away from those we care for. I get the sense you care about Jim. Am I right?"

The question shakes me to my very core.

Yes. I care about Jim. *I care about him a lot.*

I cant give voice to it, though. My throat closes around the thought of making those sounds. My jaw aches from the mere idea of saying them. I can only nod.

"All right, then. You said you were having trouble talking to him, connecting with him. And I think part of that is because it took an enormous amount of courage for you to open yourself to someone like that again. But when you were hurt, you immediately withdrew, on instinct. Even though he wasn't the cause of your pain, you are so used to having to defend yourself from those who claim to care, you fell back into old patterns. And that's okay, but if you want to maintain a connection with Jim, you're going to have to work very hard to move past those patterns."

"How?"

"Starting over and slowly rebuilding, rediscovering the sense of trust you had in him, doesn't have to be done overnight. It's something you take tiny steps towards, even if it's only an inch a week or a month. The people who truly care about you should be willing to work with you, especially if you communicate that need to them."

Start over.

I remember that first time we were together. And the second. And the next, all the way through to October. It was crazy. It was stupid and exhilarating and I still can't comprehend how exactly it happened, but it did. It's hysterically ridiculous, but if I could call him to me once, then maybe I can do it again.

"Regina?"

I look at my therapist. I can't breathe a word of what I'm really thinking. If we can start over, start from the beginning, maybe that can fix things.

Maybe he'll be "James" again.

I nod. "We probably do need to take a step or two back, to go forward again."

She smiles at me.

Chapter 14

Square One

I feel like I'm in the Army all over again. Towards the end of my career, I spent more of my time in meetings and filing reports than anything else. I'd forgotten the number of times I had to take some wet-behind-the-ears-kid into my office to play counselor, father and superior all in the same hit.

I hated doing that. I hated the meetings, the paperwork, the stress because my people were just being stupid for no damn good reason, or because the people above me weren't being fair to the people below.

There were times when I would wait until the garage was closed for the night, and I'd spend a few hours in a bay, by myself, completely against regulations, to putter around on a vehicle my people just couldn't get to that day. Mostly I just changed the oil, or replaced a spark plug or something small. Sometimes I'd take out all the nuts and bolts I could easily reach, and then just put them back again. Not really fixing anything, just trying to not bring the bullshit home.

If my people had seen me doing that, they would've thought they were dreaming. I rarely had time to even walk through and check if the floors were clean. Some of those kids probably didn't even realize that Sarge actually knew something about motor pool beyond chewing on their asses.

I cannot describe how many times I have wanted to pull my truck apart, completely strip the engine, and put it back together since Valentines' Day.

When I saw Mikie behind the counter looking like he was going to puke, I knew it was his buddy who'd held up Regina. The little punk had been picked up the day before, and the story was in the paper the next morning. No names or pictures, because he's not eighteen, but enough details to know he'd been local.

I thought Mikie was going to shit his pants and pass out when he realized I'd followed him out of Java Books. He was waiting for his dad or mom to come pick him up when I snapped the cigarette from his mouth and flicked it to the pavement, grinding it under my boot.

"I swear to God I didn't know!" He practically pled for his life, his eyes rooted to the gun on my hip. It didn't register to him that we were right in front of the windows of Java Books, with light from the store covering the both of us. If I'd wanted to do something to him, the best time and place would've been when he took the trash out the back—there's barely any light, and rarely anyone around back there to be a witness.

But he doesn't think tactically. He's a kid. All he could think about was the guy with the gun who might be royally pissed at him. Of course he was terrified. He may be young, but if he isn't dumb. If Honesty hadn't figured it out before the robbery, then everyone sure as hell has figured it out now—I care about Regina, and I'm probably the wrong guy to piss off when it comes to her.

"I know," I told him. *"You had a dumbass friend who thought he could get away with it. It happens."*

I think he agreed with me, but he was too spooked and relieved to make much sense. He realized it himself after a few words, and tried to pull another cigarette from his coat when I yanked that one from his hand too. His hand was shaking so much, I didn't think he'd be able to light the thing, but I wanted to make a point. the radio. I broke the cigarette, and held out my hand for the rest of the pack. He didn't want to give them up, but it's hard to argue with a man who has a gun when you're still in high school.

I crushed the pack, chucking it in the trash near the door. *"That crap will ruin your voice,"* I told him. *"She knows you're a good kid. I know it. Sometimes we just pick the wrong friends."*

I left it at that, and went back inside.

That was two weeks ago. He's still jumpy as all hell, but at least he smiles a bit at work now. By the end of school, he'll be back to trying to outmatch the radio again while working the counter.

Kids. Things are a lot less complicated at that age.

Unlike my age, where everything is complicated.

Most of the time "complicated" is about the normal stuff: bills, appointments, figuring out what constitutes socially acceptable levels of stalking—all these things I can handle.

Regina has managed to turn my world on its head again, and now things have suddenly gotten very complicated.

I missed it coming out of my house this morning. I was late, and needed to get to Java Books before Regina even thought about getting out of her car. She's been getting more defiant lately, which I hope is a good sign, but it makes things a damn sight harder to help.

She seemed like she was in a better mood. She smiled at me a few times, even touched my hand once. She was nervous as all hell when she did it, but it still happened. I felt a load lift from my shoulders.

She's coming back to me. Slowly, but she's still coming back.

On my way home, I'm happier than I've been in weeks. I can actually feel my shoulders release, and I'm whistling when I get out of my truck, spinning my keys in my hand. I even notice there are some plants struggling to grow, despite the bone dry dirt. They're little green buds poking through the sand and gravel, determined to try and make a go of it.

At my door I see it, and my good mood goes to hell.

There's a small black box on the railing around my porch. Inside is a tiny charm shaped like a Mardi Gras mask. I know she must have left it on my porch sometime after I'd gotten her home last night, and I'm pretty sure it's an invitation for tonight.

Ironically, it's April thirtieth today. I remember that being an important fertility date when I was looking into the pagan stuff. Or maybe it's not ironic. Maybe she's planned it that way. It doesn't really matter. I've received an invitation. A summons.

Until this morning, I thought I was fighting a losing battle. She barely speaks to me. After the gun business, she wouldn't even look at me until this morning.

I can't blame her, though. I can only imagine what life was like with fucktard, and I knew I was going to have to at least give her a taste of it again to get my point across about carrying a gun. I felt like a royal shit for doing it, but I didn't think she would believe me any other way. Most people just don't understand that a gun doesn't do a damn thing if you don't have the will to back it up.

I would've been thrilled to hear the dry "click" of the trigger being pulled. I would've been ecstatic that she could at least pull the trigger even if the gun was pointed at the floor.

But that's not what happened. She dropped it before I'd even gotten close enough to touch her.

I know it took a hell of a lot to walk away from fucktard, but that doesn't mean she's ready to carry. I want her to be safe, but she's got to be willing to hit back. Hell, even if she'd tried to hit me with the gun like it was a club, I'd have been happy.

It isn't necessarily a bad thing, though. Some people can pull the trigger. Most can't. I was drilled so hard in the Army that when the time came to do it, I didn't think about it, I just did it.

When I finally did have a chance to think about it, I had nightmares. That guy hadn't been much older than me, but at the time, it was either him or me. More than thirty years later, through hell and high water, that face stays with me. It haunts me, but I've learned to live with my ghosts.

I just don't want Regina to be one of them. And if she drops that gun when she needs it most, she probably will be.

So the invitation implied by the little mask charm surprises me.

It also makes me angry. I still wear her bracelet, and I will be damned if I hang that trinket anywhere near her hair.

I don't want the no-strings sex. I want to talk to her. I want her to talk to me. To have coffee with me in the mornings, and to bitch about her day at night. I want her to laugh at my jokes, and complain about my morning breath when I try to kiss her. I want to kiss her lips to shut her up because she's talking too much.

I want her to talk too much.

I push the box around my dining room table with a finger, while I rest my chin in my hand. I want so many things this invitation isn't offering. How would she take it if I don't show up? It took an incredible act of bravery to do what she did last summer, even if it was stupid as hell.

Of course, I wasn't much smarter, and it's too late to be pointing fingers, now.

We'd come so far, and then the robbery set us back. I know she's trying to start over. I know she's trying to turn back the clock, but if I show, I'm worried I'll send the wrong message—that I'll confuse her because I'm not being clear about what I really want. If I don't show, I'm worried she'll take it as a full rejection.

Shit.

I can't take that chance. Not if I want her to come back. She smiled at me this morning. She's expecting me to start from the beginning with her again.

Okay. Let's see where this goes.

When I help her close that night, I don't say anything about her little gift. She's more energetic than usual, and drills into the bag like she means it. I can see it in her eyes that she's trying to make me proud of her.

I give her a few pointers, and briefly compliment the effort she made, but that's all I say. I see her chew her bottom lip as we walk out to the parking lot. Was she expecting more from me? Did I miss a cue for a new rule?

If there's a new rule, then she's going to have to open her mouth and say something, dammit.

At two in the morning I get up to make myself presentable. I turn on the bathroom light to shower and shave, because if she can't handle seeing the light, then maybe it's best that she doesn't show at all.

I turn on the music because I need it. I'm irritated. I'm frustrated. I'm terrified.

But I'm also determined. Heavy metal is pretty good at boosting that.

It's breezy outside, and chill as all hell. I stomp the ground, pacing to keep the shivers off. The grass isn't just pathetically dry, it's turning to powder with every step I take.

Even if I was in the mood, I think the temperature would be enough to turn me off, no matter what she does. I don't hide behind the scrub oak. I've got my robe and loafers on, and, of course, that stupid mask that got me into all this in the first place. I'll go that far for her, but if she wants more, she's going to have to give me more.

She's going to have to speak.

Her door opens and closes, and she comes to our spot holding the blanket I gave her. I kiss her hand, and take the blanket from her, enveloping the both of us inside it. I don't try to take her robe off, but I do hold her. I hold her, and rest my head on hers for as long as she'll let me.

When she's ready to go home, she pulls away. I try to stop her, I try to make her stay with me, but she taps her fingers on my lips, shaking her head before she leaves me with the blanket.

Shit.

At Java Books, she won't even look in my direction, and I won't talk to her any more than I have to. I'm not angry, but I'm going to get something out of her. Anything. I don't care. Even if she throws a pot at my head, screaming at me to leave, that would be something.

That evening, she pounds on the duffle bag until the

seams I haven't wrapped duct tape around pop. She won't even call me names or glare at my chin. I coach her form like I usually do, but that's it. I catch her eyes a few times, and they brim with tears, but she will not talk to me.

It goes like this for a week.

At our next meeting, she manages to slip her hands into my robe while I wrap us in the blanket. The blanket falls from our shoulders as I take her hands in mine, pulling them firmly down to our sides. Any idiot can tell that my body is interested and ready to go, but I'm the one doing the thinking this time, not the other guy.

It's shivering cold, but I won't let go of her hands to pick up the blanket. Playing "chicken" is something Army grunts learn to do well. I'm not going to flinch. It isn't until we're both violently shaking that she concedes defeat, and retreats to her house. I had to drink an entire pot of coffee before I could stop shivering that morning.

At her shop I can see she's confused. She doesn't understand why I'm holding back. During the week I'm in the store a few times when Deputy Dawg shows up for his kiddie drink. He can smell the tension between us. I can practically see his tail wag when he talks to her.

I want to kick the shit out of him. The body isn't even cold yet, and he's already sniffing around.

Greedy prick.

Her sparring improves, and she's getting aggressive. She beats my duffle bag like she wants to go through it. Like she wants to beat the hell out of me, but she still won't meet my eyes or say a word.

I know that just falling back into the wild nights routine we had last summer would be an easy fix. She'd get her confidence up, and things would start rolling back to where they were before.

The problem is I think it's just a worthless hankie on a broken leg. I'm not willing to screw her over like that. I want her to be able to walk again without a damn crutch, and I can only carry her so far. If she wants sex, that's fine, but she's going to have to talk first, even if all she says is "I want to get laid."

She has to speak first.

At our third meeting I hold her face in my hands, trying to put everything I have in my eyes. Everything I feel, everything I want. *I love you.*

The words shock me when I hear them in my head, but they don't scare me. A million possibilities run through my mind, and the only one I think that has a chance of making her realize how serious I am, means scaring the hell out of both of us. I want her enough I'm willing to bend.

I flinch.

I drop my hands to take hers, and draw the antler ring off her right hand. She starts shaking and bites her lip. I lift her chin, and shake my head slightly. Before I can lose my courage, I slip the ring back on her hand.

The ring finger on her left hand.

She frowns at her hand, perhaps thinking I'd gotten it on wrong. She gapes when I fall to one knee holding her left hand.

I can feel her fear. Or maybe it's mine. I don't know who's more scared but something slithers off her face. She freezes as it falls whispering to the ground.

Her mask has come off.

She rips her hands from mine. I rocket to my feet, tearing off my own mask, grabbing her shoulders. "Regina, stop! Talk to me!"

I flinched again, breaking my vow to make her talk first, but I don't care. I'm done with all this silly shit. I seize her head so she can't move, and push my lips into hers, stealing the kiss I'd always wanted her to just give me.

If this were a cheesy romance novel, she'd melt into my arms, and we'd make love until sunrise.

She doesn't melt. She jams her knee into my crotch, and runs away from the evil fiend of the woods.

As I clutch at myself, desperately hoping my balls won't come out of my mouth, a very tiny part of me is actually proud she did that.

Chapter 15

Learn from History

When I left the charm on Jim's porch, I worried he wouldn't know what it meant. My alarm went off but it didn't wake me—I'm so spun up I didn't sleep a wink. In my bathroom I take extra care when I wash and shave, making certain that every touch of his will be met with as perfect a body as I can make it.

From my kitchen window I see a light from his house through the trees. It's a tiny window, but now I know how he discovered my woodland frolics the first time. He must've been using the bathroom, and saw me by pure coincidence because he didn't turn on the light.

The light is on now, so I know he's awake, getting ready to meet me.

I desperately want a cup of coffee to steady my nerves, but I don't want to ruin the magic with coffee breath. He probably wouldn't mind, but I want things perfect.

I want to start over.

I look at the antler ring on my right hand. He didn't give it to me until months after we'd first started. Should I take it off? My hand feels naked without it at work. The thought of taking it off to meet my knight of the woods feels wrong. If he doesn't feel it on my hand when we meet, he might be hurt and leave. I don't want him to leave. I want him to stay with me, to make me forget dawn is coming, and the real world is full of disappointment.

The light from his bathroom is off now. I know he's coming. I hope he's coming. What if he doesn't want to start over? What if he shows up fully dressed? My stomach flips; my heart is fluttering when I make my way to the back door holding a blanket. My blanket. Our blanket.

"Fucking slut," I hear from the back of my mind.

The windchimes tinkle and clang in the night. I take a deep breat,h and rip open the door before I have time to think about what I'm doing.

The weather is still cool, but we've had sex in chill weather before, so that shouldn't be a problem, especially since I'm bringing our blanket.

What if he says something? What if he isn't wearing the mask? I don't think I can do this without the extra trappings of drama. In a mask I can pretend I'm someone else. I'm someone stronger, someone braver and more capable than who I really am.

My knight isn't hiding behind the bushes. He's wearing a robe, house shoes, and his mask, but he's pacing to keep warm, stomping on the ground like he's angry at it. He stops when he sees me, and holds out his hand for mine, but stays clothed.

It is chilly out. Maybe he's waiting until we're in the blanket. I give him my hand, and he kisses it as he did the first time. An electrical tingle zings up my arm and down my spine. He takes the blanket from me, wrapping us in it, but when he wraps his arms around me, there's nothing sexual in it.

All he wants is to hold me.

I can feel he's hard against me, but he doesn't slip a hand under my robe. He doesn't caress or tease me through the fabric. He doesn't kiss my neck, or even try to speak. He just holds me, resting his head on my own.

I don't know what to do. I want to start over, but it's obvious he has another idea.

He doesn't want to let me go when I'm ready to leave. He catches my hand with the ring and holds it, silently begging me to stay. I touch his lips with my fingers, suddenly wanting to kiss them.

I hated kissing Larry. He never cared for it after we married and his true colors started to show. When he did, it was rushed and slobbery, nothing like what our kisses had been before. What I thought a kiss should be. What I wanted it to be.

Would kissing my knight be different? I'm afraid to find out it wouldn't be. That despite his ability to know exactly what I want, that one thing would be a disaster, reminding me of Larry all over again.

My knight cups a hand on the side of my face, touching my own lips with his thumb, and I know what he wants. He wants me to break the rules. He wants me to speak. As much as he wants the rest of me, he wants that more than anything.

I want to die.

I shake my head and leave before I cry.

***

He doesn't say anything to me at Java Books while he's hanging around for business to pick up enough to feel comfortable enough to leave me. When he comes back to close, he stays quiet until it's time to leave. Then he's all business, coaching my punches, telling me to mind my footwork.

But he doesn't ask me about my day like he used to. I can see he wants to, but he holds himself back. I do my best to beat the hell out of the duffle bag, do my best to make him proud of me, but all he'll do is nod, and say I'm getting better, before it's time to go.

It goes on like this for a week and it drives me insane. My employees even notice I'm kattywampussed. I overhear Steve talking to Cheyenne about how to make a proper fist. He's obviously using it as a way to ask her out, but I have to hide in my office, and bury myself in paperwork or I'll collapse, screaming and crying.

I didn't know they knew what Jim and I were doing after hours. Do they know about any of the rest?

My next meeting with my knight, I get my hands into his robe before he can fold me in his arms. The blanket falls and he's shivering, but he grabs my hands and holds them at our sides, twining his fingers with mine. He shakes his head slightly, not willing to let go even to tie his robe closed again. I try to step nearer, to push myself against him and share my body heat. I hope maybe it'll be enough to begin a seduction.

He knows what I want, but won't let me have it. Not until I give him what he wants, first. I try to wait him out like some kind of staring contest, but despite the chill, and the increasing shivers we both have, he will not give up.

I have to leave or we'll both get hypothermia. In my house I slam an entire pot of coffee, and wear a sweater to work because I'm so cold. It being May, I can get away with it here in the Rockies. Back in Virginia, someone would've noticed and asked if I was all right.

If someone asked me that now, I would probably fall apart.

When Cheryl comes back from college for the summer, I offer her a closing shift three nights a week along with her schedule. I tell her it comes with a raise, that Jim would be there to help her about an hour before to see her safely home. She's hesitant until I tell her it's an assistant manager position, then she jumps for it.

I hadn't intended to create an assistant manager position, but I need a break. The schedule I'm running is grinding me into the ground. I have to have at least a few nights without silent Jim, tearing my heart to pieces without a single word.

Deputy Travis has noticed something's changed. He offers to talk with me after work, or take me to his gym for formal self-defense classes. I wish I could believe he's just being nice, that he's just concerned, but I know a set-up when I see one. He can see something has driven Jim and I apart, and he'd be more than happy to help wedge that rift open further to get a foot inside the door.

When I see Jim glaring at Travis' back one day, I spitefully consider going out with him just to get a rise out of Jim. I can't do it, though. I'm honestly not at all interested in Travis, and faking it would just hurt all of us in the long run.

I want my knight from the woods.

I sit at my kitchen table before our third meeting, wondering how I can turn things around. I could go out in jeans and a shirt, bringing a thermos of coffee, and offer to watch the stars with him, but that would mean talking.

Why can't I talk to him? I was doing so well before.

"It's normal, Reggie," I hear my brother saying. *"If you want it back, you're going to have to take it."*

Is that what Jim's doing? Making me come and take it?

"Do you understand what it means now?" He'd held my hand over his tattoo when he asked. I remember the feel of the whisker burn on my palm from when I slapped him.

That's exactly what he's doing. I tap my nails on the table. I've been keeping them longer than I usually do, anticipating their use for my nights. He can see what his silence is doing to me. To us. How far is he willing to go to make his point? Maybe I should just give up.

The ring on my hand feels heavy. I stand, moving with purpose to my door. No. I am not giving up. I will not be that woman. If he wants me to take it, fine.

I lose my resolve when I see him in the dark. There's a sliver of moonlight left in the sky, but it's enough to see his eyes. He holds my face in his hands, and I can see the pain in his eyes. He so desperately wants to hear my voice.

If I talk to him, that will mean he'll have to see me, sooner or later. Playing in the dark won't be enough for him. I can't handle the thought of him seeing me, really seeing me, and making me feel stupid.

He sighs, dropping his hands to mine, pulling the ring from my finger. *"Rings mean something to guys,"* Will told me. I can see my bracelet on my knight's wrist. I know he's going to give it back.

I don't want to give up, but I can't say that it probably isn't for the best. I can't stop the tears, though. He lifts my chin, shaking his head, before putting the ring back on my finger, but it's on the wrong hand.

It's dark, so maybe he made a mistake. When he drops to one knee, silently holding my left hand, I know he didn't make a mistake. It's unbearably romantic and ridiculous and more terrifying than the thought of talking to him has ever been.

I can't do this. I can't deal with this. I don't know what to do.

I must not have knotted my mask tight enough, because I feel it fall from my face. I panic, tearing my hand from his, frantically catch-grabbing at my mask in the dark like it's a magic talisman. I have to have that mask. I need it. It's too real out here with him in the dark without it.

He leaps to his feet, tearing his own mask off, trying to stop me from replacing my own. "Regina, stop! Talk to me!"

He spoke, and it's like a fist against my chest. Whatever magic the masks and the dark gave me, it's all gone now. I don't know how to deal with this. I'm really here and so is Jim and I'm so scared I don't know what to do next.

He pulls me into rough embrace, pushing his lips against mine. His kiss is passionate and desperate, totally focused on me. Everything I thought a kiss should be.

It's nothing at all like Larry's, even if it is forced on me.

It's too much. I slam my knee as hard as I can into him. I know he's stronger than me, I know he can hold me here no matter how hard I fight, unless I can drop him quick.

He falls with a hissing cry. I seize my mask from the ground, then run to my house, my windchimes laughing at me. I slam my door, and flip the deadbolt before sliding to the floor, screaming and sobbing hysterically for a good hour before my alarm goes off for work.

I force myself to stand. I have to open. I have to get ready for work. I fall on my bed, crying more with no idea why. The ring on my finger feels heavy.

I tear it off like it's a slug or a creepy millipede, flinging it away as I steel myself to get dressed for the day.

I'm running late by the time I get to my car. I tear down the road to the highway that leads to Honesty proper. Jim's truck pulls into the parking lot of the tiny shopping center where Java Books is located as I turn the locks to open the door.

I burn myself four times before he comes in, dressed as he always is in jeans and boots with a long-sleeve button shirt over a t-shirt. I can see the gun and its holster on his right hip. He steals the paper from a café table where I dropped it in my rush to get in, and pulls it out of the plastic bag. He sits in the overstuffed chair without comment, moving carefully.

I frantically pray that he's not going to repeat Valentines' Day, staying throughout the day until closing. Mikie and Cheyenne come in the door at seven, and the store is already packed. I glance up at where Jim had been.

He's gone.

I'm a nervous wreck all day. When Cheryl shows up, she must've had a whispered conference with the other two because she politely, but firmly, tells me to go home.

"You don't start closing by yourself until Sunday," I remind her.

"I want to start tonight. The crew will fight me as assistant manager every step of the way if you're here with me."

She's lying, and we both know it. Even without the title of assistant manager, she still has seniority, and the others listen to her without question. She bullies me, threatening to call Deputy Travis and have me escorted home if I don't leave. I know it's a bluff, but I leave. The girl is doing me a favor, and we both know it.

At home, I clean. Frantically. I'm drenched with sweat,

and it's dark outside before I even realize it. My house is so clean I could eat off the floor. I even scrubbed my walls, and pulled the appliances out to get under and behind them.

My bedroom is the only room I didn't clean. I should've at least made my bed in my cleaning spree, but I couldn't bring myself to even go into the room until I was so tired I couldn't think.

Jim's ring is still where I left it on my bed.

I don't want to touch it.

~~~

When Larry proposed, I was seventeen, and he was a Junior in college. He was my first boyfriend. He proposed in my mother's diner for all the world to see, and my mother was over the moon, giving everyone there a free desert because she was so happy.

I was happy too. I was delirious. A college junior asked me to marry him, and we'd only been dating six months. The wedding plans had been a whirlwind, and the day after I graduated high school, I was pronounced Mrs. Whitaker at eighteen.

Almost a year later was when I found out who it was I'd really married. He asked me to wait to go to college, until after he'd finished his degree. I was a teenager in love, so of course I agreed.

My marriage started out as perfect as I imagined it would be. Then, little things began to fall out of my pretty picture. He would be late coming home from school or work. He stopped with the spontaneous embraces and flowers. He was never a good kisser, but when even the kisses fell off, I wondered if I'd done something wrong.

I caught him in the university library when I went to
~~~

surprise him for Valentines' Day. I thought that would fix whatever was wrong. He told me he'd be home late because he was studying. I knew the 400-level chemistry classes were difficult, because he'd complained about them more than once, so him saying he couldn't make it home in time for dinner on Valentines' wasn't shocking. Upsetting, but not shocking.

Instead of cooking the elaborate dinner I had planned, I decided to jump him in the library instead. I made myself up, and took the bus to the college, wearing the most fetching dress I had. I remember being unable to control the smile on my face as I prowled the third floor science stacks for Larry, imagining his face when I attacked him. I had wicked plans for coaxing him into a broom closet or a bathroom or something, when I saw him one row over with his hand up her shirt.

I froze, at first thinking it had to be a mistake, but it wasn't. My view between the shelves let me see everything. His hand up her shirt and under the bra, pinching her nipple despite her hushed , giggling, whisper not to. Her protests weren't worth much, because he bent and took her breast in his mouth, sucking at it as she pulled his head in closer.

I remember him pushing her back against the wall, hitching her skirt up, and plunging a hand into her panties. I couldn't move as I watched her gasp and bite her lip, her hips rocking to the rhythm his hand demanded. I heard her panted breaths, begging that he fuck her right now.

I saw him bite at her nipple one last time before standing straight to whisper something in her ear. She giggled, and turned to face the wall. She bent over, bracing her hands on a stepstool, kicking one foot out of her panties. Larry didn't even hesitate—he unbuckled his pants, and seized her hips to him.

I remember thinking it was some horrible nightmare. That I must have fallen asleep at home, and I was just having a nightmare. It couldn't be Larry.

It was Larry. How could it be Larry? He guided her hips against him faster, and more violently with each thrust. I watched her grind against him as her hand shot to the wall to keep from smacking her head, trying to suppress the tiny sounds of pleasure that escaped her lips.

When they finished, they straightened their clothes, talking about the class they were studying for. I heard him tell her it was a good break from the books, and how he couldn't wait for their next one. She winked, and slapped his ass as she strut past him, warning him about too much study taking him away from the old ball and chain.

He laughed, grabbing her back, thrusting his hand up her shirt again from behind her, whispering that his wife was just a child, and maybe a threesome could teach her a thing or two about how to please a man. She wriggled her ass against him slow circles, promising that she could show me all sorts of things.

I listened numbly, my eyes unseeing as he promised to meet her after class again on Wednesday as they moved out of the stacks together. Even after they'd left, I couldn't move. I couldn't make a sound. I was stunned.

Then I was angry. Despite the anger it still took me another day to build up my courage to confront Larry about it, to tell him what I'd seen. I told him if he couldn't stay faithful to me, then I wouldn't stay at all.

He laughed, and grabbed my arm.

That laugh heralded the start of a bad week, but the first night was the worst. I fought and bit and scratched until he punched me in the face and stomach. I remember lying on the floor, struggling to breathe with the far away sensations of my clothes being yanked from my body, before the tearing pain brought me screaming back into the present.

I ached inside and out. I reeled from the shock that my husband had raped me. I hadn't realized that was possible. I didn't know that kind of thing happened, ever. No one talked about it then like they do now.

The next morning was more of the same, and that afternoon as well. Then the night after that. And again, when he decided to skip classes, and again that evening, and again and again . . .

Until I stopped fighting him.

What could I do? My mother was convinced Larry was made of gold. My little brother was just starting high school. My father had died years earlier. My friends thought I was so lucky to have married Larry. No one would believe me if I told them what happened. Even the law didn't recognize it was possible back then.

I decided I could survive. I learned the rules. If I did what he wanted, if I didn't raise a fuss, if I didn't say what he didn't want to hear, he was nice to me. Life was tolerable, but it wasn't living.

Looking back, there were signs even before we got married. There were the dates he missed because he had to study, or because his car broke down. There was his temper when he'd grab my arm, leaving bruises from his fingers because he thought he'd caught me flirting with another boy.

Jim never touched me like that. He never let me down, he never hurt me, even after I kneed his crotch. He's gentle, patient, frustratingly persistent, and even sometimes an asshole, but he's never hurt me.

Jim's ring stares at me from the bed.

I pull a blanket from my linen closet, and cry myself to

sleep on the couch.

Chapter 16

Cross the Bridge Before You Burn It

When I show up at Java Books to spar and escort Regina home, she's not there. Our morning was tense, to be polite about it. Regina was shaking the whole time I was in the store. I didn't push the issue about what had happened a few hours earlier, in part because I know she's scared out of her mind and needs time to sort things through.

I'm a little scared myself, to be honest about it. And still feeling very delicate.

School's out now, so I leave when the kids start showing up for their shifts, and come back at my usual seven in the evening. Since it's May, the sun is still up, so it isn't as dangerous for Regina to close, but we've got a ritual, and I was hoping to talk to her, now that we've both had a chance to cool off. Even if I'm the only one to do all the talking, I at least want her to hear me out.

The girl with the hair who went to college is closing tonight. Now that summer break is on, I expected to see her at the café soon, taking orders and breaking hearts all in the same breath, but I'm surprised to see her with no sign of Regina anywhere.

I point at her. "Cheryl, right?"

She nods. "The Boss said you'd be here to help close for the night."

"So she's not here?"

She shakes her head. "No. We changed the schedule up for while I'm home. I close Sundays, Wednesdays and Fridays."

Regina didn't tell me.

Cheryl prattles on about enjoying the added responsibility without the soul-crushing hours. She's hoping Regina will let her help interview some of the new applicants.

Regina didn't tell me.

I can't very well leave Cheryl alone to close, now that I'm here. I don't know the kid, but I still don't want anything to happen to her, and I'd bet money that Cheryl's parents didn't go for the shift change until the nightly bodyguard was thrown into the deal, so I stay and help like I always do.

When Cheryl comes out from the office, she looks at me with a hand on her hip. Her hair is a bright candy-cherry red that makes me want to paint a big red blotch over her nose to match. "Are we sparring tonight?" she asks.

"I'm sorry?" I'm still thinking about Regina not telling me about the shift change.

"We've been watching, you know," she says, looking at me like I'm an idiot. "Pretty much all of Honesty knows what happens here, after hours."

Not suggestive, just factual. I shrug. "We can spar if you want, I guess."

She shakes her head. "Not really. My parents are

making me take a self-defense course at the community center."

Regina didn't tell me. I want to storm her house, slam the door open and make her talk to me. "That's good," I say.

"Deputy Travis is trying to get her to take some formal lessons. In the same gym he trains in."

She didn't tell me. "It might not be a bad idea."

Cheryl squints at me. "Are you even listening?"

I shoulder the duffle, and turn for the door. "You're a nice kid," I tell her. "But you have no idea what's going on." I push the door open with an angry shove. "I have to get you home."

***

I say nothing when I help Regina open the next morning. I go about my routine, and she does hers, and then I go home and wait. It's Saturday. The Boss doesn't work Saturday day.

Her car throws up dust and rock from the dirt road as she comes home just before lunch. I watch my backyard for another thirty minutes, giving her time to settle in. I want her mind at least mostly off of work when I go over.

Further west there's a cloud rising up in the sky. It looks like it's covered in dirt, and I realize I'm looking at the plume of a forest fire, but it's impossible to tell how far away it is. It could be just over the ridge or another three back.

I decide it can't be that close. Someone would have already started screaming evacuation orders if it were. I know the entire mountain is a tinderbox because the winter was so dry, but it's a distant fact to me. It isn't something I care about.

Birds are singing, and some squirrel is barking in that weird squirrel chitter that they do when I stroll up the road. I'm weirdly detached. No jitters or nerves like the first time I went to her door. There's nothing embarrassing to talk about. We need to talk, yes, but this isn't like the first time when I felt like I was dealing with my mom after she'd caught me with skin mag.

Regina's windchimes are clanging in the wind as I knock on her door. She doesn't answer. I do it again. And again. And again. There's a new, big frickin' windchime right near the door, and it's making my ears ring. I remember reading somewhere that windchimes were originally used to scare off evil spirits.

I'll be damned if I let windchimes scare me off. I'll go deaf from those things before I give up. I knock on her door. And again.

"I'll knock until my knuckles bleed, Regina," I tell her.

I knock again. I have to kick the door a few times to give my hands a rest, but I don't damage the thing.

It finally opens, and I'm confronted with Regina glaring at me. I prop my hand on the door to keep it open, and hold up a finger. "First, kneeing a man who is off his guard because he's feeling romantic is cruel, evil and vicious. I'm proud of you."

She blinks and her mouth opens in surprise.

I shake my head with a rueful smile. "I don't think you would've had the guts to even try that six months ago." I hold up another finger. "Second, if a man is feeling at all aggressive towards you, a crotch shot isn't going to work. We've grown up learning to defend that part of our anatomy, so we're usually on guard."

She still doesn't know what to say. I notice she's not wearing the ring.

"Now that we've got that out of the way, I think you owe me an explanation," I say. "What, exactly, did I do?"

"You hurt me."

I nod. It isn't what I want to hear, but it's something. "How?"

Her body shifts. I can see the words coming before she drags up the courage to say them.

"Don't you dare say *it's not you, it's me*," I growl.

"Well what the hell else do you want?" she demands. "I can fuck your brains out in the pitch black, but I can't say a damn word that means anything."

"You were doing fine before the robbery," I point out.

"It's-" She cuts herself off, tears in her eyes. It's heartbreaking as all hell, but I can't let that stop me.

"It's not just you," I tell her. "It's us. This is us. He didn't just hurt you, he hurt us. He hurt me."

She gets pale when I say that, but she doesn't say a thing.

"You promised you would tell me if I hurt you," I remind her. "Now you tell me what I did."

"I wasn't expecting you."

"What?"

"I wasn't expecting you to see me. I wasn't expecting you to come. I wasn't expecting a ring or New Year's or any of it!" she shouts.

Shit. Now the tears are falling, and part of me wants to do whatever it takes to make her stop.

And the other part of me is pissed. "I'm too real? Is that it? I'm too close to what you want?"

She doesn't say anything. She's got her hand over her mouth, and she's looking at our feet.

Now I'm not just pissed. I'm hurt. Which just makes me more angry. "If all you wanted was a goddamned toy, why the hell didn't you just buy one and stay inside?"

"You think I didn't-" she snaps her mouth closed, and takes a deep breath, clenching her fists at her sides. "Trust me. They aren't the same as the real thing." She waves at her yard. "Even rolling around in the grass alone with my imagination is better than batteries."

I can't believe she actually said that. It's something I never thought I'd ever hear any woman say.

"Fucking prick." Her voice is filled with hate and pain and the door slams shut, narrowly missing my face.

At home, I stare at my table. I feel a range of emotions. Anger. Pain. Desire.

I hate the masks. Both of them. All of them.

The phone rings. I pick it up, and don't even get out a full "Hello" before the automated message starts. "There is a fast moving wildfire in your area. Your area is under mandatory evacuation orders. Please leave your home immediately, and head East on US Highway 24."

Everything in my gut turns to cold water. It's only May. Fire season doesn't usually start until June. The message repeats itself. "There is a fast moving wildfire in your area."

Most of the paperwork is in the last drawer in the office desk. "Your area is under mandatory evacuation orders."

I have a suitcase in my closet. "Please leave your home immediately, and head East on US highway 24."

The phone drops from my hand. I race into my bedroom for my suitcase. I'd been so preoccupied with Regina, that I hadn't put together a new go-bag for the fire season. I'd emptied my duffle to use as punching bag, but hadn't packed the bigger suitcase to replace it. I slam clothes in it without thinking. I haul it to the dining room, and throw it on the table, spilling my coffee everywhere. Most of my paperwork is in my desk, but I can't find my insurance policy. I grab a random sheet from each of my bill folders, tossing them into the suitcase. The power goes out.

I freeze. There's something terrifying about the power going out in an emergency. "They always cut the power in a wildfire, Shit-wit," I mutter. I throw a photo album into my suitcase, and bring it all out to my truck. I can see the plume rising like some hateful cloud of dirt and ash. A wave of heat pushes against me—there isn't any time left. The roaring, crackling sound of it from behind my house fills my ears.

Regina's car is still in her carport.

Flames swirl on treetops not more than a few acres away from the far edge of my property. Sirens are shrieking their way close. I get in my truck park just behind her car.

There's no movement.

I can't leave until I know she's gone.

I leave my truck with the door open and the engine running, to tear down her path again and pound on her door. "Regina? Open the door, Regina! We gotta go!"

"Fuck you!" comes the muffled curse.

She probably didn't even answer the phone when it rang. She probably just picked it up, then hung up. She probably thinks the power outage has something to do with a fallen tree. The sirens belong to an ambulance for a neighbor in distress.

Why is it women never do what you want them to do, when you want them to do it?

It's been a long time since I've had to do anything like a house clearing op, but the growing smell of smoke doesn't allow for anything else with finesse. Emergency vehicles are tearing up the road. A fire truck pulls up to a hydrant across the street from Regina's, and a cop car skids to a halt nearby.

I grab a small log that hasn't been cut to firewood from a stack near the porch, and ram it on the door, slamming it open in a shower of splinters and broken hardware. Regina runs into the foyer, fear etched on her face. I seize her hand, and pull her struggling along behind me.

She claws at my arm with her free hand and kicks my legs. Her voice is filled with fear, though I'm not paying attention to the words. She gets violent, and her strikes come harder. Her heel clips my knee hard enough to make grind my teeth.

I can't pull her out like this. I hear someone yelling, feet pounding down the path to her house. "There's no time, Regina!" I shout as I wrap my arms around her waist and bodily pick her up, pulling her out the door.

The heat and smoke are like a bucket of cold water on her senses. She yells something about having to get things, but I don't care what she needs. The fire is too close. There isn't enough time.

I can't not save her again.

There's more shouting from firemen. Cars are racing by as neighbors evacuate, looking to break speed records, heedless of the crews in the road.

Regina's still fighting me, squirming and swinging. It isn't a move my body likes, and I know I'll hurt in the morning, but I haul her over my shoulders to carry her to my truck, brushing by Deputy Travis who's already making tracks for his car, now that he's seen her house is empty.

I shove her in the cab. She stares in horror out the window. The fire hasn't gotten to our properties yet, but it is definitely knocking on the door. Someone yells to get my truck the hell out.

I'm already moving. Regina twists around in the cab to look at the scene as we retreat. I can't do anything but drive.

There's a road, and I can focus on that. If I look for the flames, even in the rearview, I know I'll stop.

I bought that house a year before I retired.

Jenny died six months after I retired.

***

"Dad, I want you to stay with us," Lucas says. "We've got plenty of room."

"You've got a baby that screams at six in the morning, every morning," I say. "I'm too old for that crap."

Not too old to get up at two in the morning, hoping for an intensely emotional and intimate chat, but too old to deal with a baby.

Lucas huffs. "Dad-"

"Regina doesn't have anywhere to go," I tell him. "Even if she did, I don't think she would."

"Dad-"

"I told you about the robbery, right?"

"What does-"

"I can't leave her, Lucas. I can't." My voice shakes. I don't want it to, but I can't keep it steady.

I can envision Lucas shaking his head, but he stops arguing. "I understand." He sighs. "Is there anything we can do?"

"Do you think you can scratch up some spare clothes? Regina's about five-seven, maybe one-seventy, one-eighty. I hustled her out with nothing but the clothes on her back, because there wasn't any time."

"I'll get on it. Anything else?"

"A bourbon."

Lucas goes very quiet.

"It's a joke, son."

He takes a deep breath. "Are you sure?"

I desperately want a drink right now, and that's how I know I can't have even a whiff. "I can't screw this up, Lucas." Tears are leaking out. I press my fingers into my eyes, trying to find the spigot and shut it off. "I've screwed up too many times. I can't do it again."

There's a relieved sigh on the other end of the line. "Okay, Dad. I'll have Missy get some things together, and I'll drive them up as soon as it's ready. If you need anything, A-N-Y-T-H-I-N-G, you call me."

"Yes, sir."

***

When I find Regina again, she's in the gym at the high school in Manitou, listening to whatever updates come in. All of Honesty was evacuated and almost all four hundred and some-odd of us are here. I sit next to her on the bleachers, and put the large shopping bag Missy packed at her feet.

She looks at me. I shrug. "I hustled you out before you could even grab decent shoes," I say, nodding at her bare feet. "The least I could do is get you some clothes."

Her face looks like it's about to crumble. Her hand covers her mouth. A reminder not to speak? Or just too much emotion to convey?

She might not be so appreciative when she sees what's inside—a few pairs of shorts and t-shirts, a fresh package of underwear and a pair of flip-flops. I made sure all the tags were clipped off, and the shirts looked a little too cutesy for what Regina normally wears, but at least she isn't stuck dropping cash on a new wardrobe because I wouldn't let her bring anything.

I take her free hand. She's trembling, and clenches so tight it hurts mine. She starts crying—great, heaving sobs. I wrap her in my arms. She clings to me like she drowning, like I'm the last thing left in the world.

I don't know how much strength I have to get through this, but if she needs it all, then that's what I'll give.

Deputy Travis comes in. I don't know if he's there officially or not, but he is in uniform. He looks a little rough for wear, and I don't doubt the last ten hours have been hard, to say the least. He sees me holding Regina, sees her practically collapsed on me.

Men are typically referred to as being dense as doornails, unable to understand basic communication, but really that's only when we're trying to understand women. When we're dealing with each other, we've got grunt-and-scowl communication down pretty well.

On Valentines' he knew I wasn't going to step aside just because he wanted me to. Now, with a glance he knows that while things have been rough, I'm not leaving Regina without one hell of a fight.

His mouth quirks. He nods, and moves on.

***

It's nearly two weeks before we're allowed home. Fire mitigation is almost a religion in our neighborhood, and there's a good reason for it. When driving back, Regina and I could see the mountains scorched on either side of the highway. There's whole areas where the ground is nothing but an eerie black covered with white powder. In places where there were trees, there's not much left. Stubby black poles without their limbs jut up from the ground like broken claws. The sun looks weak, shining through the damage, even though there isn't a cloud in the sky.

The dirt road through our neighborhood is a journey through an unfamiliar world. We can't take the main entrance into ShadowPines, because the fallen trees haven't been cleared yet, but the back way is still open, which means we have to wind through scenes of total devastation with our neighbors before we can see how badly we got hit.

Everywhere is blackened charcoal and pure white ash. A scorched stone chimney and patio is all that's left of the Munn's big house. I saw Gordon and his wife, just standing there, staring at what was left, holding each other as Regina and I drove by.

Simmons has a twisted lump of wood and metal at the center of his property where his horses were stabled. He'd taken them out a day or two before the fire, something about a show and a wedding in New Mexico, so he and his ponies survived. The shape of his property looks so different with the damage that I can't even begin to guess where his house was.

I have no idea how the grumpy Santa is going to take it when he sees what's left. He wouldn't do much more than grunt when I'd called him. He's got a daughter in Colorado Springs, and he said she'd been calling him with updates, checking on him every few hours.

Some people in ShadowPines lost everything. Regina holds her hand over her mouth as I drive, too horrified, too numb to comprehend the damage. Every once in a while we pass striking halos of greenery. Places where you knew firemen took a stand, and held back the flames. Regina's house is one of those lucky islands of paradox surrounded by destruction.

I've seen things like this before. You don't spend a good portion of your life as an enlisted man and not see it.

But it's different when it's your house.

I'm too overwhelmed to think. My house is scorched all up the back, and the windows are broken. The roof is shot on that half of the house, and there's water damage inside, mostly in the kitchen and utility room, although the master bedroom looks like it got a little soggy. I won't know how bad it is until I peel up the carpet. Other than that, my house is still pretty solid. Nothing a lot of sweat and cursing can't fix.

After surveying the damage to my own property, I go to Regina's, intending to ask for a shovel since my shed is well and truly burnt to ashes, but I do want to see what might be left behind under the debris.

A lot of her windchimes are on the ground, melted plastic threads coiled around metal tubes, stomped into the dirt by large bootprints. A few windchimes are still up though, tinkling as I knock on the remains of her doorframe. I feel shitty about the fact that the only real damage I can see to her house was what I'd done. I'm thinking about offering to hang a whole new door for her as the old one drifts open, and I see her mask just inside the threshold. I don't know what it's doing there. I don't remember her holding it when I broke down her door, but I hadn't been looking for it either.

I can remember the days we spent at the shelter together—holding hands, playing cards, talking, trying to do anything to distract ourselves from the reality of what was happening, unable to go anywhere or do anything other than wait.

I thought that as bad as it was, the fire was bringing her back to me. I thought we didn't need the masks anymore. Even if our houses and everything we owned went up in flames, that was a price I was willing to pay if it meant she would come back to me.

Now there's that mask again, waiting like a smug bastard in her house, and I realize the whole time we were at the shelter together, despite everything we talked about, we never actually said a damn thing.

She steps into the foyer, drying her hands on a towel. I stalk in, deliberately trampling the mask under my boot. She closes the door behind me, probably more out of habit than really expecting it to stay shut. "Sure, come on in," she mutters sarcastically. "Can I get you anything?"

I slam my hand against the foyer wall to block her way into the house, and grab her wrist. She twists in my hand, and I let it go.

"What the hell is the matter with you?" she demands.

I point at her. "You. You're my problem."

"Look. I am sorry about your house but-"

She doesn't get to finish because I've pinned her to the door, my mouth hard against hers. She manages to push me away slightly, her arms crossed over my neck. I push back. "I'm not leaving until you tell me."

"Tell you what?" She's afraid. She's confused.

So am I.

"I've had every part of you except for this." I wiggle my hand between us and rest it on the center of her chest. I rest my forehead on hers. "It's not fair that you've got mine."

I know there's a very good chance that she has no idea where this is coming from. I'm not sure I know, either. I shake my head, closing my eyes. I can feel her nose barely a few hairs away from mine. "No more masks. No more rules. If I can't have it all, I don't want any of it."

I'm scared. I know this wasn't the best time to confront her about everything. We're both still reeling from the fire, but I can't wait any longer.

I feel her arms move. I don't want to hear her say "no." I

don't want to hear her say she's still not ready to at least talk to me. I don't want to give up, but I know I'm going to have to.

"You are such an asshole, James."

My eyes fly open as she kisses me.

She called me "James."

True, she also called me "an asshole," but I can live with that because she called me "James."

Her kiss is deep and breathtaking and I want her, but she breaks away. Then she takes my hands in hers, leading me into her house.

My head is still buzzing before I realize where she's taking me. I freeze just outside her bedroom. She looks at me shyly, with a crooked smile on her face. "It's a little more kinky than anything we've done before," she says. "But I've heard it's a lot of fun."

I don't wait for another invitation. I step inside and shut the door behind me.

Chapter 17

Starting Over

For two weeks he stayed with me at the shelter when he could have stayed with his family in Colorado Springs. He told me bad jokes, played gin and canasta with me until I thought he'd go insane, and held me throughout every crying jag I had during the fire. Today, he drove me home through the devastation, and told me he'd be right next door if I needed anything.

Then he barged into my house, pissed as all hell, demanding an answer to a question I haven't had the emotional strength to consider for the last two weeks.

I'm not sure if calling someone an asshole and then kissing them is considered "healthy intimacy," but James seems to think it is.

I don't care. I want my knight.

I'm mentally exhausted. I'd been sitting at my kitchen table after retreating from the reeking, disgusting fridge, staring at the dishtowel in my hands when James had barged in.

The fridge needs to be replaced. Rotting food and mold clings everywhere inside it. Just the smell enough to make me gag when I'd opened the door a tiny bit.

But it's too much to think about. I feel like I'm drowning under a heavy fog. Even though my house survived unscathed except for a single broken door, I'm overwhelmed. Five months of pressure and pain have wrung me out. I'm relieved, but I don't know why. I'm angry, but the anger isn't focused. I want to lash out, but I don't have a target.

My focus returns when he kissed me, and it was such an obvious answer. I need my knight, rusty armor and all. I can't lose him. I can't.

He gets a goofy grin on his face when he sees my bed, and he closes the door behind us before taking me into his arms, kissing me again. I'm thrilled he's in my room. I'm delirious he's willing to follow me into something so mundane after the more exotic fare we've had so far. I feel like I can do anything, now that he's here.

That's when I remember there's a skylight over my bed, and no way to make the room dark until after sunset. I can feel my heart pound. I try not to think about what will inevitably happen. I try to lose myself in James, to make him surrender to frantic passion, roughly yanking his shirt over his head.

But he doesn't want to play that way. Not this time. He grabs my hands when I begin on his pants.

He smiles against my mouth. "What's the rush? You got a hot date after this?"

There's nothing I can say. There's no way to hide. The sun streaming through my skylight is like a spotlight and there is no way to turn it off.

James takes his time, running his hands under my shirt, indulging himself with my lips. He draws off my t-shirt and I tremble. I can't look at him. I'm too ashamed.

A thoughtful thumb strokes the scar on my left shoulder. "Was this him?"

"Surgery," I nod, looking at a corner of my room. "Dislocated shoulder."

His finger follows my arm down to the elbow and drifts to the scar on my ribs below my right breast, peeking out from under my bra.

"He wore a heavy college ring," I say. "Lots of squared off edges." I sniff, remembering the doctor's face when I gave him my excuse of tripping the wrong way and slamming into the end of a stair railing. "Six stitches."

He takes a shuddering breath. There's no help for it now. The last secret I could hide in the night shadows won't stay hidden much longer. Not if James stays.

Part of me wants him to go. I don't want him to see. I don't want to be ashamed. I don't want to hear my brother's words tumble from his lips. *"Why didn't you leave? Why didn't you ask for help?"*

I turn to face my door, pulling my arms in tight to my chest, exposing my back.

James hisses.

"What part of you thought this was okay?" I can hear Will demand. *"You had options! Why didn't you come to me?"*

"It didn't happen often," I say, my voice tiny. "And he was smart enough to not hit my face when he did, most of the time."

James' fingers are trembling as he traces the scars crisscrossing my back.

My heart is thudding in my ears. "If he was feeling

nasty, he'd use part of an extension cord, with the end he'd stripped the insulation off of." I can't believe I'm saying this out loud. I can't believe I'm letting James hear this, see this.

"When you talked back?"

I swallow hard and nod. "I learned. I don't talk, I don't fight, and he won't hit. Most of the time."

James kisses my shoulder, his arms slipping around my waist. "How long?"

"Twenty-seven years."

Something wet tickles my shoulder. James' arms tighten around my waist. "What made you leave?"

The words are shaky and mumbled against my skin. I don't hear my brother's accusations in his question. James wants to know what changed. He wants to know how I went from a doormat to. . . to what? What am I now?

I lean my body against the door, suddenly too tired to think, too tired to be ashamed, too tired to hide. "He left for six months. Work in Richmond. He came back on weekends at first, but then he stopped."

I draw in a shuddering breath. "Then he came back, out of the blue, in the middle of the week. He was angry. His newest girlfriend found out he was married, and kicked him out. He drove three hours to take it out on me."

He's crying.

James is crying.

My lips are numb. I don't want to tell the story, but I have to. He's tried so hard to get me to talk. If I don't now, I don't know that I ever will. I'm afraid if I don't, James will leave. I'm afraid if I tell him everything, he'll leave anyway.

I screw up my courage. "When he finished, he left again. I called an ambulance, and afterwards called my brother."

"The cop?"

I can feel the cool wood of the door warming against my cheek as I nod. "He lives in North Carolina so he hadn't seen much of the bad times. He knew my marriage wasn't a winner, but he didn't know how bad it was, until he saw me in the hospital bed."

I remember that day. The sun coming in from the room window felt false and uninviting and there was a chain of curses from my brother when he saw my face.

"He-he. . . " I stutter. The words are stuck.

"It's okay." James' arms are tight around me, his head resting on my shoulder. "You don't have to tell me if you don't want to."

I shake my head. I have to tell it. It took me three years of therapy before I trusted Dr. Beas enough to say it, and I pay her to listen to me.

James wasn't getting a dime, and he had wanted to hear me. Wanted to know my story. He wanted me to talk. More than he wanted my body, he wanted me to talk.

"My brother filed charges for me. He helped transfer me to another hospital out of state, then kept me in his house while the divorce went through."

I remember sitting with the lawyers and Larry, everyone arguing about what my alimony should be. I remember feeling a foot stroke my leg under the table, playfully, seductively. When I looked up, Larry was slouched back in his chair, a small smile twisting his lips.

For the first time in my life I stood up. I stood up, and told everyone at the table that I didn't want a fucking dime from him, and if he was ever in the same room with me again, I'd kill him. I then stormed out of the office with all the righteous anger I could muster to keep me moving.

I didn't leave the firm's bathroom for hours. My lawyer's secretary came in to check on me, to talk with me through the stall. She had to leave, and come back with paperwork for me to sign, sliding it under the stall door.

She kept telling me not to sign anything, just yet. That she was only bringing it in for me to see how close I was to ending it all with him. She said it wasn't ethical to have me sign anything with the state I was in, that the bastard should pay through the nose. That even the "good" divorces are an emotional train wreck, and decisions made in haste could hurt me down the road.

I remember repeating over and over again that I just wanted out. That I would leave the state and never come back. That I would do anything to never see him again. That just the clothes on my back were good enough to start over. That I wasn't going to leave that bathroom until the paperwork was signed and done.

It would've been a hilarious scene if it hadn't been so pathetic, so tragic. A paralegal on her hands and knees, explaining each paragraph through a stall door, and handing me a pen to initial and sign each page to end my marriage with Lawrence Daniel Whitaker III, Esquire.

There were a few more court appearances before a judge to finalize it, but I was able to attend remotely. I think the judge decreed alimony for me, but I can't remember. I haven't gotten a dime from Larry, and I don't want one.

For all intents and purposes, I ended my marriage in a bathroom.

A damn bursts, and James is on the receiving end of it. The words fall out of my mouth in a rush. They're coming so fast, I don't even know if they're in the right order. My face is pressed against the door and I'm sobbing. I can't move. I can't speak.

I feel lips on my back. Tender, gentle, lingering kisses softer than butterflies on my scars. He kisses my shoulder, then turns me to kiss the scar under my breast. Falling to his knees, he holds me around my waist, pressing his damp face into my stomach and holding me.

I stroke his hair quietly. I don't know what to do. I've never had a man act like this. I sink to the floor, and rest my head against his chest, his arms wrapped around me with no thought of sex, or running away. His only thought is to give me what I never had.

A shoulder to cry on.

I can feel the tears coming again, but I can't handle another crying jag. I don't want to do it again. Not today. I slip a hand up his arm, and circle my fingers over his tattoo. "James?"

"Yes?" His voice is quieter than mine.

"Will you do something for me?"

He has to pull back a little to meet my eyes. "Anything."

"Make love to me. Now."

He blinks. I think he was ready for me to ask him for anything except that. My lip starts trembling. "I don't-don't want to cry a-again, today."

A light hand caresses my side. "Are you sure?" His words are filled concern. "We don't-"

"The first time I ever, actually, made love to anyone was with you, just before Halloween," I interrupt him. The tears are starting to spill down my face. "I want that again."

He smiles, his own eyes glistening. "It's hard to make love to a crying woman," he admits. "But I'll give it a shot, if that's what you really want."

He guides me to my bed, a rumple of sheets and blankets because I only make my bed when I change the sheets, and I haven't at all since before the fire. He kisses my face, blotchy, pale and covered with tears, each kiss meant to take a tear away. He kisses each scar as he undresses me, not at all hurried or frantic as our meetings in the dark have been. I fumble with his pants as he presses his mouth to mine, kissing long and deep.

In my bed, he slowly slides his hands up my legs, my sides, my arms, drawing my hands over my head, gently pinning them to the mattress, twining his fingers with mine. Our love-making is slow and sensual and lazy, making me feel like I'm the only one in James' world.

Afterwards, we lay there, in my bed. Just lay there, holding each other. The sun in my skylight is fading into ribbons of purple and orange and scarlet.

He's stretched on his side, and glances up at the failing light. "Shit."

"What?" Did I do something wrong?

He smiles at me and strokes my face. "The day's almost gone." He takes a deep breath. "You showed me your scars, it's only fair I do the same."

He tells me about his wife, Jenny. She sounds like a woman I would've liked to know. "She had a lot of fire in her," he says. "A lot of spark." She died six months after his retirement, leaving him with a teenage son, and no compass to steer by.

"They try to prepare you for retirement," he says about the Army. "But nothing can make it real until you're there. No orders, no routine, no experience hunting for a job. A wife is sometimes the only thing that holds a military man together until he finds his feet when he retires, and. . . she was gone." I can see him struggling to find the words. "I've been in a few hellholes, not knowing which way was out, but I'd never been lost like that."

He'd started drinking. Before then, he'd only taken an occasional beer, but after Jenny's death he fell into the bottle. It wasn't until Lucas went to college, and didn't come back for the holidays, that James realized he would lose his son.

One of our neighbors, Simmons, helped him back to sobriety when James had asked.

"It was the roughest year of my life," he said. "I was sick for the first six weeks, and felt rotten for another year after. I had to dry out. I had to mourn. I had to relearn how to be human. Even boot camp wasn't that hard." His expression is unreadable, his eyes are far away.

It took years for Lucas to be willing to talk to him again. If it hadn't been for Lucas' fiancee—now his wife, he might still not be talking to James. She insisted on meeting her future-father-in-law. She wanted to give him a chance to be a part of their lives. "It took a while," James says, "but he finally saw that I'd moved out of the dark times."

My room is dark now. The moon isn't up yet, but I can tell he's crying. He's taking deep breaths, trying to breathe through the pain in silence.

I know what that's like. I've done it many times.

I kiss his face, pushing my body against his. I don't say anything, because I don't know what to say. He pulls me close, crushing me against him, burying his face in my shoulder. I can feel his back jerk as he cries. With pain for lost years. With relief that he hadn't lost everything. With regret because he feels stupid to have ever made that mistake in the first place.

Also things I know about.

He calms after few minutes, roughly wiping at his eyes.

His stomach growls.

We both snicker. It's been such an emotional day it's hard not to laugh at something so utterly, ridiculously common. "It's been a while since I ate," he admits.

I nod, my own stomach deciding to speak up.

"Breakfast, for me."

"Dinner?" he suggests.

"We'll have to go out unless you want canned soup and crackers. The power-out spoiled everything in my fridge."

His stomach growls again. "Crackers and soup sound pretty good."

Chaperr 18
Sonesty May Not Be the Best Policy

For the fourth of July, I pull into my son's driveway and look at Regina. "Nervous?"

She blows air from her mouth for a long moment and nods. I squeeze her hand. "So am I."

She laughs.

"Don't worry," I tell her. "They'll love you."

"And if they don't?"

I barely heard her, but I lean over and give her a kiss. "If they don't, they're just going to have to deal with it," I murmur. I kiss her again, and the thought of perhaps being an hour or two late to my son's barbecue might not be a bad idea.

I break our kiss even though I don't want to. "I don't think that's going to be our biggest concern tonight, anyway."

She giggles, and we leave the truck.

My son welcomes us into his house, and Missy is overjoyed to meet the mystery woman she's heard almost nothing about. We're ushered inside, Rosy immediately laying claim to Regina's hand, toddling her off to the living room with Missy not far behind, already peppering my lady with questions.

"Go easy on her, Missy," I tell her. "It isn't like we're going anywhere. You've got time."

Missy looks at me. "You shush." She waves her hand towards the kitchen and the door leading to the backyard. "Go help Lucas or something. This is girl time."

I look at Regina. She smiles nervously, but nods her head. "Yes, Ma'am," I say, and leave the room like I'm told.

Lucas has already started the grill out back, and he's holding his hand just over the grate to figure out the hot spots when I wander outside. He doesn't even glance at me. "Got kicked out of the house, huh?"

"I was informed I did not have enough estrogen to participate," I say, tapping the top of a soda I pulled from the refrigerator.

Lucas laughs. "She was pinging off the walls when she heard you were bringing Regina to meet us."

I open my soda, taking a cautious look around. So far, Tommy hasn't heard it. "Well, I was going to have to sooner or later, right, Dad?"

Lucas snorts. "We just want to be sure you're not hanging with the wrong crowd."

I fetch the meat from the refrigerator, and shuttle dirty plates and trash back inside while my son cooks. We talk about the fire and my house. He thinks he can scratch up some hands from his church to help me fix things, if I can give him a date to be there.

Missy stomps through the back door, outraged. "You're married?"

My son spins, and stares at me. I raise my hands in

surrender, one holding my soda. "It was three days ago?" I offer.

Lucas gapes at me. "You got married?" he asks incredulously. "You just got back from the fire a few weeks ago."

"She didn't want to wait." I say. I'm still surprised by it, myself. We haven't yet figured out how to combine our houses, and if we should call one "the house," and the other a guest house, or a warehouse, or a really damn big shed, or sell it, and which will be which. So far, she's got me over a barrel because my house is still damaged from the fire, and all hers needed was a new front door, which she now has.

On the other hand, Simmons needs a place to stay, and she isn't willing to leave him out in the cold, either.

One thing I know is going to change is the bed. She's got a queen, and as much as I love my wife, I like to sprawl when I sleep. We're getting a king sized bed, so I don't have her arm on my nose in the morning.

Lucas stares at Missy and my wife, Regina, behind her.

"A J.P. Can you believe that?" Missy is fit to be tied. I can tell she's angry, but I can also see the glee dancing in her eyes. She's happy for me, and trying her best not to show it.

"I was the one who wanted it," Regina admits, holding Rosy, and making faces at the giggling girl. Rosy could care less about being left out of our wedding plans. She holds her chubby little hands on my wife's cheeks, tying to make Regina's faces even funnier for her own amusement.

"If it makes you feel better, her brother wasn't so happy about it either," I say. "I have to present myself for inspection no later than Christmas."

"You passed the background check, so I don't know why he's upset," Regina says. She sticks her tongue out at

Rosy, crossing her eyes. The blonde girl shrieks with glee, her little blonde pigtails bouncing on either side of her head.

"Background check?" I ask Regina.

"He's a cop, remember?"

"Oh." I'm going to have to track down one of my first CO's, if he's still alive. I now realize just how much I owe him.

I wasn't trying to lie to Regina, I just forgot about it until the words "background check" came up. I'm pretty sure she'll understand. It wasn't horrific, but it certainly would have popped on an official check if it had been properly reported.

I'm trying to envision her face when I tell her how I the day after my divorce, I got ripped, and was picked up by the MP's while urinating in the gas tank of my former best friend's car. After I had thoroughly soaked the leather upholstery.

He loved that car. I never saw it parked with the top down and the doors unlocked ever again.

I suck in my lips to not laugh at the memory. Missy doesn't take it the right way. She thinks I'm trying not to laugh at her.

She points an imperious finger at me. "This is not over," she warns me before shooing Regina back into the house. I just hope that whatever Regina agrees to, it won't cost too much.

"We're going to have to get married again, aren't we?" I ask my son.

"If you want Missy or I to ever speak to you again, yes." Lucas says.

I slump. "Does it have to be in a church?"

"It's going to have to be a ceremony with an officiant of some kind, and family present," he tells me. "I can probably talk Missy out of the rest as long as she gets to take Regina dress shopping." He frowns. "Missy might want the kids involved, too. Petal flinger, ring bearer, that sort of thing."

"I'm sorry, am I marrying Missy?" I ask. I see Tommy make his way through the dining room towards us, no doubt sent this way by his mother.

"No," Lucas admits. "But do you really think you can stop her?"

Tommy seats himself in my lap, trying to sucker me out of my soda. I absently spin the antler ring around my left ring finger. It matches Regina's, and she wouldn't hear of going to a jeweler. I'm planning on making her a new one, something fancier with leaves on it or something as a Christmas gift. I've already watched some videos on carving, and deer antlers are cheap enough that I can practice before making the real one.

Lucas suddenly turns to face me. "You don't think this is too fast?" he asks me. "You're still dealing with the fallout from the fire and all that."

I let Tommy have some soda. "Sometimes you have to burn a bridge to find a better road," I say. "I think we'll be okay, son. We'll have our share of rough spots, but I think we'll be okay."

He turns his attention back to the grill. I can tell Lucas is concerned, even hurt I got married without telling him, but he doesn't tear into me.

I have to snatch my soda back from Tommy. The little thief is trying to get off my lap with it, thinking he could finally have an entire soda to himself if he's just sneaky enough about it.

I've been told that any cavities resulting from my giving him sweets will result in the bill being sent to me, so I'm not so keen on that aspect of spoiling the boy.

"It wasn't personal, Lucas," I tell my son's back. "I told you about-" I catch myself before I say *"fucktard"* in my grandson's presence. "Her ex." I look at my soda. "When she said she didn't want to wait, that she wanted to be married that day, I couldn't say *no*."

Lucas sighs. "I can see that." He waves his grilling spatula at me. "You're going to have to say no every now and again, you realize."

"Didn't you just buy Missy a new car on her say-so?"

"That's different, Dad."

"Uh-huh."

He glares at me. I smile at him. Was I ever that young? "She won't get the moon, son. But I won't mind spoiling her when I can."

Lucas pinches his lips together, then turns back to the grill. I feel bad that I upset him with all of this. Maybe I should've pushed back when Regina said "now," but to be honest, I wasn't thinking about Lucas and Missy.

Given that it took her two hours with me holding her hands before she had the courage to call her brother and tell him about it, I don't think she was thinking much about other people until after the fact, neither. "Are you willing to be my best man?" I ask Lucas.

"That's not even a question," he fires back. "You don't have a choice about that."

"No strippers for my bachelor party," I say.

He snorts. "You'd probably die of a heart-attack. I was thinking maybe steak and a movie. With her brother."

"What's a stripper?" asks Tommy. Lucas chokes at the sound of his son's voice.

"A really scary clown," I say without missing beat. "Go find your squirt guns so we can play." Tommy scampers off before his father can stop him.

"Are you trying to get me killed?" Lucas demands.

I shrug. "You let him watch shows with zombies using the exact same explanation."

I wince as Regina's voice comes from deep within the house. "James Marshall Beaumont!"

My son winces too. "All three names. Ouch."

"Guess I'm sleeping in my house tonight," I say as I stand. I stick my head in the door. "What?" I shout inside. No man in his right mind will go into a house when all three of his names have been used in a single outburst.

"*Scary clowns?*"

"Well, what do you want me to say?" I ask. I don't get an answer, but I do hear Tommy being chewed on by his mom, before I retreat back to my chair.

Lucas and I start laughing at the same time. It feels good.

After a few minutes Lucas manages to clear his throat. "So, Dad. You never did say how the two of you met."

I drop my soda.

Shit.

***

Jim's daughter-in-law is a hoot. She wasn't nearly as mad about our shotgun wedding as she played at. Her reaction was almost like Cheryl's. Shock. Concern. Uncontainable glee.

Missy sighs when I show her my ring as I tell her a very edited version of his proposal. A midnight stroll, a bended knee.

She starts talking about dresses and wedding ideas, and when can my brother and his family come out for a formal ceremony, shushing me when I tell her I don't need all of that. Tommy runs past us and dives into the bathroom. "This is more for Lucas. I'm more forgiving than he is. He'll come around, but he needs-"

"Grandpa and I are going to shoot strippers in the backyard!" Tommy shouts excitedly as he runs past again, each hand carrying a neon colored squirt gun.

"Thomas Scott!" his mother snaps in that tone guaranteed to bring a child back into a room, cringing. Tommy's eyes are wide as he looks at his mother. "Where did you hear that word?" she demands.

"Grandpa said they were scary clowns, like zombies."

Missy's mouth drops open.

"James Marshall Beaumont!" I call.

"What?" He hasn't come all the way inside. He probably just stuck his head in the door to answer. Coward.

"*Scary clowns*?" I ask.

"Well, what do you want me to say?"

I look at Missy. "He's got us, there."

She recovers, and admonishes Tommy to never use that word again before sending him back outside. Laughter floats in from the patio. Missy looks at me. "I'm certain it was just a bachelor party joke."

"He knows I'll poison his coffee if it isn't," I say.

Missy laughs. Rosy giggles between us on the couch, enthralled by the soft ballerina doll I'd brought for her. "Oh, Mom, you'll fit in fine," Missy says.

Mom.

I never thought I'd ever be called that. My hand shakes on my mouth.

Missy smiles at me. He smile gets broader and her eyes sparkle with an idea. "What if we did the ceremony where the two of you first met? Wouldn't that be fun?"

My face is suddenly very hot.

"Are you okay, Mom? Your face is getting red."